CW01024847

'The Director's Cu
and the views exp
responsibility of the

The Director's Cut
Published by KDP

Also available as an audiobook

© 2021 by Lucas Tobin
Cover design © 2021 Lucas Tobin c/o Book Cover Zone

First published 2021

ISBN: 979-8-598023-80-8

THIS BOOK IS DEDICATED TO MY INCREDIBLE FAMILY.

You make me who I am.

CHAPTER 1

George Mason completed his final checks. The nameplate on the lid, matched the information on the wrist tag, which in turn matched the various paperwork. The clothes being worn, matched the entry in the Personal Effects Register, and most importantly, the clingfilm wrapped package, containing the severed arm, he had placed in the coffin, remained completely unseen as he screwed the lid down for the final time.

As George left the mortuary room, his team knew it was the signal to enter, and move the coffin to the rear of the open hearse in readiness for loading. Rubber matting was placed on top of the coffin lid, and the double ended spray of flowers in autumnal colours was put in place.

Loading a coffin onto a hearse is a four-person operation, and as always, the team knew their roles without further instruction. As bearers, Holly and Charlie stood either side of the foot-end of the coffin, closest to the back of the hearse, and Tommy took position at the head of the coffin. As the hearse driver, Tommy was the second in command during any funeral, and responsible for the safe loading of the coffin onto the hearse.

Tommy gave the instruction to lift in his broad Scottish accent, and all three lifted in unison. As they did so, Theo, the fourth, and most junior member of the crew, removed the wheeled bier from under the coffin, and it was loaded onto the rollered deck of the hearse and gently pushed towards the front, until it reached the stopper.

Tommy secured the coffin in place with the rear stopper, screwing the mechanism against the head-end of the coffin until it was tight, ensuring it didn't move during the ride to the crematorium. He closed the rear door of the hearse and the team gave a small bow to the coffin as a mark of respect before it began its final journey.

While the hearse was being loaded, George was in his office, changing from the everyday jacket to the long tailcoat traditionally worn by Funeral Directors. He brushed his top hat with a clothes brush to remove any specs of dust, and placed it firmly on his head.

The antique ebony shafted walking cane, topped with the solid silver globe, was, as always, resting in the wooden umbrella stand by the door. It had been handed to him by his father, four years earlier when he knew he was terminal. He had in turn, inherited it from his father, the original George Mason, after whom George was named, and whose name still adorned the frontage of the funeral home 'Geo. Mason and Son'.

CHAPTER 2

D ominic 'Nic' Watson watched mesmerised, as the fire quickly engulfed the doorway of The Old Barn pub. The flames reached up, out of the door's broken window, and licked beneath the door, like a flaming dragon's tongue, thirstily lapping at the petrol he had poured in, just moments before.

There had been a 'wumpf' when he had thrown in the flare - more of a feeling than a sound, as the petrol's fumes instantly ignited. Now, just seconds later, wallpaper and curtains started to smoke as a ball of flame rolled along the ceiling, dripping hot debris onto the carpet below.

Nic watched the fire grow steadily for a few minutes, until the super-heated air inside the bar area caused the optics to explode in spectacular fashion. The various alcohols adding high energy fuel to the fire. Even from his vantage point, behind a parked car on the opposite side of the road, he could feel the heat from the fierce flames. The sounds of glasses, bottles and windows breaking, were lost to the roar of the fire as it continued with its inevitable growth, totally consuming everything it touched.

Nic didn't know the reasoning behind why the pub had to burn, but he didn't let that bother him either. He knew that he had to perform three tasks to prove his worth, and now he was already one third of the way to achieving his goal of being accepted into the toughest and most notorious gang outside of London, The Mad Hatters.

He didn't yet know the details of the next trial, but he wouldn't have long to wait.

CHAPTER 3

T he greatest and worst day in any young boy's life is when they first beat their father at something, whether it be a one-on-one sport such as squash or snooker, a test of strength such as arm wrestling, or in George's case a battle of the minds and nerve, in the form of a game of chess.

His father had taught him to play chess from the age of eight. It was frustrating for both of them at times, but slowly the pieces, moves, and forward thinking necessary to play, started to make sense.

George was eleven, and as had become tradition, they were playing chess on a Sunday afternoon. He was sure that his father had chosen that time to start their chess games, just to get out of doing the washing up following the usual Sunday roast cooked by his mum, but she always appeared happy pottering in the kitchen, listening to music. Later George realised that this was probably just her way of giving him and his father some time together. Just one of the many small unspoken sacrifices his mum made for the love of her family.

Young George had been bought an expensive set for his tenth birthday, the pieces were made from crushed stone, and depicted the 1746 Battle of Culloden. He asked his father, that now he had a serious chess set, rather than the cheap wooden one they had used previously, would he promise to never pretend to lose against him again. He agreed, and needless to say, at least for a while, George became very accustomed to losing.

The game in question started as any other, with some piece-for-piece capturing on both sides, and even now, George can't say when the turning point was, but towards the end of the game he knew that the tide had turned, and his dad was on the run. George moved his knight into position in readiness to trap his opponent's king, and they both knew that the game only had one inevitable ending. George didn't credit his father at the time, but after playing many subsequent games, he later realised, that he could have resigned by knocking over his king, but continued playing, allowing George to experience the full joy of getting him in checkmate, for the first time ever.

Two moves later, George moved his rook into place and the deal was done, check mate! It was at that exact moment that he felt what psychologists refer to as the 'Bipolar Paradox'. George had beaten his hero! He was elated that after so many years of trying, and experiencing so many defeats, he had finally bettered his dad at their competition of choice. At the same time, he was devastated! His father wasn't infallible. This man who was his inspiration and his tutor had been beaten. Not by another adult, but by him!

George thought that he would never feel the effects of such a strong paradox again, but twenty-three years later, when his father called him to his study to ceremonially present him with the ebony cane he had used, when conducting many hundreds of funerals, his mind was transported back to that eleven-year-old kid and his paradoxical check mate.

The cane was his. The symbol which embodied Alan Mason F.D. was being handed from father to Son, as was the company his father before him so proudly established, and he himself had built upon through both good and bad times.

As a family business, George knew that one day it would naturally pass to him, and he was very proud and excited that it finally had, but at the same time, his father was telling him that he was becoming too frail to continue to do something which he had loved doing all his life.

Just three months later, his father, Alan Mason,

died in hospital after having a stroke. Naturally, George arranged and conducted his funeral, paging proudly in front of the hearse, using the ebony cane with the silver globe top, just as his father had done for George's mother five years earlier.

Now, standing in the cloakroom, George forced his hand to reach for the cane, and willed his arm to pull it from the hat stand as if it weighed far more that it physically should. He cannot bring himself to even look at the silver globe. This symbol of justice, pride and honesty, once held by great men, is now in his hand, and he feels as if his very touch will tarnish it, just as the truth would destroy the Mason name forever.

The irony of the origins of the Funeral Director's cane is not lost on George. Historically the 'Guardian of the Dead' as they were known, used his stick to physically protect the deceased in the coffin from grave robbers and young vagabonds, now here he was, using it to protect himself with a form of camouflage, hiding behind the virtues of great men. Not after stealing from a coffin, but after adding things which should never, ever have been there.

CHAPTER 4

G eo. Mason & Son Funeral Directors, is based in a former coaching inn, near the centre of town. Records show that the oldest part of the building dates back to 1726, and has been added to over the years.

The office and chapel occupy the main frontage of the building, with the workshop, mortuary, and garage, behind. The double doors of the garage, opening up onto a central courtyard, which once echoed to the sound of horse's hooves.

The old stables used to house the mortuary, but this was modernised and relocated into the main building, in the mid 1980's. The now, out-dated equipment is still in place, but no longer used.

Across the courtyard from the business buildings, adjacent to the old mortuary, sits a converted, double storey barn, which George and Julie proudly call home. The exposed oak beams, visible in the kitchen, give a hint to the building's former existence.

Julie Ann Mason enjoyed her morning routine. Sure, sometimes it wasn't easy getting out from under the covers, but then she'd never been a 'leap out of bed full of sunshine' kind of person, and she firmly believed they only actually existed in TV commercials for breakfast cereal or cat food.

Mornings were usually hectic, sometimes a struggle, but always rewarding.

Throughout her childhood, and even into college, it was fair to say that Julie Dupree had been known as a bit of a tomboy. Growing up with two older brothers, meant weekends were usually spent playing football, being chased by the farmer for building scrap wood dams across the local stream, or playing made up, rough and tumble games, such as Death Ninja Squad. Traditional girly games didn't feature highly during Julie's childhood.

During the first week at junior school, Thomas Scott, the class clown, thought it would be fun to tease Julie about her name, calling her Julie Dopey. Her reaction sent him to the welfare office with a bloody nose, and only enhanced her rough and ready image.

Young Tommy Scott, and indeed anyone from Julie's past, would never have imagined that the girl with the scraped knees and the handy right hook, would now like nothing better than preparing breakfast for her Husband, and spending the day with Oliver, their 10-month-old Son.

Marrying George caused a profound change in Julie. She realised, that despite her boyish upbringing, she actually had quite old values when it came to how a marriage should work. As the owner of the family's funeral business, George had a stressful job, and Julie knew that by managing the running of the house, she was doing her bit for the family business. She had helped out in the office for a while, but the sights, sounds, and occasional smells, of the funeral industry aren't for everyone, so now she does what she can by supporting her family from the relative comfort of their home.

This morning was no different. By the time her Husband had showered, shaved and dressed in his dark grey pin striped suit, Oliver was in his highchair at the table, more wearing his cereal than eating it, and George's place was set with his breakfast of warm croissants and black coffee in the mug she'd had made for him for Valentine's Day the previous year, decorated with the words 'I want your body, isn't such a turn on, when your Husband is a Funeral Director.'

Julie knew that George wasn't much of a

conversationalist in the mornings. The pressures of running the funeral business, as well as the usual stresses associated with organising and carrying out any funeral service, usually meant that breakfast time was fairly quiet, but no matter what was going on at work, he always made sure he spent breakfast time with Oliver, and watching the two of them together, chatting away in their own unique way, it was clear to Julie that Oliver wasn't just the apple of George's eye, he was the entire orchard!

CHAPTER 5

It is said that some families only come together for three things in life - hatch, match and dispatch. A birth, a wedding, or a funeral.

One of the many things George's dad taught him, is that funerals are similar to weddings. One is a celebration of a union, whilst the other is a celebration of a person's life.

Families need to organise dates, venues, music, catering, flowers, outfits, even photographers, vehicles, churches, ministers, balloons, doves, horse drawn carriages, who is staying where with whom, and how people are getting to the venues.

You could spend thousands of pounds on either, or as little as possible, for a simple registry office wedding or simple cremation, it makes no difference, you won't be any more or less married, or dead than the next person.

The amount of money spent on a funeral is not a gauge for how much that person will be missed by their friends and family, and neither should it matter to the Funeral Director. Duty of care extends to the family, not just to the person who has died, and a good FD will treat everyone the same. Wise words which George always remembered, especially when arranging funerals for his less salubrious clients.

One such client was a man called Joseph John Harris, but only his mum got away with using his full name. Other close members of the Harris family got to call him Joe or JJ, but most people who knew him, knew him as Trigger. The police knew him as trouble.

George met Trigger three years ago when he came to the funeral home to speak to him about arranging the funeral for his mum, who had died just two days earlier, in hospital. He wanted the best funeral he could afford, but that wouldn't be a lot, as they had no insurances or funeral plans in place.

Trigger had been led through to the arranging room located next to George's office.

The arranging room was decorated in neutral colours. A couple of paintings, one of a vase of flowers, and another of a countryside scene, added some subtle colour to the walls, and a grey carpet with white flecks covered the floor.

A glass fronted cabinet housed shelves of hand written journals, detailing funerals carried out by Geo. Mason dating back over many years. The invoice for the first funeral George's grandfather ever conducted, when he was just twenty years old, was framed and hanging on the wall above the now purely decorative fire place. It details the funeral for a Mrs Mabel Olive Jordan whose funeral took place on 24th June 1947, costing £21 15s 6d.

Other than the cabinet, the room contained a dining table with six chairs that wouldn't have looked out of place in a farmer's country kitchen, and two cream 2-seater leather couches off to one side, to allow more informal chats, depending on the client's preference.

Trigger was definitely a leather couch type of client, as sitting at the table would have been too formal for his liking. George gestured for him to sit and offered him a drink.

George liked to leave clients alone for a few minutes, so they could feel more comfortable in their new surroundings, before discussing often very traumatic details. He left Trigger for a few minutes and made the cup of tea with four sugars that he'd requested, and returned to find him leafing through a coffin brochure, not showing any interest in the prices.

George had taken to Trigger almost immediately. He was a simple man with simple needs, unfortunately, one of his simple needs was to have what other people owned, without paying for them, which frequently tended to put him on the wrong side of the law. Not a man with exemplary morals. But what he did have, was a deep respect for death and anyone associated with it.

Throughout the arranging process, George soon realised that Trigger hadn't been ignoring the prices in the catalogues because money was no object, because clearly it was, but because he simply couldn't read. George didn't make a fuss about this, he just completed the forms as much as he could himself, then passed them to his client for signing. This didn't go unnoticed by Trigger, and once the meeting had ended, he shook George's hand, and simply said "You're a good man Mr Mason, you've done me a solid. I'll never forget that."

CHAPTER 6

T he text message was short and to the point
'The Dungeon, 10pm'

It had been just over a week since Nic's arson attack on The Old Barn, but now he was already being summoned for his second trial.

In its previous life, The Dungeon had been a glitzy nightclub known as Chyna Beach. The road it was on, was set back from the main thoroughfare, and throughout the 80's and 90's had been popular with teenagers attending the two local colleges. An urban redevelopment plan had been initiated at the start of the new millennium, and the introduction of trendy bars, restaurants and coffee shops, had brought a new style of socialising to the high street. The redevelopment swept up the high street like a Mexican wave, one trendy shop giving birth to the one next to it, as people saw the trend changing and wanted to be in the right place at the right time.

Unfortunately, Chyna Beach, being on a road

parallel to the high street, but one row back, remained largely untouched by the new money upscaling the area, and it soon started to look its age. The owners sold it and moved on, and the club became The Dungeon. The demographic of the clientele changed from young college kids looking to piss their bursary up the wall, to more alternate tastes such as Goths, Emos, and Manson wannabes, both Marilyn and Charles! Although still a club, The Dungeon was now anything but glitzy.

Nic arrived almost an hour before his deadline, and watched the entrance from the secluded doorway of a charity shop opposite. He squatted low in the doorway, and couldn't be spotted; hidden from view behind a couple of black sacks of donations, clothes by the feel of them, left there for the shop's volunteers to take in when they opened up the next morning.

As he waited, watching the club for any signs of activity, he nervously wondered what would be in store for him, behind its doors. Was his second trial in there, or was it just a place to meet, or pick up instructions?

According to the local news, no-one had been in the pub at the time of Nic's arson attack on the Old Barn Pub, but the owner's two Alsatian dogs had died. The smoke probably killed them before the flames got to them, but their charred remains had been recovered by the fire crew. Nic wasn't affected by the loss of the dogs, he'd never had any pets growing up, and didn't share other people's affinity toward them. He was however, quietly relieved that there had been nobody at home, although he would never admit it openly. Such a weakness would have been exploited and punished.

With just a few minutes to spare, and not having seen anyone enter or leave the club, Nic left his hidden vantage point, and walked to The Dungeon's front entrance. The black double doors were decorated with pictures of chains, skulls and strange runes, and as Nic opened one of the doors, he couldn't help but wonder just how prophetic the club's name would be.

The dimly lit hallway, with its fake industrial pipework and steampunk themed décor, led directly to a wide staircase, descending to the main body of the club. The hallway and staircase were deserted, and the only noise Nic could hear, was the squeaking sound his Reeboks made as they lifted from the grimy parquet floor with each step.

Nic wasn't surprised that the club was empty, it was mid-week, and even Goths had day jobs to worry about, but he also had no doubt whatsoever that it wouldn't have mattered if it was the club's busiest weekend, and The Cure's tour bus had broken down directly outside, if the Mad Hatters said the club was to be empty, then empty it was. A request from the Mad Hatters wasn't something to be taken lightly. A lesson that the owner of The Old Barn was learning the hard way.

When it came, the attack was fast and vicious. Nic was young, fit, strong, and knew how to fight. He had been fighting all his life and rarely came out worse off than the other guy, or often guys, and his attackers knew this.

The first thing that happened, just as Nic reached the bottom of the stairs, was a bright light, shining directly into his face. Instinctively, he raised his arms to shield his eyes. That's when the point of the baseball bat was driven into his solar plexus, much like a police SWAT team breaching the door of a crack house.

Nic's reactions were good, but he could do nothing to prevent the bat from delivering the debilitating blow. Falling forward to his knees, Nic desperately tried to gasp for air to clear the overwhelming nausea that he now felt. Before he could take a breath, a second blow, this time across the top of his shoulders, sent him crashing to the floor.

Nic's attackers wasted no time in raining blows down on him. Fists, bats, and feet were battering him all over. He knew he had to move. Staying down on the floor left him defenceless and open to attack. Despite the onslaught raining down on him, Nic managed to get to his hands and knees, ready to push himself up, and vault forward, confusing his attackers for the briefest moment, and giving him the opportunity to get to his feet. The opportunity never came. Nic saw the movement as just a blur, too fast for him to react in his prone position. The bat made a sickening noise as it connected with the side of his head, and he was once again, flat on the floor.

Before the sweet relief of unconsciousness overtook him, Nic heard an unfamiliar voice. "See, Dominic Watson ain't all that".

~~~~~~

Nic had pissed blood for three days following the attack at The Dungeon. His body had been battered and bruised, his nose and cheek bone fractured, at least two ribs had been busted, and his right hand must have been stamped on, as two of his fingers needed resetting. The combination of his ribs and nose had made it difficult to breath or sleep for a while, but he had slowly regained his strength, as bones knitted, and swelling subsided. One thing was for sure, whoever attacked him didn't want him dead, or he'd not have regained consciousness. That could only mean one thing – his second trial was over.

CHAPTER 7

George had been born into the funeral business. Growing up with conversations over dinner about new embalming techniques, coffin manufacturing, or the best ways to dress a deceased person affected by skin slip, were just as normal to him as other families discussing the latest crime thriller on TV, or chatting about the weather. Death was never a taboo subject in the Mason house, in fact it was rare to go a day without it being discussed at one point or other.

This, sometimes, caused problems at school. Kids would tease George that his house was haunted, or that his dad was the Grim Reaper and carried a scythe when he went to people's houses at night to steal their souls. He knew a lot of it was ignorance, and always struggled to understand why most people were afraid to discuss the only thing that is guaranteed to happen to every person on the planet.

Because the funeral home was, in part, attached to their home, young George was no stranger to the back-of-house workings. Even though he was never allowed in the same room as a deceased person, by the time he was eight-year-old, George understood well enough the processes involved from the time a person dies to the day of their funeral.

When he was eleven, George's dad took him to the joinery workshop, and showed him different techniques for dressing coffins, explaining the various emblems to place on the head-end of the coffin, depending on the person's belief or religion. A simple rose for most Church of England Christians, a crucifix, RIP, and sacred heart for Catholics, as well as the Sikh Kanda, Hindu Om, and Square and Compasses for Masonic funerals.

When the workshop was quiet, and he was allowed, George would practice dressing coffins of different sizes and qualities, under the ever-watchful eye of Tommy, his dad's second-in-command. They ranged from delicate little caskets designed for babies, to large, full sized adult coffins that were too big for him to even move. One time, the workshop had a coffin in it that was so big, it looked like a wardrobe, and took 3 people to move it when it was empty, but Tommy wouldn't allow George to practice on that one, in case it fell on him!

On his fifteenth birthday, George's dad handed him an envelope containing a contract his parents had written. As long as he kept up with his studies, and it never interfered with his schoolwork, he could spend time in the workshop during the weekends, and would now be allowed to dress coffins that would actually be used on funerals. George would be paid for his work as long as Tommy agreed that the quality was good enough. George knew that wouldn't be an issue, 'Make it like the bairn' was Tommy's way of berating other members of the team if they'd miss dressed a coffin.

Although George still wouldn't see a deceased person for another three years, his journey into the world of working within the funeral industry had begun. It would teach him many things, and as he continued to study at school, then college, George's real skills were being learned the more time he spent within the walls of the business that bore his name.

The one indisputable fact that George learned is that everybody dies. That sounds obvious, but only people working in the funeral industry truly understand just how much of a game leveller death really is. It doesn't matter if you're a millionaire living in a mansion with staff catering to your every need, or you struggle to make ends meet each month and live pay day to pay day. No matter your religion, beliefs, skin colour, sexual preference, abilities or disabilities, some day, when your time is up, you will die.

You may be a law-abiding citizen, a criminal, a drug dealer or a nun, a King or a man who has nothing, and living on the street, it is all irrelevant once your time comes. Certain lifestyle choices may affect the timing of the inevitable, but nothing on this earth can prevent it.

CHAPTER 8

Francisco Juliano had emigrated to the US from the sleepy fishing village of Marzamemi in Sicily in 1971. For as long as he could remember, Francisco idolised the likes of Franco Columbu and Muhammed Ali. Larger than life sporting heroes who had been driven enough to achieve their goals.

He was in his mid-twenties when he arrived in Venice, California with nothing more than the clothes he wore, and a dream of opening his own gym. The whole world had become fitness obsessed, and this is where he wanted to make a name for himself.

Unfortunately for Francisco, reality was a harsh mistress, and it wasn't long before he found himself working in the engine room aboard a Norwegian owned cruise liner, bound for England. The work was hard and the pay was poor, but the work kept him fit, and at least he had a roof over his head, even if he did have to share a cabin with five other staff. Francisco's Sicilian charm and toned body didn't go unnoticed with the women working on board, and the galley staff were only too happy to keep him well fed, as long he returned the favour by catering to their needs too.

After working tirelessly aboard the ship for 6 months, Francisco was in the best shape of his life, which is why he decided to once again pursue his dream of opening his own gym, only this time, he would try his luck in the UK.

Hard work, dogged determination, and a large amount of good fortune, meant that within 18 months of arriving in the UK, Francisco Juliano opened his own boxing and fitness gym.

Over forty years later, much had changed in the world of fitness. Isometric cross-training equipment, computerised treadmills, pro fitness Pilates reformer equipment. None of which were worth the cost of the paper the operating instructions were printed on, as far as Francisco was concerned. If you needed more than gloves, a punch bag, a skipping rope, free weights and a boxing ring, then 'Julie's' as it had affectionately become known, was not the place for you.

Even though he was now close to seventy, Francisco still opened up the gym at 5am and closed it at 10pm. Just like the gym that bore his name, he was dated, battered, and showed signs of wear and tear, but despite that, he could still hold his own with some of the guys half his age.

Dominic Watson had been a regular at Julie's for the past seven years. Francisco had seen promise in him from an early age, as he had seen something rare in someone so young, and it wasn't something you could easily teach. Nic simply had no fear. He would train and spar with people older and stronger than him, and he would simply not quit, no matter how many times he was bruised or blooded. His drive and determination reminded Francisco of himself as a young man.

CHAPTER 9

T heodore Weston is 20, energetic, enthusiastic, and eager to impress. He is also very naïve, trusting, and green around the gills. Most of the team call him Theo. Tommy chooses to call him Dory. The big Scotsman once explained to George that it's because he just seems to move around in circles, forgetting everything.

Today, Theo would be spending his time with George, in the actual mortuary. Facials, embalming, and the removal of pacemakers, are all key elements of the funeral business, and George liked every member of his team, to have, at least witnessed the processes first hand. How can you be expected to answer a grieving family's questions regarding these processes, if you've not seen them for yourself?

Today was Theo's chance, and he had been counting down the days, ever since George mentioned it to him just last week.

Tommy, of course, had not been quiet about

the subject, and had been ribbing Theo about it all week, but even the big Scotsman's horror stories about arterial spray, noxious gases and injecting embalming fluid directly into eye balls, had not quashed his excitement.

Theo put on the surgical PPE that had been left out for him. Latex gloves, plastic apron, sleeve protectors, and a full visor face mask, then knocked tentatively on the mortuary door.

George opened the door. "Come in young man, and say hello to Mr Nicholas Smith."

George always encouraged his team to talk to the deceased people in their care. It helped them to keep in mind that the people they look after, are still someone's loved one, and should be treated with great respect.

Theo walked past George, into the room, and said "Hello sir" to the deceased gentleman lying on the mortuary table.

"Nicholas, this is young Theo," George turned to face the room after closing the door, "he will be joining us on our little embalming adventure today." Then in a theatrical whisper, directed at the deceased Mr Smith, added "He's a little green around the gills, but don't worry, I have high hopes for him."

"So, Theo, as you can see, I have prepared Nicholas here, by stripping and washing him with disinfectant, then laying him on the table, with a sheet covering his lower half. He may be dead, but still deserves to keep his dignity."

Theo looked at the man lying on the stainless-steel mortuary table. He looked to be in his seventies, about 6 feet tall, and had various tattoos on his arms and hands. By the designs, he was probably in the navy at some time in his life.

George talked Theo through the embalming process before he made the first incision, so he had an idea of what was about to happen. He explained to Theo that he was about to witness some unusual sights and smells, and if he felt faint at any time, just say so, and leave the room. There's no bravado in the mortuary. Theo agreed, so George started the process by using a scalpel to make an incision in the right side of Mr Smith's neck.

Theo had seen quite a few dead bodies in his relatively short time at Mason's, but this was the first time he'd seen one being cut open. He took a big gulp of air, and moved closer to watch George raise the Carotid Artery, then use some surgical equipment to hold it in place, and clamp it after cutting a small slit with his scalpel.

George described the workings of the embalming machine as he worked, explaining the different chemical solutions to use in different circumstances, and different mixtures to achieve various results.

George inserted a metal rod into the artery, from which, a clear rubber tube led to the glass jar on top of the embalming machine. Once the machine was switched on, George released the clamp, and blood started to flow along the tube into the jar.

"Once we have drained about 90% of the arterial system, we will reverse the flow and introduce the embalming liquid," George explained as Theo watched the jar fill with red liquid, "we will then continue to the next stage, which is to aspirate the internal organs. For that, we use one of these."

George held up, what looked to Theo, to be a pointed, hollow metal pole, about 2 feet long, with holes drilled in the end.

"This is called a trocar, which besides being a great word for Scrabble, is what we use to aspirate the internal organs. The tubc is attached to this end, and the embalming machine extracts the fluid from inside the chest and stomach cavity as we go."

As he talked, George continued with the embalming process. The peach-coloured embalming fluid was now flowing from the machine, into the tube in the side of Mr Smith's neck. George massaged Mr Smith's arms, hands and fingers, to aid the flow of chemicals through the bloodstream. Theo watched amazed, as the he saw veins fill with the liquid, and he could even see skin gaining a healthy colour as he watched.

Once the first stage of the process was complete, George clamped the artery and removed the tube and rod. He then attached the tube to the trocar in preparation for the second stage.

George again, took his scalpel, but this time made an incision in Mr Smith's belly, a few inches to the side of his belly button.

"OK Theo, we will now use the trocar to aspirate the internal organs. This is the only time you can ever use force, or anything resembling violence, towards a deceased person. If you're going to feel a bit iffy, then this is the time."

George picked up the trocar, and placed the tip into the incision in Mr Smith's belly. "I will demonstrate, then I want you to have a go, so you understand the process fully." With that, he pushed the stainless-steel rod into the incision, up towards the upper chest.

"We want to aspirate the upper cavity, moving in a fan like movement, before changing position and doing the same in the lower half. Our first point though, is to pierce the right atrium of the heart, so from here, I aim at the person's left ear, and that will find the heart."

Theo watched, as George forcibly pushed and pulled the metal poker, back and forth inside Mr Smith. The sound of the embalming machine sucking the liquid along the tube as George continued puncturing the internal organs, reminded Theo of the suction tube the dental nurse uses, to remove excess spit from his open mouth.

The chemical smell of the embalming fluid made Theo feel a little nauseous, and his eyes stung a little, but he didn't allow it to distract him from the fascinating sight before him.

"OK young man, it's time for you to have a go." George removed the trocar and handed it to Theo. "There's a knack to it, but you'll soon get a feel for where the tip of the trocar is. You'll need to put some effort into it, but you'll get the idea."

Theo placed the tip of the trocar back in the incision and tentatively pushed it upwards, into the chest cavity.

"Give it a bit more force Theo, but not too much. You need to pierce the organs, but not come through the skin. That's better." George double patted Theo on the back. "See Nicholas, I said you were in good hands, Theo's a natural."

After a few minutes, George took over control

of the trocar again, and continued to aspirate the lower cavity; as before, working in a fan like movement to ensure full aspiration. As he did so, he explained the process of removing a pacemaker, which is vital if the person is to be cremated, as well as the much more difficult process of embalming someone who had been to a coroner and had a post-mortem.

By the time George had finished explaining the complexities of embalming a PM case, as they are known, he had finished embalming Mr Smith.

"Just a few stitches, then another wash and hair wash to do and we're all done. While I finish up here, how about you go and stick the kettle on?"

Theo removed his PPE and placed them in the clinical waste bin, before leaving the mortuary. As he walked to the tearoom, he knew he wouldn't forget the name Nicholas Smith in a hurry. After all, it's not every day you get to legally stab someone in the heart.

CHAPTER 10

T o most people, a Funeral Director is a large, often bearded, rotund character, wearing a black suit, a black top hat, and waving a stick around as he walks in front of a hearse. A person most likely to be portrayed in a film by the late, great James Robertson Justice.

While it is true that this is the public image most people see on the day of a funeral, Julie was well aware that working in the funeral business is a 24/7 job, and it is not a career or life that is suited to everyone, or their families.

If a person dies in a hospital, they are transferred to the mortuary to rest in a temperature-controlled environment, until the doctors have completed the necessary paperwork, and the funeral director has been instructed that the deceased person is clear to be transferred into their care.

Care homes, nursing homes, and most hospices are not equipped with mortuary rooms, and definitely no private address has one, so a

Funeral Director has to be available at all times of the day and night to be ready to transfer a deceased person into their care, as well as offer help and advice to families who had just lost their loved one.

Julie had become all too accustomed to holding-off serving up dinner because George was going to be late home, or being woken up in the middle of the night by him gently telling her that he had been called out.

Today was just another example.

George walked into the house just before 6pm. Julie had seen him approaching the house through the kitchen window, and was pouring his coffee as he walked through the door. As usual, George's first words upon entering the house rang out "Where's my Oli-phant?"

Oliver gave a shrill noise from his baby seat at the kitchen table on hearing his dad's voice, and George immediately walked over and picked him up for a cuddle.

Julie walked over, kissed her husband, and placed his steaming coffee on the kitchen table.

"Work OK hun?"

Between gargles, goo-goos and raspberries, George replied to his wife's question.

"Let's just say I'm glad it's Friday. It's been a fairly steady week, and nothing's gone wrong, but I am very much looking forward to spending some quality time with my number one guy." Oliver squealed as George tickled his belly as he spoke.

"Just him, eh?" Julie asked in a mock hurt voice.

George looked at his wife over the top of Oliver's head, "Oh I think I might be able to spare a minute or two for you too Jules," he joked, "it all depends how good that coffee is!"

"Oh yeah, coffee comes first," Julie flicked the tea-towel at her husband's back and continued the banter, "get your priorities right after all. I know better than to compete with a good cup of coffee!"

George spoke to Oliver in a stage whisper, "A good cup? Mummy would be lucky to compete with any cup!"

"I heard that, George Mason!"

"Oh no, Oli, we're in trouble now, Mummy's using Daddy's full name, let's run!"

George ran comically around the kitchen table, with Julie chasing after him. It looked like a scene from a slapstick comedy film, and little Oli was giggling as they ran.

After the third lap, Julie grabbed hold of their son, and they pretended to play tug of war with him. Eventually George let go, and picked up his cup. Tasting the coffee, he quipped "Mmm, not too bad, I might keep you around for a bit longer!"

Now it was Julie's turn to 'whisper' to Oliver "Sounds like Daddy wants to sleep on the couch tonight! Yes, it does!"

"Oh Jules, before I forget, I just need to pop out and pick up some photos from Mrs Collins. It won't take long, but she'll only be home this evening and she's got no transport."

"No problems hun, could you grab some milk while you're out?"

Before George could reply, his phone rang. He checked the caller ID and recognised it immediately. The police control room.

George grabbed the pad and pen from the kitchen side, and walked into the lounge to take the call. He never liked discussing work in front of Oli.

After a few minutes, he returned to the kitchen, and Julie knew their plans had just changed.

"Sorry babe, it's a coroner's, and it sounds like a

difficult one. Charlie and Theo are on call, but I'm going to need to go with them as it will be Theo's first time."

"Of course, hun, you need to be with them. Do you want me to pick up the photos from Mrs Collins for you?"

"That would be a great help if you can, I'll write down her address."

Julie bounced Oliver in her arms as she spoke, "We don't mind do we Oliver? We need to get some milkies anyway, don't we?"

George wrote down the address details, then called Charlie, then Theo. They would meet back at the yard, and all travel out in the ambulance.

George tore the piece of paper from the pad, and handed it to Julie. He kissed her on the lips, then kissed the top of Oli's head.

"Thanks Jules, sorry about this, I'll be back as soon as possible." As he walked out the door, he turned back and added, "Save some of those cuddles for Daddy, big man."

CHAPTER 11

N ic massaged his hand as he walked to the showers. Just over two months had passed since his last meeting with the Mad Hatters, and he was nearly back to full strength. After a heavy session with the punch bag, the ache in his hand was the only reminder of the beating he had received. Rather than see this as a negative, Nic remembered the humiliation of feeling helpless and used it to fuel his training.

Modern gyms had state of the art shower rooms, with pulsing shower heads, steam rooms and of course, complimentary, soft, white fluffy towels and hair dryers. Francisco's philosophy differed – if you want a shower at Julie's, either bring your own towel, or stay wet.

After his shower, Nic sat on the wooden slatted bench with his towel on his lap, and drip dried for a while. It was then that he noticed the red flashing light on his phone indicating he had a text message. Without giving it a second thought, he touched his fingertip to the sensor to open his phone, then tapped the text icon with his thumb.

'The Kenyan Cafe. Friday @ 6pm. Bring wheels.'

Nic read the text, then read it again to make sure he was seeing it right. He was starting to think that something had gone wrong, and the Mad Hatters were done with him, but here it was, his call to the third and final trial. He had three days to prepare himself, and clearly, the first thing he needed to do, was find himself a car.

Nic had stolen plenty of cars over the years, sometimes for profit, sometimes for fun, and once just to piss off a teacher who had told him he would never amount to anything; and he had employed various techniques to get the job done.

His teacher's car had been a simple case of going into the school car parking area, and punching a screwdriver through the lock of the driver's door. The car was an old Vauxhall Cavalier, built before central locking and car alarms were fitted as standard, and it was the work of just a couple of minutes to find the correct wires and hotwire the ignition. Nic aimlessly drove the car around for the rest of the afternoon. By the time the car had run out of petrol, it had two punctures, and the bodywork had been redesigned by several walls and knocked over sign posts. Nic simply abandoned it on the side of the road where it stopped.

Stealing random cars for money, or specific cars stolen to order, meant using a technique that wouldn't cause any damage to either the locks or windows of the car. Damage meant less profit. Carjacking was an option, but the possibility of the unknown, meant it wasn't without its dangers.

One guy called Herbie, who lived in Nic's neighbourhood as a kid, had once tried to jack a Merc in a supermarket carpark. He had approached the car just after the woman got into the driver's seat after placing her shopping bags in the boot. Unfortunately for Herbie, he got his timing wrong, and the woman had already started the car. In the struggle, she managed to get the car into gear, and it lurched forward, slamming the driver's door against a wall, knocking him under the rear wheels of the car. His resulting broken ankle and pelvis meant he spent several weeks in hospital and three years in Bedford prison. His limp would last the rest of his life.

The easiest way to steal a car is to have the keys. No damage, no alarms, and no suspicious witnesses. All it takes is knowing the right place to look.

~~~~~~

Nic lived on the Kirkwood Farm estate, on the

East side of town. A mixture of flats, terraced and semi-detached houses. A few of the council houses had been privately bought, and the front gardens had been converted into driveways, so the owners could park their cars as close to their front doors as possible, but the majority of the cars were parked in garage blocks, in separate areas, at the ends of the roads. This made the garages an easy target for thieves, but were unlikely to serve Nic's purposes.

Nic checked he had everything he'd need before leaving the house, then walked down the road and along St James' Road, which took him to Darwin Park which sat between the council estate of Kirkwood Farm and the privately owned houses of the more affluent Ann Boleyn Estate.

Nic walked past the play park with its vandalised swings and slides, and around the heavily graffitied skate park. Tags from various gangs were displayed among the usual football team names and rude slogans. At the highest point on the skate park's half pipe was a triangle of letters. The letter M above an A and D, the upper points of the M serving as the points of a crown. The unmistakable tag of the Mad Hatters.

A line of evergreen trees neatly dissects Darwin Park, and there is no mistaking on which side you are standing. As Nic walked through the trees, he emerged onto a well-lit playing field, with a basketball court on one side, all weather tennis courts on the other, and an immaculate, fenced off, bowls green and club house near the Western edge of the park.

Nic exited the park through the open wrought iron gates, and walked up Woodley Avenue into the heart of the private estate, where the detached houses with their private drives and porches, were hidden from the road by well-maintained trees and hedges.

The residents of Ann Boleyn Estate include local councillors, doctors, solicitors, and at least two football players. Crime was low, gardens were lovingly manicured by teams of private contractors, and the roads were new, well maintained, and cleaned twice a week. Clearly having councillors living in your road comes with certain benefits. Then there were the cars! BMW, Mercedes, Audi, VW, Porsche. There was a reason that Ann Boleyn Estate was better known as Little Berlin Estate. Apart from the occasional Jag or Tesla, the German car market had done very well in this part of town, and that suited Nic perfectly.

It took Nic just over an hour to find what he was looking for. The car on the driveway to the side of the house was a two-year-old, white, BMW 540i M Sport. Nic didn't know what the

Mad Hatters had in store for him, so a powerful saloon seemed the best option.

He had originally seen a 2 litre Audi A5 that looked like it could be useful, but the driveway had become brightly lit by security lighting as soon as he'd approached.

The house with the BMW couldn't have been more ideal. No security lighting, or alarm box on the front of the house, and after careful observation, Nic was comfortably sure there were no dogs in the house. Keeping to the shadows, Nic made his way nearer the house so he could see into the porch.

The owners of this house had obviously never been victims of a burglary before, and had become lazy and complacent. No alarm, no PIR lighting, and exactly what Nic had hoped for, a set of keys sitting on a cabinet in the porch. Easy to pick up on the way out of the house, easy to drop back onto the side as you pass through the porch on the way back into the house. Easy for someone with Nic's skills to steal, without the owner's knowledge.

The exterior door was upvc with double glazing, and would be fitted with at least a three-point locking system. Not easy to get past, without causing serious and loud damage. The window on the side of the porch was of similar design, so again would be difficult to open without alerting anyone inside.

Nic knew that most exterior doors had one fairly obvious security flaw. A large hole at a convenient height, with no locks and no security.

Nic lifted the outer cover to the letter box, and propped it open with a piece of wood he had bought with him. He placed a rag on the bottom lip of the letterbox to help deaden the sound and pushed his extended telescopic magnet through. Originally intended to help mechanics retrieve screws and bolts accidentally dropped into inaccessible parts of a car's engine bay, Nic had replaced the original magnetic tip with a neodymium magnet, meaning it could now comfortably manage to lift up to three kilos. It took him less than a minute to silently retrieve the keys from the side, and use them to drive his newly obtained car off the drive.

CHAPTER 12

A fter stealing the BMW, Nic drove straight to Barker's car lot on Priory Street. Nic had stolen cars to order for Micky Barker in the past, and knew he had several lock-ups tucked out of the way of prying eyes.

Micky had been known to strip a stolen car down to its component parts, and have them boxed and ready to be shipped in less than eight hours, but Nic knew that a car stored there for the Hatters would be perfectly safe. Micky might be dodgy, but he wasn't stupid.

~~~~~~

Nic spent Friday morning trying to stay as relaxed as possible. Half of him wanted the hours to fly by, so he could begin his ultimate trial, and the other half wanted time to slow to a snail's pace, as he tried to imagine what form the trial might take.

An hour's bag session at Julie's helped to focus his thoughts. He visualised the attackers involved in his previous trial with each punch, elbow and knee planted on the patched up, leather punch bag. The pain in his hand, a reminder of what he had already endured in order to achieve his goal.

Nic stood in the shower following his work out, his head bowed and his hands stretched out in front of him, pushed against the wall of the cubicle. He let the steaming water fall on his shoulders until his skin complained about the intensity of the heat.

He had been working towards this day for almost four years. He was finally one step closer. All he had to do was to get through whatever lay ahead of him today, then bide his time for the right opportunity. His promise to Kelly would soon be fulfilled.

Nic took hold of the silver St Christopher pendant that he wore around his neck, and raising it to his lips, said a silent prayer. He then gave it a kiss. "Love you Sis"

At 1pm he wandered past the train station, to Netty's Café. He didn't know what was ahead of him, or when he'd next get the opportunity to eat, so thought he should be prepared. An all-day breakfast and two cups of tea should do the trick.

Netty's was a typical greasy spoon café, catering for most of the building trade in town. People who had walls to build, floors to lay and scaffolding to erect, who wanted high calorie fuel at a reasonable price.

Netty provided this in abundance, and was much loved for it. The flat above the café had once flooded and caused water damage to the café's walls and electrics. After the word hit the grapevine, the café was up and running again within 24 hours. New electrics, new plastering, and fully redecorated.

No-one would accept a penny from Netty for their work. She has never forgotten the generosity, and certain people still get an extra sausage with their order, and free refills on their drinks.

There was never any trouble at Netty's. Partly due to the fact that the usual clientele were builders and plumbers with hammers and wrenches attached to their tool-belts, but also because Netty herself was rumoured to have had a bit of a chequered past, and was well known in certain circles.

Nic never knew just how true these rumours were, until he tried to pay for his breakfast. As he placed his money on the counter, next to the till, Netty placed her hand on top of his. "No charge today Dominic," she said, looking him straight in the eye, giving his hand a comforting squeeze, "it's your big day".

Nic arrived at Micky Barker's car lot just before 5pm. He had an hour before he needed to be at the Kenyan Café, and he didn't want to chance the car being spotted before then.

Micky saw him crossing the sales yard, and came out of his hut to meet him. "Today's the day huh?" Micky said in his unique accent, which seemed to waiver somewhere between Welsh and Spanish. Nic had never known where Micky was from, he just knew to always check his fingers after shaking hands with him, to make sure his rings were still there.

Despite Micky being a foot shorter than Nic, it didn't prevent the odour of stale fags and cheap coffee from invading his nostrils.

"I've checked the fuel, oil, and water, and changed the plates so you're good to go" Micky said, as he half skipped next to Nic to keep up with him as they walked towards the lock up. "The tracking unit and remote immobiliser have been deactivated too. We don't want any excuses, do we? I'm having her cleaned now"

Nic ignored the not-too-subtle dig. There won't be a need for excuses. It didn't matter what the Mad Hatters had in store for him, Nic had made a promise to Kelly, and nothing on this earth was going to stop him from keeping it.

Nic reached the double doors of the lock up

just as the man who washes Micky's cars came out. Nic knew he had some sort of nickname, but never had bothered remembering it. He just knew that he washed cars, and always seemed to scurry around like a rat or a ferret.

~~~~~

The Kenyan Café may have the same business classification as Netty's, but that is where any similarity ends. No self-respecting plumber is going to be seen ordering a gluten free, maple and pecan pinwheel pastry and a grande, half-caff, mocha latte, especially considering you can get a full English breakfast with tea and extra toast at Netty's, for the same price.

The modern, boho chic furniture, and 60's patchwork gypsy design, appeals to young professionals who want to feel a connection to a decade even their parents weren't alive for, and who worked in industries that didn't even exist ten years ago, let alone back in the era of free love. Professions such as App Development and Internet Security. Of course, the café provided free Wi-Fi to encourage the right sort of people to stay longer. Why rush back to the office when you can continue to work from the comfort of a genuine vintage Camden tan leather couch, and eat overpriced pretentious pastries?

The Kenyan Café is now completely unrecognisable from its previous incarnation as

'The Plaice To Eat' fish and chip shop, and although no longer used as a storage room for sacks of potatoes and drums of oil, the back room is still accessed by a side entrance once used for deliveries, completely separated from the main café itself.

It is in this room, that a select few members of the Mad Hatters now wait for the arrival of one Dominic Watson, gang initiate.

CHAPTER 13

It was only a short drive from Micky's car lot to the Kenyan Café, but Nic didn't drive straight there. Instead, he turned away from the high street, and drove to the top of East Street to visit his sister. He parked the BMW in the allocated parking area, and walked over to see her. He regularly kept her updated with news about his life, and had told her about each of his initiation trials, knowing she alone would understand his reasons for wanting to join this notorious gang.

Nic openly chatted with Kelly about what may lie ahead. Telling her how he felt, and asking her to pray for him, and help him to find the strength he would need to make it through the next few hours.

After finishing off with his customary 'Bye little Sis, be seein' ya', he stood up, brushing the cut grass from his knees, leant forward, and kissed her headstone.

Dominic and Kelly Watson may have been

physically separated by six feet of earth, but as he walked along the cemetery path back towards the car, the first solar-powered lamps that were dotted around on various graves, flickered into life as the daylight dimmed. Strings of fairy lights, like blue fire-flies, led the way along the path, and Nic knew in his heart that his sister was right there beside him.

CHAPTER 14

N ic parked on the opposite side of the road to the rear entrance of the café, leaving the car pointing down the hill towards High Street. He crossed the road, side stepping a large, silver Mercedes with blacked out, privacy windows, that was parked at the curb, and approached the inconspicuous looking door that led to the back room of the cafe. He knew where the entrance was, everybody did, but no-one dared to use it without a direct invitation. Nic opened the door for the first time, and walked through. At the end of a dimly lit, short alleyway, there was second door, and this one had someone standing in front of it.

Nic knew that there was no turning back now, not that he would have done, even if his life depended on it, which as far as he knew, it did.

At 6' 2" Nic's athletic frame didn't leave a lot of passing room in this tight space, so he knew that this person would have to move, either by choice or by force, as there was no way he was going to show weakness by backing up. As

Nic approached the doorman, looking straight through him to show him how inconsequential he was to him, the guy put his hand behind his back.

For a couple of seconds there was no movement from either man. Nic showed no expression on his face, whilst at the same time being very alert to this guy suddenly pulling out a knife, baseball bat or even a gun from behind his back. The doorman paused long enough to see what Nic's reaction would be to this perceived threat. When none came, he gave a small nod of his head, then turned the handle that was behind him, opening the door to the back room.

Upon entering the room, Nic was met by further members of the gang. The doorman stayed outside. The smell of testosterone was palpable.

Nic was pretty sure he had seen all of the people in the room before, either at the gym or just on the street, but there was one person he recognised in particular. He had remained perfectly calm when faced with the possible threat of a doorman with a weapon, but now, standing just feet away from this man, Nic felt an adrenaline rush that made him catch his breath.

Four years ago, as his sister lay before him, dying in a hospital bed, Dominic Watson had made a promise, that he had spent every day since, working towards fulfilling. The reason for that promise, was now sitting at a table, talking to someone on his mobile phone, and it took every ounce of Nic's self-control not to discard his plan, leap over the table, and mule kick this mother fucker straight in the face, snapping his neck in the process. If Nic could guarantee that he could reach his target before the two giant slabs of meat that sat either side of him could react, then that is exactly what he would do, regardless of the resulting consequences.

Nic knew that the man in front of him was actually called Victor, but it would be a very brave or stupid man who called him that. He was Hightop. Sitting at the table, wearing a grey two-piece Tom Ford suit and £800 Santoni shoes, he wouldn't have looked out of place dining with city bankers at The Ivy. His designer suit and expensively managed hair, may allow him to move in high class social circles, but Nic doubted the society elite were aware of just how callous and ruthless he was. Hightop had been the leader of The Mad Hatters for the past 10 years, and no-one keeps that position for that long without making, and breaking a few enemies.

Hightop wasn't the sort of person who had 'been there, done it, and got the t-shirt', he was more 'Having seen someone wearing the t-shirt, had him dragged off the street and beaten, to find out where he'd bought the t-shirt, then ransacked the shop and left it in flames so no-one else could have the same t-shirt'.

Hightop gestured for Nic to sit down in the seat opposite himself and his crew, and he did so without question. At least being sat at the table would remove Nic's temptation to ruin his chances of redemption by making a rash move.

Nic sat quietly for a few minutes while Hightop continued with his phone call, nodding his head occasionally whilst listening to the person on the other end of the call. He barely acknowledged that Nic was sitting opposite him.

Classic assertion of power. Nic even wondered if the phone call was real or just a ploy to assert dominance in the situation. Nic knew that he would be waiting for as long as Hightop wanted.

Nic took the opportunity to take in his surroundings. He was sitting at a large, round wooden table, with four, very large men sitting opposite him, two either side of their ignorant boss. The room was large, and had an industrial quality about it. Several pieces of mis-matched furniture were dotted around the room, and off to one side was a dart board and pool table. A kitchen area displayed cupboards, a sink, fridge, and a kettle and coffee machine. Clearly this was an R&R area for the Mad Hatters to chill after a busy day extorting, dealing, and violence.

Immediately to the right of where Nic had entered the room, was a set of stairs, leading up to the next floor. Nic guessed that this was where Hightop would normally be found, at the heart of the nest, with his workers protecting the access points.

After several minutes, the phone call was ended by Hightop hanging up. He had barely said a dozen words all the time Nic was waiting, and now he looked at Nic as if seeing him for the first time.

"So, you are Dominic Watson," Hightop said in a slow and controlled manner, no doubt more intentional power play. Nic knew it was a rhetorical question and remained silent.

"I don't personally know you, but I've heard things, but I'm sure you've heard of me."

Nic didn't know whether to feel relieved that this designer suit wearing prick didn't recognise him, or to be more enraged that he clearly had no recollection or remorse regarding the events that ultimately led to Nic now sitting opposite him.

Nic didn't give a verbal reply, just a slow nod as he was certain the statement was just more rhetoric, and there was no actual intention for him to be part of the conversation.

Hightop continued his monologue in the same

measured tone.

"So far, you have successfully completed two trials. The first was to test your ability to carry out a simple task without question. The landlord of the Old Barn won't give us bullshit excuses for missing a payment again.

The second trial tested your strength and resilience, and served as a reminder that no man is too big or tough to be put in their place."

Hightop held his hand out flat as he spoke, and the guy to his left placed a white box onto his palm, about the size of a cigarette packet.

"Now there is just one small task standing between you continuing as a small-time punk, or joining the elite brotherhood of the Mad Hatters, and the next few hours will decide whether you've got what it takes. Not that failure is an option, no-one alive has ever failed the third trial."

This brought about a brief round of laughter and mumbled comments from the rest of the gang members in the room.

Hightop opened the box and pulled out a pack of playing cards, placing the empty box on the table.

As he continued speaking, he casually shuffled the cards. If this was another tool to assert dominance, it was lost on Nic, but neither could he understand the relevance of the cards. He didn't know what this fucker had planned for him tonight, but was fairly sure it wasn't going to include a cold beer and a game of poker.

"This final trial will test your allegiance to the Mad Hatters, and in turn to me, and will tie you to us forever."

Hightop placed the shuffled pack of cards face down on the table, and fanned them out like a magician performing close up magic. He slowly waved his hand over the cards, and looking Nic straight in the face, said "Pick a card Dominic."

CHAPTER 15

George called Charlie to let him know that he'd just taken a coroner's call, and, as it looked a bit tricky, he would be coming out too, and he'd meet them at the yard. He then went into reception, grabbed the ambulance keys off the hook behind the desk, and went to check the necessary equipment was on board, knowing that Charlie had followed procedure, and phoned Theo to alert him of the call.

Fifteen minutes after receiving the call, Charlie drove into the yard, having picked up Theo on the way. They could see George in the driver's seat of the ambulance, already starting to fill out the necessary paperwork, so they both climbed onto the bench seat in the passenger side.

"Evenin' lads," George said after he'd finished transferring the information he'd received from the police call centre, onto the official paperwork kept in the ambulance, "I hope you don't mind me tagging along for this one, I don't want to cramp your style."

Charlie laughed, "Not at all. If it's as bad as you think, the more the merrier."

Theo just sat between the two of them, wide eyed. Not quite believing that his first coroner's call, might be more than just an old lady who'd fallen in a care home.

George had already put the address into the sat-nav, so he set off, and updated the two lads with the information that had been passed to him.

"It looks like a suicide, and a bit of a messy one too. It seems as though a man has checked in to one of the rooms at the Sunnyside Inn, and decided to redecorate it a nice shade of red." Charlie and Theo both scrunched up their faces at the thought of what will greet them.

George continued to follow the electronic voice, instructing him which turns to make. He knew the way there without thinking, as he did for most areas of the town. You soon learn the back streets and short cuts when you drive an ambulance, but he was teaching by example, and asked the team to always use a sat-nav when on coroner's calls. They only had an hour to be on scene from the time of the phone call coming through from the control room, and having up-to-date traffic information, was essential sometimes to meet the deadline.

"The police on scene have said that although he looks to have taken his own life, they can't be sure until the coroner has examined him, so they will be escorting us to the mortuary."

As George drove, he explained to Theo that in the majority of cases, they simply collect the deceased person from wherever they are, and transfer them to the hospital mortuary, so the next day, the coroner can perform a post-mortem exam.

Sometimes, as with this case, the police have suspicion to believe, or can't rule out, foul play, so once they have transferred the deceased onto the ambulance, the police will escort them to the hospital, to ensure the chain of evidence remains intact.

"Or, to put it another way," Charlie said with a grin on his face, "if I've just murdered someone, what's to stop me from holding up the ambulance, shooting the crew, and destroying the incriminating evidence on the body?"

"Maybe a little extreme Charlie, but I suppose anything's possible. OK, game faces on, we're here."

As soon as the ambulance stopped, Charlie jumped out, and opened up the side door. Theo joined him, and they started to don their PPE.

After a quick chat with one of the police officers, George joined them, to do the same.

"OK, our gentleman is in his room, laying face down, on the floor." George turned to Theo, "If this were a house, flat, or the middle of a field, we would do a dynamic risk assessment, so we could work out if there were any hazards to avoid, and what equipment we would need to access tight spaces. As this is an hotel, and one we have visited before, we know that there are lifts big enough for our stretchers, and the corridors and doors will allow us straight access to the room."

Charlie walked to the rear of the ambulance, "This way Theo, I'll show you which equipment we'll need."

The young lad followed, and joined his teammate as the rear door of the ambulance swung upwards.

"We don't yet know the size of the person, so we may well need the bariatric stretcher, so we'll take that, as it has the removable hand carry built in anyway, should we need it." Charlie removed the pin securing the stretcher to the bed of the ambulance, and pulled it out, the wheeled legs automatically unfolding as he did so.

"We'll definitely need a couple of removal sheets, and I'm going to take a few extra just to be sure." He placed a handful of the tightly woven, cotton, disposable sheets onto the stretcher, along with the coroner's pack, which contained extra pairs of disposable gloves, shoe covers, masks, and body bags.

"It is room 320, so we'll take the lift to the 3rd floor." George said as he joined them at the rear of the ambulance.

George and Theo walked into the reception, closely followed by Charlie, pushing the stretcher.

The Sunnyside Inn is part of a nationwide chain, and anyone visiting them, knows exactly what to expect. The ground floor houses the reception area, dining area, and bar, and the décor is the same, no matter which of their 240 hotels you visit. Mainly used by travelling business people throughout the week, and families attending weddings and other family functions at weekends.

They are also visited by Funeral Directors on more occasions than they would like to admit.

CHAPTER 16

Fifty-one cards now lay face down on the table in front of Nic. He didn't understand why this twisted fucker was apparently showing him a cheap parlour trick, but knew that to get through tonight, and eventually complete his four-year promise to Kelly, he had to go along with it.

The card he had selected from the fan was now laying face up in front of him for all to see. The relevance for now, lost to him.

Nic hadn't uttered a single word since entering the back room of the Kenyan Café, and apart from leaning forward to select a card, he hadn't moved in his seat. He didn't understand the bizarre ritual or know what lay ahead of him, but he remained outwardly calm, despite the feeling of pure hatred he felt for the man sitting opposite him.

This changed as he returned his attention to Hightop after turning his card over to show its face value. Nic immediately sat bolt upright as a wave of panic spread over him. He had no doubt it had shown on his face, as clear as a beacon.

Hightop was still sitting in his chair, and nothing had changed, apart from he was now pointing a gun directly at Nic's face.

~~~~~~

"This Dominic, is a Glock 19. One of the most reliable 9mm handguns ever made. It holds fifteen rounds in the clip, and one in the chamber, and is the preferred sidearm of the majority of law enforcement officers, due to its compact size and reliability."

All the time Hightop was talking, the barrel of the gun remained perfectly still, just four feet from Nic's face.

Nic immediately regretted his decision to stop at Netty's before coming here, as his stomach was now threatening to show his all-day breakfast to him for a second time.

Was Hightop on to him? Had this all been a bluff? If so, what was the playing card all about?

The gang leader could see he had Nic rattled, and he gave a little chuckle, knowing he had ultimate dominance of the situation.

With a quick movement of his hand, Hightop flipped the gun around, pressing the magazine release button with his thumb as he did so. The clip slid from the gun's handle and he caught it with his left hand, before placing them both on the table in front of him.

Nic took his first breath in what seemed like an age, and relaxed slightly in his chair. Looking at the gun, he could clearly see the black polymer grip and 'Glock 19 Austria 9x19' written along the side of the slide. He could also see that the magazine housed no bullets.

"I know you're keen to join us, and I've heard good things about you," Hightop said, noticing Nic look at the magazine, "but I don't know you well enough to pass you a loaded weapon. You will receive the bullets in good time."

Nic had acted as hired muscle a few times to frighten people into paying or confessing, and he had used a replica gun before, but purely for show to put the frighteners on people, but he had never actually used a real gun before.

He did know however, that Hightop handing him a loaded gun would have been the last mistake of his life, as the temptation and opportunity would have been too great to resist.

"You've now got the three components you need to complete your final trial, Dominic. You've brought the car, I'm supplying the gun, and you've drawn your card. Now listen close, as

I explain the rules."

CHAPTER 17

N ic pulled open the door and pushed past the guy waiting on the other side. The sound of laughter echoed after him as he stumbled down the short alleyway, to the door that led out onto the street. He pulled it open, and just got over to the car before he threw up. The gun in his jacket pocket hitting against the side of the German car as he bent beside it.

He thought he had been prepared for anything, but so much had changed in just the short time he was in that back room. The goal Nic had been working towards for four years was within his grasp, and sitting across the table from the man who had caused him to start on this journey, had added fuel to the fire that had burned inside him for so long. He had to finish this……. but at what cost?

Nic sat for ten minutes in the car, as per Hightop's instructions. As he sat there, he held on to the St Christopher around his neck and talked to Kelly. Asking her for her guidance and strength to continue with the trial he knew he had to complete, and asking for her forgiveness for what he was about to do.

The knock on the driver's window made him jump back into the here and now, and he turned to see a pair of tree-trunk sized legs. He craned his head up to see one of the giant slabs of meat that had been sitting at the table.

Nic was over six feet in height, but this guy towered over even him, and he was nearly as wide. If a rhino stood on its hind legs and put on a suit, it would still be less menacing than this guy.

Nic pressed the button on the arm rest and the window quietly lowered.

"You'll need these." The man mountain said in a surprisingly high-pitched voice, completely contrasting his physique.

The guy was holding out a hand the size of a bunch of bananas. In it was a red and black box, and a piece of folded A4 paper. Nic took them both without saying a word.

"Don't get any ideas. Just do as you've been told. We'll be watching."

Nic pressed the up button on the window controls as the guy walked back across the road. He placed the box on the passenger seat, and unfolded the piece of paper.

On it, were simple instructions. Set off at 7pm, head along The Embankment and turn right into Church Street. Right again onto Piper's Avenue, then take Hunters Hill back down to the river. Normal speed. Back to Barkers when done.

Nic had grown up in the area and could picture the roads in his head. A circular route of about three miles. No cameras or speed bumps to worry about. No petrol stations or supermarkets with external security cameras, just a couple of independent stores along the river. Their security cameras would be facing inwards towards the till, not out at the road. Someone had clearly considered the route carefully.

The clock on the dash showed 12 minutes until 7, so Nic turned his attention to the box sitting on the passenger seat.

The logo on the box was a black and white eagle on a red background, and the writing left no doubt as to its contents.

'American Eagle, 9mm Luger, 124 grain Full Metal Jacket.'

Nic opened the end flap and slid out a white plastic tray. In it there were 10 rows of 5 slots, each designed to house a single bullet. A full box would hold 50 bullets, but only 6 slots of this box were occupied.

Pulling the gun from his pocket, Nic looked at the 6 golden opportunities that sat in front of him.

Would he be able to end this now? He looked across the road at the door that led to the short alleyway. There were 5 people on the other side of that door, and one standing on this side, and he had 6 bullets. Just a coincidence or a test?

What were the chances that he could get to Hightop and still have a bullet in his gun?

He knew rhino man wouldn't be armed. No gun had a trigger guard big enough to allow his giant fingers to pull a trigger, but Nic suspected that it might take all 6 bullets to take him down alone, and even then, it might only serve to piss him off.

He had to be sure that the time, opportunity and circumstances, were exactly right before he fulfilled his promise to Kelly.

Reluctantly, he pressed each bullet into the gun's magazine, and slid it into place. He still couldn't get his head around the events that were unfolding, with him in the middle, but he put the car into gear, and pulled away from the curb.

CHAPTER 18

As instructed, Nic drove the BMW along The Embankment. The river to the left of him reflected the Victorian lamps that lined the water's edge, and the street lights shone their light onto the road.

The road alongside the river was a popular cut-through for those people in the know, as it bypassed the two sets of traffic lights in the town centre, that were always gridlocked during rush hour. At 5pm, Nic's car would have been sitting nose to tail with several others, all waiting to filter out onto the high street. Now, just two hours later, there was barely a car in sight.

The only car Nic saw approaching on the other side of the road, hadn't reached him before he turned right onto Church Street.

Church Street climbs lazily up from the river, and runs parallel to High Street, but is a slight misnomer, as there are in fact, two churches situated along its length.

The Catholic Church of St Joseph sits on the

right-hand side of the road. The front of the church marked by a 20-foot-high illuminated crucifix.

On the opposite side of the road, and about ½ mile further up the hill, stands the impressive Priory Church of St Peter. Its arched doorway and grotesque gargoyles highlighted by halogen spotlights.

Just as Nic drove the Beamer past the gated entrance to St Peters Church, the driver of a white delivery van flashed his headlights from the opposite side of the road. The game had begun!

At the end of Church Street, Nic had the option of either a left or right turn onto Pipers Avenue. The road was clear, but he sat at the junction for longer than was necessary. Turning right would mean following the rules of this sadistic and twisted game. Turning left would mean something worse.

As Nic sat at the junction, contemplating his options, a car tooted its horn from behind him. Nic jumped at the sound, and looked in his rear-view mirror to see two gang members in a silver Merc. They were mocking him with over exaggerated hand gestures, waving left and right, as if they were reading his mind.

'Wankers!' Nic thought to himself as he put

his foot on the accelerator and turned right. The Merc didn't follow, but instead, turned left, but Nic now knew that he was indeed, being watched as he performed this sickening ritual. He also remembered what Hightop had said in the back room of the Kenyan Café – 'No-one alive had ever failed the third trial'. Nic really had no choice, but to continue with this macabre game.

Pipers Avenue is one of the more sought after addresses in town. The wide, tree lined road, gated driveways and art deco architecture make it very desirable among those who can afford to live here. Residents include both lawyers and doctors, and as Nic drove along, he wondered which of these he would be needing the services of, after tonight.

By the time he had reached the turning for Hunters Hill, Nic had been flashed by three further vehicles – two from cars approaching him on the other side of the road, and one from the car behind him. The unmistakable Angel Eye headlights of another BMW flashed several times in his rear-view mirror as the driver tried to warn Nic that he was driving in complete darkness. As he turned onto Hunters Hill, Nic could see the BMW driver throw his hand up in despair as he carried along Pipers Avenue, never knowing how fortunate he was.

From the high vantage point of the top of

Hunters Hill, Nic could see that there were no other cars on the road, so he was confident that he would reach The Embankment without his flash total increasing. As he cruised down the hill, Nic still couldn't believe what he had to do to get through tonight. It was almost incomprehensible, but he was sure that his life, and the memory of his sister, depended on him finding a way to complete the horrendous task ahead of him.

About half way down the hill, Nic saw a flash of light off to the left side. A bright yellow Smart car had started to pull out from one of the side roads, to turn right, up the hill. The car's driver had spotted the dark shadow of the unlit BMW just in time to prevent a collision. Not so much seeing the actual car, more sensing the absence of light from behind it. The car's headlights flashed again as Nic drew level, and the driver leaned heavily on the horn. Nic could see the female driver gesticulating wildly at him as he passed, no doubt calling him every name under the sun.

As he reached the end of Hunters Hill, and turned right back on to The Embankment, Nic could see a car parked on the left side, near to the river. The front interior light was on, no doubt to catch Nic's attention. It was the same silver Mercedes that had been parked by the Kenyan Café, and Nic had no doubts about who would be sitting in the back, probably laughing at him behind the blackened windows.

The urge to pick up the Glock from the passenger seat and fire all 6 bullets into the rear window of the Merc, was almost too strong for Nic to resist. His hand moved from the steering wheel, and his fingers wrapped themselves around the black polymer grip of the gun. The thought quickly disappeared as night turned to day, and for a split second, Nic couldn't work out what was happening. He dropped the gun back onto the seat, and raised his hand to shield his eyes from the blinding light in front of him. Just as quickly as the light had come on, it disappeared, and Nic blinked hard a couple of times to try and regain his night vision.

The headlights and halogen spotlights mounted on top of the cabin of the tow truck driving towards Nic, flashed again as the driver tried to warn him of the one thing of which he was very aware, that he was driving around the dark streets, with no lights on.

As the tow truck driver passed by, he made a mental note of the car, as he was sure he would be seeing it again later, as he loaded onto the back of his truck, after winching it from the river, or unwrapping it from a lamppost.

Cursing the missed opportunity to put an end to this madness, Nic drove along the side of the river, to begin his second lap of this bizarre and deadly assault course.

The illuminated crucifix adorning the front of St Josephs' Church shone down on Nic, as he once again turned right into Church Street. Over the past four years, Nic had had many conversations with the man looking down at him from the instrument of his crucifixion. During different stages of the grief Nic felt following the death of his beloved sister, he had begged, pleaded with, sworn promises to, cursed and sworn at, any, and all Gods that he thought were listening. He hoped that tonight, none of them could see his actions.

Nic was very aware that six people had flashed at the driver of the BMW who had supposedly forgotten to turn his lights on. Six very helpful, and very lucky people, who had no idea that their very own guardian angel was watching over them tonight.

A car, coming down the hill, but further up, by the Priory Church, flashed its lights, once, twice. Two very quick flashes, not the usual prolonged flash that Nic had seen tonight. Did that count? Were they flashing him? Then Nic saw a red car pull out from a parking spot at the side of the road, and flash its hazard lights as a thank you to the helpful driver who had signalled for them to pull out. Not an addition to Nic's tally then.

As both cars continued down the hill, Nic

watched them very closely as they approached. The inside of his performance vehicle seemed incredibly quiet, and it was only when the red car's headlights flashed a warning, that Nic realised he had been holding his breath. As Nic exhaled, the second car, a grey Ford, also flashed a friendly warning to him that he had forgotten to switch on his lights.

The grey Ford was the eighth car to flash. If the kind person driving it hadn't let the red car pull out of the parking spot, it would probably have been the seventh. But they had, and that made them the eighth.

Nic felt light headed, and had to swallow hard to prevent himself from being sick again. His stomach was cramping as he turned on his lights, and swung the car into the Priory Church car park. He drove a tight circle, then pulled back out onto Church Street, this time, heading down towards the river.

The BMW's 3 litre engine roared into life as he accelerated to catch up with his mark. He had caught a quick look at the number plate after he had been flashed, and saw the last three characters, a private plate, ending in 'MFD'. It was, after all, a matter of life and death to get the right car.

Nic was soon directly behind the small grey Ford. This sick game, and four years of waiting, training, and planning, was now just minutes away from coming to an end.

Nic tried to distract his mind from over thinking what he was about to do. By allowing the red car to pull out in front of them, this person had unwittingly become his stepping stone to gaining entry to The Mad Hatters. Once in, his ultimate plan could finally be put into action, and Kelly could, at last, rest in peace.

CHAPTER 19

T he driver of the small grey car turned right at the end of the road, and continued along the Embankment, until it met the high street, then took a left. Nic knew he had to stay close, but not look too obvious. Anyone can get spooked if they think a car is following them. He kept the BMW at a safe distance, so as to not arouse suspicion, and even signalled for the driver of a black Range Rover, to pull out of a side road, and join the traffic in front of him. Good cover.

The high street changes name after the roundabout on the edge of town, although Nic didn't know what to. He expected the grey car to turn right down Station Road, then continue on towards the various housing estates past the station, but instead, it continued straight on and took the road out of town. This was an unexpected development, but definitely one that Nic welcomed. Very few houses, poor street lights, and light traffic. He couldn't have asked for more. The Range Rover turned right, leaving just predator and prey travelling on the remote rural road.

Nic knew his opportunity was approaching. After another half-mile of winding around fields, the road would straighten and go up hill, and as it does, it opens out into a short dual carriageway. Designed to allow cars to pass slower moving vehicles, struggling with the steepness of the hill.

Nic thought it was a bit of a cliché, but time really did seem to slow, almost to a stop. Was he really going through with this? He was fairly certain that the person driving the car in front, was a woman. Not something he had reckoned on. Should it make a difference? Will it make a difference? He had to exact his revenge on Hightop. He had thought about little else since Kelly's death. He had no choice.

As the road started its steady assent, Nic pressed the button to wind down the passenger window. As the road widened, he pushed his foot down on the accelerator, and the powerful BMW easily drew level with the smaller car. With all the thoughts that were going through his head, Nic hadn't actually worked out the logistics of how to fire the gun. The target was to his left, and he was right-handed. The Glock was designed to be operated left or right-handed, and Nic could hold his left arm straight and brace it against the passenger seat back rest, but he knew that was a weak firing position, especially when firing from one moving vehicle to another.

Nic picked up the Glock in his left hand, and passed it into his right, swapping his hands on the steering wheel as he did so. With his right arm bent in front of him at ninety degrees, and with his left arm straight, gripping the steering wheel at the 12 o'clock position, he was able to rest the butt of the gun on his upper left arm, creating a much stronger frame from which to shoot.

The down side of this position became very apparent as soon as he squeezed the trigger, sending the first bullet flying from the barrel of the gun. The noise was deafening! Nic squeezed the trigger again. Four times, five times, six? He wasn't sure. He dropped the gun onto the passenger seat, and quickly swapped hands again on the steering wheel. Calling out in pain, as his left hand automatically came up to cover his left ear. His eyes were streaming through pain and the gun smoke in the car, the smell of which filled his nostrils.

Nic floored the accelerator, and the German saloon roared up the hill. He looked in his rear-view mirror, and saw the small grey car swerve right, then sharp left. The front wheels made contact with the kerb, and the laws of physics took over. The front of the car was launched upwards, just as the rear wheels met the kerb at a more of an acute angle. The effect was to send the car spinning up and sideways, into the trees that lined the road. All the speed and energy that was being conveyed by the car as it flew through the air, stopped abruptly as the car slammed into a large oak tree. A dead stop.

The BMW raced up the hill. Nic's right foot pressed down on the accelerator as if he were trying to push it through the floor. His pulse was racing. He was half blind with tears and smoke. All he could hear was a high-pitched screaming, caused by the explosions of the bullets leaving the gun. The car was still accelerating. The three-litre engine had power to spare and Nic's right foot was demanding to see it all.

The BMW's wheels scraped along the kerb, and branches hit the bodywork as the car sped along the winding road, which had now narrowed once more. Tyres screeched as the car tried to negotiate a tight turn, but it was going too fast, for even the German car's high tech safety features, to keep the vehicle safely on the road. The left wheels mounted the kerb, and a low tree branch smashed into the windscreen. The passenger side mirror was torn from the door, and a large crack appeared across the front screen, like a bolt of lightning flashing across the sky.

The noise of the tree branch was almost as loud as the bullets as they left the Glock, and it shocked Nic into action. He lifted his foot from the accelerator and slammed it onto the brake pedal. The back of the car fishtailed from the soft grass, back onto the road. The BMW went from over 100mph, to a safe stop in less than three seconds, and Nic sat in the driver's seat, his heart pounding, breathing as if he'd just beaten The Bolt in a sprint race, and shaking from head to toe.

He sat for a few minutes, just staring ahead out of the front windscreen. He had done it. He had actually done it. Nic looked at his hand, then down at the gun that was lying on the passenger seat. It seemed so surreal. Did it really happen? A car was approaching along the road from behind, and its headlights flashed briefly into Nic's car. He realised that he was blocking the road, so had to move before the other car got too close. He didn't want anyone seeing him.

CHAPTER 20

After squeezing themselves and the stretcher into the lift, the three men eventually exited, onto the third floor. They were immediately met by a police officer who was guarding the lift to make sure people didn't inadvertently see anything that would upset them, and she pointed out the direction of room 320.

After so many years attending coroner's calls. George knew most of the police officers in the local area by name, and today was no exception.

"Officer Nick Cunningham! What's the story?"

"Hi George, it looks as though we have a young man who has taken his own life in quite a dramatic fashion." The police officer led the team through the doorway, into the hotel room. "As you can see, there's a lot of blood, due to him apparently having re-designed his own neck with a broken bottle."

George made sure he went into the room first, and had been blocking Theo's view so far, until he had assessed the situation for himself. He turned to the young lad.

"Are you OK Theo? Remember this isn't the place for heroics, if you feel nauseous at any time, just say, and leave the room."

"I think I'll be OK, thank you, boss."

George stepped aside, and Theo saw his first coroner's incident.

Although Theo had seen litres of blood being removed from Mr Smith during his embalming, he never realised that the human body contained so much of it. The white sheets on the bed were red with blood, as were the pillows and headboard. The once tan carpet looked almost black where the blood had soaked in, and there, in the middle of the floor, lay the young man in question. He was naked and face down, laying straight, with both arms up, next to his head.

The second thing Theo noticed was the tattoo. A knight in full armour, riding a horse, carrying a St George standard, covered the whole of the deceased man's back. A castle stood in the background, in grey shading on his right shoulder. Beautiful artwork that would have taken serious money, and hours of dedication, sitting in a studio to create.

Charlie assessed the situation as soon as he had a clear view, and immediately knew how best to transfer the man from the floor, to the ambulance. As always, he discussed it with his crew partner before going into action, so everyone knew the what, how, and when of the situation.

"OK Theo, first, we need a clean area, away from the blood, so we can put on our shoe covers, and put our PPE in a clini-bag once we're done." He indicated that the bathroom next to the hotel room door would be ideal.

"Next, we will lay some plastic sheeting next to the body, and place an open body bag on top. We can then roll him over, so he's face up in the body bag, then lift that onto the stretcher once it's zipped up."

Theo nodded as Charlie spoke, mentally working through the steps in his head.

"The floor area at the bottom of the bed is clear, so we'll collapse the stretcher down there, so we only have to lift the body bag a small distance, then snap the stretcher back up onto its wheels"

"OK," Theo said, "got it."

Once they had both donned their gloves and shoe covers, they placed their equipment just as Charlie had explained, before even approaching the body.

"Right Theo, everything's in place, so it should

all be straight forward. Now, what is the most important thing we do before we do anything else?"

Theo looked around the room. The stretcher was collapsed, with its straps undone, ready for the body bag to be placed on it. The open body bag was next to the body, protected from the bloody carpet by the plastic sheeting. Everything looked to be in place.

"Now we roll him over into the body bag." he said, trying to sound confident in front of the police officers.

George had been standing out of the way, listening to how the two lads worked together. He cleared his throat as Theo answered Charlie's question, and the young lad looked over to see his boss rubbing his hand around his wrist.

He quickly added to his answer, "But not before we've placed the wrist tag on his left wrist of course." he said with a grin.

"Exactly," Charlie said, raising an eyebrow in George's direction, "the wrist tag has to be in place before we even start to move the body."

The two of them carried out the rest of the procedure just as Charlie had described, and once they had placed the elasticated, purple corduroy, stretcher cover over the body bag, they went to the bathroom and removed their PPE, placing it into the clinical waste bag, which they then closed with a zip tie.

Charlie and Theo pushed the wheeled stretcher back to the ambulance, while George carried the bag of waste. Both were loaded onto the back of the ambulance, and the rear door was closed once the stretcher was secured in place. All three bowed as the door clicked shut.

"Right Nick," George called across, as he climbed into the driver's seat of the ambulance, "we'll follow you to the mortuary."

"So, what did you think of your first coroner's then Theo?" George asked, as he pulled out of the hotel car park.

"It was er, interesting," Theo answered, still trying to process the whole experience, "I just find it really difficult to understand why someone would do that."

"That, young man, is a question that is impossible to answer. I have attended too many suicides to count, and each time, I am at a loss as to why it happened."

Theo sat quietly thinking for a few minutes, before adding, "But it makes no sense. Why would someone invest so much time and money, on such impressive ink, then do that to themselves? I don't get it. Don't get me wrong, I'm not saying that the loss of the tattoo is more important than the loss of life, it just doesn't sit right in my head that someone's mindset can change that much."

"Don't worry mate," Charlie replied after he'd finished the phone call he had been making, "we know exactly what you mean. You can't always know what is going in someone's life or in their head. There isn't a set type of person, or a specific profile when it comes to suicide."

"Which is why I encourage you all to talk to each other," George added, as he pulled up next to the police car at the entrance to the hospital mortuary, "this can be a very tough job, and I don't want anyone to keep thoughts or worries to themselves. We are all here for each other."

Charlie got out of the ambulance, and rang the doorbell on the side of the mortuary door. During the day, the mortuary staff would answer within minutes, but out of hours, the mortuary is unmanned, and the ambulance crew have to wait for the night porters to make their way down to the mortuary, from elsewhere in the hospital, which is why Charlie had called ahead. The door was opened almost immediately. The porters always prioritised the mortuary, when they knew it was a police-escorted, coroner's!

Mortuaries are functional buildings that serve a specific purpose within a hospital, so are therefore nearly always very similar in design, and, because no-one likes to advertise the fact that people die in hospitals, they are nearly always tucked away, around the back of the hospital complex and accessed via small service roads.

This stark white, clean room, housed rows of fridges, each containing five stainless steel mortuary trays, sitting on rollers. Some fridges were intentionally wider than others, and some were just small domestic fridges as you would find in any home. It is a sad fact that bodies come in all ages and sizes.

Charlie and Theo wheeled the stretcher into the mortuary, and removed the corduroy cover as the hospital porter drew out a mortuary tray using the mobile scissor lift. As George transferred the deceased person's information from his paperwork to the hospital's 'Community Intake' form, Charlie and Theo transferred the deceased from the stretcher to the mortuary tray. Officer Cunningham observed from a comfortable distance.

The porter had placed the now occupied tray, back into the fridge, and was just closing the door, when Officer Cunningham's radio broke the silence. The people in the room couldn't hear what was being said, just that there was a voice in his earpiece, but the look on his face changed dramatically as the information was relayed to him.

They all heard his reply. "Roger that Control, but there's no need. He's here with me now."

CHAPTER 21

As instructed, Nic drove the BMW back to Micky's garage. As he pulled into the yard, the weasel guy approached the car, opened Nic's door, and said something to him. Nic just stared at him and shook his head. He had no idea what had been said, as he was still only hearing whistling noises, but it was clear that he urgently wanted him out of the car.

Nic stood up out of the car, and Trigger jumped in, and drove it through the open doors of the main garage, where a team of people set to work with pneumatic wrenches, cordless drills, sockets and spanners. Before morning, the car would be stripped down to thousands of component parts, destined to fulfil orders already placed across Europe.

Nic wasn't sure what was happening. He was in shock and everyone was moving fast around him. People were shouting, swearing, and pointing. He heard someone say something about a fucked-up mess. He was led over to a Luton box van, and told to climb into the back.

His mind was racing. What mess? He had done as he was tasked, and thought it had all gone to plan.

He felt like an automaton. He was just blindly following instructions, and not really understanding what was going on. Inside the van was a pile of heavy-duty boxes, empty and folded flat, a sack barrow, straps and bungee cords, and large rolls of bubble wrap. He found some removal blankets near the bulkhead, where he dropped to his knees, before rolling onto his side in the fetal position, chatting constantly to his sister as he did so. "I did it Sis, you are one step closer to being free".

A driver and passenger entered the cab of the van, and it pulled away. Nic neither knew, nor cared where they were going. He just wished this damn ringing in his ears would stop.

The van drove steadily for almost an hour, before Nic sensed they were stopping. The driver called out to someone, and they answered. Nic couldn't make out what was said. A gate squeaked open, then the van started moving again. Just a short trip this time, five minutes, maybe less. The van stopped, and so did the engine. Wherever their destination was, it appeared as though it had been reached. Both cab doors opened, then closed, and Nic could hear different voices. Four, maybe five people. The sound of the van doors closing and the sound of the voices, had a distant echo to them. Nic got the impression that they were inside a building, but the sounds were wrong. A cavern maybe?

One of the voices got louder as it approached the rear of the van. The roller door was pushed up, and Nic saw where they were for the first time.

During the mid to late 1930's the Air Ministry bought thousands of acres of farmland, and converted them into various runways and airports, to house fighter and bomber squadrons, in readiness for the growing threat in Europe. These airports were vital to the RAF during World War II, and were often targeted by German bombers. Once the war ended in 1945, those airfields that survived, were used for different purposes. Some were kept on by the RAF as training bases, some were converted back to farmland, sold to property developers for much needed new housing, and some, like this one, were bought by private investors to be used by farmers, glider clubs, or private and hobby pilots.

The hanger was vast. Looking around, Nic could see several heavy construction vehicles parked up at one end, like sleeping yellow dinosaurs, drums, crates, and scaffolding were stacked near some cabin style buildings, but the most impressive vehicle was just fifty yards in front of him. The plane was a 1992 Beechcraft 1900D, originally designed to carry 18 passengers. This one had undergone some interior modifications. Most of the seats had been removed, allowing for a larger cargo area to now exist at the rear of the plane. The six seats that remained could be positioned to face forward or back, or with just a pull of a lever, could be removed entirely to create yet more cargo space.

Nic looked at the majestic beast in front of him. With its aerodynamic design, T-shaped tail, upturned wing tips, and two large propeller engines, it looked sleek, modern, and fast. Most of all, it looked expensive. Surely the Mad Hatters didn't have access to the sort of funds needed to own a plane? Nic couldn't help but be impressed, and for the first time, he questioned whether his ultimate goal was either achievable, or indeed wise.

"Get on board then," the booming voice belonged to the guy who had ridden as passenger in the van, a large, heavy set man, with a face like a bulldog chewing a wasp, "I'm your hostess for today, but don't think you'll be getting any extras, I'm not that type of girl!" he let out a deep rumbling laugh, and turned to one of his colleagues, "Oh bless him, he's still in shock. It was his first."

Nic walked towards the plane, being half guided, half pushed by the big man. "Hightop wants you off the ground and out of the way as soon as possible, we need to draw the heat away from the Hatters. You need to disappear."

As Nic stepped up onto the stairs on the rear of the fold-down door, near the cockpit, he stammered "Wh...er, wh... where are we going?"

The big man answered in his gravelly voice, "Away Nic, just away. There's been a complication".

CHAPTER 22

F our pairs of eyes were staring intently at the Officer, as he finished his radio conversation. It was very clear that Officer Cunningham had just heard some shocking news, and it appeared to involve someone in the room. Four minds were frantically thinking, panicking, and pleading that the man in front of them, wouldn't make eye contact with them next.

"I'm sorry George," Nick said in a voice which seemed to make the mortuary even colder than it was, "but can I speak to you outside please?"

"Nick, what is it?" the panic clearly heard in George's voice.

"Can we just step outside George, I really thi. . ."

"No Nick," George shouted, his mind already dreading the worst, "just tell me what's going on."

Officer Nick Cunningham had known George for over four years, and had worked with him many times. What he had to say next, was probably the most difficult sentence of his entire police career.

"It's Julie and Oliver. There's been an incident."

George felt as though the floor had been removed from beneath him. It was if he was falling into a hole without actually moving.

George's mouth moved, but no sound came out, then it was if his brain caught up again.

"Incident? What do you mean incident? Where are they? I need to see them. Where's my family Nick?" George's frantic questions fired out of him like a gun, each one sounding more desperate than the one before.

George took a step towards the Officer, but his legs buckled from beneath him, and he fell into the stainless-steel table next to him. Boxes of gloves, folders and paperwork went flying across the floor, as George fought to stay upright. Charlie and Theo both rushed over to him, but George held up his hand, warding them off.

"Come with me George," Nick said, walking towards the stricken man, "I'll take you upstairs to Julie, she's in the ED now."

The walk from the mortuary to the Emergency Department took about 8 minutes, and the two men passed many people on the way. To George, it was like an underwater dream. He knew people were talking, but he could only hear sounds, not words, and he had no idea where he was going, even though he knew the hospital well. The part of his brain that was still functioning, just knew to stick with Nick, and that was all he was doing. It was if he were being operated remotely.

On entering the A&E Department, Nick approached the triage counter and spoke with the nurse behind the plexi-glass screen. She pointed to the left, and pressed the button releasing the lock on the door leading to the ED room.

George stumbled through the door from the public area, to the sterile smelling Emergency Room. Sounds changed from the chatter of a dozen people waiting to be seen, to beeps and hushed voices, but he still couldn't make out words, or believe this was real. Again, Nick took the lead, and approached two doctors who were reviewing a patient's charts at the nurse's station. George blindly followed, like an obedient cocker-spaniel.

Less than a minute later, George was being ushered into a private waiting room by a kind looking male nurse. He looked back at Nick as he was led forward, to make sure he was doing the right thing. His brain was just a fog. He saw Nick give a little nod, just as he entered the room.

The nurse gestured for George to sit on the

couch, and asked if he could get him a drink.

"What?" George said in a confused tone. He had only heard fragments of what was said to him.

"Would you like a hot drink Mr Mason?" the nurse said patiently, squatting on his haunches in front of George, "A sweet tea might help with the shock."

"Tea? Er, yes. Tea. Please, yes." George's brain was desperately trying to work out what was going on, and why he was here. "Where's my wife and my son? I need to see them. Something's happened. Where are they?"

"Doctor Gibson will be in to see you shortly, and he will update you," the nurse explained as he stood up and walked to the door, "I'll go and get you that tea, but I won't be a minute."

As the door closed, George looked around the room. Soft furnishings in neutral colours. Walls in similar colours, with a couple of inoffensive pictures on the wall to add just enough colour. A box of tissues sat on the small wooden table, next to the couch he was sitting on. He recognised the style of room immediately. He had one just like it, located next to his office. This wasn't a room where people had casual chats about the film they watched, or which reality TV star, was dating which. This was a bad news room. Where the fuck was this doctor!

As if answering George's mental cue, the door opened, and a female nurse walked in, and handed George his tea. She was closely followed by a tall man wearing a light grey suit.

"Thank you for waiting patiently Mr Mason. My name is Mr Gibson, and I am the Consultant Neurosurgeon here at the hospital, and I am reviewing your wife's condition."

"Wait, what?" George spat out the words as he sat upright and put his cup on the table. "Neurosurgeon? What's happened to my wife, and where's Oliver?" George stood up, and shouted, "Where is my son?"

"Please sit down, Mr Mason, I need you to remain calm, as we have a lot to discuss."

The nurse, who until now, had been standing with her back against the door, walked over to George, and taking his arm, sat down with him on the couch. She knew that Mr Gibson was a great surgeon, but also knew that he wasn't the best at giving the sort of news that George was about to hear.

"George," she said, looking him directly in the face. He voice was calm with a soft Irish tone, "your wife and son were involved in a serious car accident, which the police are investigating."

She looked up at Mr Gibson, and he nodded his approval that she continue.

"It appears as though someone fired several shots at your wife's car while she was driving, and she was hit in the shoulder and the right side of her chest." she paused and watched George's face to see if he understood what she had just said.

George just stared at her. "Shot? What do you mean shot? Someone shot my wife?" It sounded perverse to George to even say the words. This wasn't the sort of place where people got shot. There had to be a mistake.

"I know how difficult it must be to hear this, but I'm afraid it's true. Apparently, several shots were fired directly at your wife's car."

George looked into the nurse's eyes, and forced himself to ask the question that he knew he didn't want answered.

"My son was in the back of the car," his mouth was dry, and his lips were quivering as he spoke. He could see the answer in the nurse's eyes, even before he asked it, but he had to hear it out loud, "where is my son now?"

"I am so sorry George . . ."

"No, you're wrong!" George shouted as he

jumped to his feet, "You're wrong! Where is he? Where's my boy?" George paced up and down the room as he shouted out the questions.

"I'm so sorry," the nurse said again, "but I'm afraid Oliver didn't survive the accident Mr Mason. He was hit by a bullet too, and died instantly."

"Shut up! Don't you fucking tell me that my boy's been shot! Where is he? This is fucking wrong. You're all fucking wrong!"

Angela Higgins had been a nurse for over eight years, and this was the one part of her job that never got any easier. Apparently, she was good at it, which is why most of the doctors asked her to accompany them when news of a death had to be given to a relative. She wished she wasn't. She always wanted to be a nurse. Helping people, caring for people, and healing people. Right now, she failed to see how any of those words applied to the broken man in front of her.

Angela knew that no matter how bad she felt right now, it was the mere tiniest fraction of how George felt. She would finish work, go home, and have a very large glass or two of the Shiraz that was sitting on the side in her kitchen, to help her to manage with getting up again tomorrow and facing another day. George on the other hand, was facing the end of his world. When he awoke this morning, it was just another day. No different from the other 364 days of the year, but now, this date will forever have meaning. There was no tomorrow for George, just the cold, hard, painful facts of today.

George slumped back down into the couch. His strength was gone. He just sat, staring ahead, not hearing anything that was being said. A thousand thoughts and questions jumbled in his head, all fighting for his attention.

The Consultant must have been saying something, but nothing registered. He didn't exist. The room didn't exist. Blackness and stillness, and a head full of slow-moving thoughts, as if trying to think through treacle.

One word invaded George's inner sanctum as he sat there, lost and alone. Something the Consultant was saying.

"...Julie..."

As if a light had been turned on, George span around in his seat to face the nurse. "Julie! Does she know? Can I see her?"

Angela already felt bad about having to tell George that his son had died, but now there was more. How much could this poor man take? "Julie was shot in the shoulder and chest, and one of the bullets is still in her. It is lodged in a very precarious place, so we have had to place her into a medically induced coma, for her own safety. Any movement could cause the bullet to move, with the potential of causing further harm."

George seemed to be looking through Angela as she spoke, as his brain tried to understand what was being said.

"Mr Gibson is our leading Neurosurgeon, and is in charge of your wife's case." George turned his head to see where the nurse was looking, and seemed to see the consultant for the first time.

"Mr Mason, I am very sorry for the situation you and your family find themselves in today. I cannot imagine how you feel right now, but I need to explain your wife's condition to you. Are you OK for me to continue?"

George stared at the floor for a few seconds, then looked back at the consultant, giving him a nod to continue.

"As you know, the spinal cord is protected by the spine, which is made up of vertebrae. The area that we are concerned with is the cervical region, which sits between the very top of the spine, and the bottom of the skull. Of the seven vertebrae making up the cervical region, the most dangerous, in terms of damage, is the atlas, which we refer to as C1. The C1 vertebra is the uppermost vertebra and connects the spine to the base of the skull, forming the atlanto-occipital joint, allowing a person to nod their head up and down."

Mr Gibson didn't know how much information George was taking in, but he continued telling the story of his wife's injuries.

"It would appear as if one of the bullets has struck the acromion area of your wife's right scapula, and ricocheted upwards to become lodged between the C1 and C2 vertebrae of the spine."

Mr Gibson looked across at Nurse Higgins, unsure whether George had taken in anything he had said.

"Do you understand what Mr Gibson has told you George?"

George felt as though he had fallen down a very deep well, full of water, and his mind had to swim desperately to the surface before he could answer. In his mind's eye, he was reaching for the surface and frantically kicking his legs. As he pictured himself finally breaking the surface, he physically took a deep, gasping breath, and focused his attention on the suited man in front of him.

"So, you're saying that Julie has a bullet in her neck, and it is dangerously close to the C1 vertebrae. How dangerous are we talking? Can it be removed?"

116

"At this stage, we are unsure as to the exact extent of the damage already caused, but we do know that your wife has had to be placed into a coma, to prevent any further damage. We are in the process of obtaining detailed images, so we can better understand the severity of the situation. The path the bullet took after striking the scapula has already caused some damage to the C2 vertebrae, but again, until the detailed imagery comes back, we are unsure as to what extent."

"So, what are we talking here, speech loss, having to use a wheelchair, total paralysis, what?" George asked desperately.

"It's not possible for us to know yet George," Nurse Angela said calmly, "but we will know more very soon once the computer images are completed."

George appeared to be on pause for a few seconds, not moving, not blinking, just frozen. The practical side of his brain was already redesigning their house to be wheelchair accessible. He was repositioning furniture and building ramps to allow Julie free movement. His business brain was telling him to get a message to the mortuary, so the guys didn't hang around, waiting for him. The emotional part of his brain was feeling as though it had been run over several times by a large lorry, and was trying to somehow process the news about Oliver. All parts of his brain agreed on one thing.

"I need to see Julie."

CHAPTER 23

M r Gibson and Nurse Higgins led George to the ICU. The first set of double doors sucked open as the consultant held his ID badge up to the scanner. Only once they were all through the doors, and they had fully closed, did a second set of doors open ahead of them.

George was shown to a changing room, where he had to put on surgical grade PPE, consisting of overshoes, a gown, disposable head cover, gloves, goggles, and face mask. He was no stranger to full body PPE, but these somehow felt very alien to him.

The exit door was remotely controlled, and once he was ready, he pushed the green mushroom button to the side, and the door opened, again making a sucking noise as it did so. Like before, a second door opened in front of him once the first had closed.

Mr Gibson was similarly dressed, and waiting for George, beside the door to a separate room.

"I know that given your job, you are used to

seeing things which may cause alarm, but I still need to explain something before we go in," Mr Gibson 's voice was muffle through his face mask, "Julie is in a very serious condition, and is being very closely monitored. She has been intubated, and an ET tube is in place, so the ventilator can assist with her breathing, due to her being in a coma. Once we are in there, I cannot stress enough, just how important it is that your wife is not moved. As difficult as it may be, I urge you to keep your distance."

George nodded that he understood, and both men entered the room.

Julie was lying in a single-bed ICU room, surrounded by several pieces of equipment, each with a screen displaying lots of numbers and graphs, and emitting various beeping sounds.

Initially, George was afraid to approach for fear of tripping on a wire or stepping on a tube. The room looked like something out of a sci-fi fantasy film, but instead of a human/cyborg hybrid lying in the bed, it was his one true love. At first, it was hard for him to even recognise the beautiful woman he had kissed goodbye to, on his way out to the coroner's call. Electric leads were stuck all over her, and her face was obscured by the face mask and breathing tube. Her eyes were closed and looked badly bruised from the accident.

Part of George's brain kicked in as soon as he had that thought. The cold, prehistoric part, that lives at the back of everyone's mind somewhere, always there, but rarely given a voice. It was angry, and it was shouting. This was no accident! Someone deliberately did this to Julie, and to Oliver! Someone will pay dearly for this!

George looked at Mr Gibson and he motioned that it was OK for him to step forward. He gingerly approached the prone figure of his wife, lying on the bed, being kept alive by the various technology around her.

"I am so sorry my angel," George said quietly, his voice barely a croak. He cleared his throat and continued, "if I had gone to get those stupid photos from Mrs Collins instead of you, you would still be at home now, and Oliver would . . . "

George was unable to finish his sentence. His brain wouldn't allow him to say it out loud, as it would then be real. He wiped the tears from his face, and sat down in the chair positioned beside the bed. His face just inches from Julie's.

"What happened baby? Who did this to you? How is any of this real?" Another wave of tears fell from George's eyes, and he was powerless to stop them. Mr Gibson watched helpless, as George sobbed uncontrollably for several minutes.

"I Love you so much Mrs Mason, please be safe. The doctors say that there is a possibility you will be OK, and will walk out of here, but I just want my Jules back, no matter what. I am so, so sorry. Once the doctors have seen exactly where . . . ."

Again, George was unable to finish his sentence, but this time it was because of several loud alarms that suddenly screamed from various pieces of equipment. Lights and numbers were flashing on multiple screens, and within seconds, ICU staff members came crashing through the door.

Everything happened at once. Mr Gibson grabbed George by the arm, and hustled him out of the door. George heard commands being given by the ICU team leader, "Clear the room please!" and "Check BP" before the door closed behind him, leaving himself and Mr Gibson in the ICU corridor.

"What's going on? What's happening to my wife?" George frantically shouted through the mask, "Tell me what's wrong!"

"I don't know George," Mr Gibson said, letting go of George's arm and turning to face him, "your wife's vitals have dropped, but the ICU crash team are doing everything they can to make her stable again. I won't know more until the team leader apprises me of the situation. Even I'm not allowed in the room when the crash team are working."

George was pacing the corridor like a caged tiger, with both hands, on top of his head, elbows out to the sides. "This is too much, just too fucking much, what is going on?"

Two more members of ICU staff ran along the corridor towards Julie's room. Mr Gibson tried to ask one of them a question, but they ignored him and entered the room, as if he wasn't there.

"I'm really sorry George," he said, gesturing defeat with his hands, like a waiter carrying an invisible tray, "all we can do is wait until the team leader is in a position to talk with us."

Time stood still for George. He put his back against the wall, and slid downwards until he was sitting on his haunches. There were noises, voices, and people moving around, but they were all in a different world and a different time. George no longer existed in their world. How much more could he take? There, slumped down in an ICU corridor, with the world moving frantically around him, George did the only thing he could do to help – he prayed.

"George."
"George!"

George looked up from staring at the floor between his knees. He didn't know if he'd been there a minute or an hour. Time meant nothing. As he looked over to the direction of the voice calling his name, he saw Mr Gibson just finishing a conversation with another doctor. Beside him was Nurse Angela, barely recognisable thanks to her full PPE.

On seeing her, George knew it wasn't going to be good news. He looked over, pleading with his eyes that it wasn't true.

From the second that Mr Gibson turned from his conversation, and spoke to Angela, the body language said it all. No words were necessary.

George's world crashed.

Blackness.

CHAPTER 24

George was aware of noises. People talking. Footsteps. A distant phone ringing. He opened his eyes to find he was lying in a hospital bed, in a private room. Looking around, trying to get his bearings, he saw Holly sitting in a chair beside him, with a magazine on her lap.

"Mornin' Boss," Holly had thought about what to say to George, and how to say it. How can words ever do justice at a time like this? She decided familiarity was best, and hoped it wasn't the wrong thing to say, "are you well?"

"Holly? What happened? Why am I in hospital?"

"You passed out in the corridor, and hit your head on the floor. The doctors just wanted you in for observation." Holly felt out of her depth, being the first person George spoke to after losing Julie. Nervously, she added, "Tommy is here too, he's just gone to grab a coffee, you know what he's like!"

George's head was spinning, and his throat was

dry. "Er, yeah" he replied, a little unsure of what was going on. Then he noticed the tears that Holly was desperately trying to hide, and like a tsunami wave, his memories came crashing back. Julie!

"They didna' have tomato soup, so I got you a hot chocolate, I hope that's . . ." Tommy was talking as he entered the room, carrying two vending machine drinks in plastic cups. He was walking backwards, pushing the door open with his back, but stopped suddenly when he turned and saw where Holly was looking.

George was sitting up in bed, with his head in his hands. His fingers where white with pressure, as he pulled at his hair. Raw emotion was balled up inside him, and as the details of Julie's death hit like a hammer to the face, he screamed! It sounded like a large wounded animal. Primal, urgent, something from another time. Holly screamed at the sound.

Tommy quickly placed the drinks on the side, and ran over to George. He wrapped his arms around the screaming man, as if trying to hold him together for fear he would break apart. Holly joined them, and the three of them cried together, rocking gently on the hospital bed.

The doctors were reluctant to allow George to leave the hospital without conducting further tests, but Holly witnessed first-hand, just how persuasive her Scottish colleague could be, and after just a cursory check-up, George was released into Tommy's care.

Tommy drove George back home, while Holly rode her motorbike back to her place. She didn't really know how to help George at the moment. He was her boss and her mentor, and he was in pieces. Tommy said it was OK, as he knew it would be a difficult thing for her to have to deal with. The fact was, he didn't exactly know how he was going to deal with it either, and didn't want anyone else around to witness either George, or himself, floundering.

The following week passed in a haze for George. Tommy took on the running of the business, which was only right, given his position as George's right-hand man, and the rest of the team worked hard to make sure every client received the very best service as always. George had lost everything in his world, except for his business, so they were damn sure he wouldn't lose that too.

Holly dealt with the paperwork, and Tommy acted as Funeral Director for the two funerals they had that week. Three other local Funeral Directors offered whatever help was needed, so there was no shortage of bearers when needed. So many people made contact with offers of help and support - crematorium staff, grave diggers, celebrants, religious leaders of all faiths, care home managers, cemetery workers, and so many families from previous funerals, stretching back years, sent flowers, cards and gifts of condolence.

George didn't leave his house that week, he spent his time mostly sitting on his bed staring at the ever-present Julie shaped void, whilst holding Oliver's favourite toy, a cuddly koala bear. Tommy moved into the house, sleeping in the guest room, so George wasn't alone at night, and all the team checked in on him throughout the day, to make sure he was at least eating and drinking. Holly's mum, Laura, made sure he was never without a casserole, curry, apple pie or bread pudding.

Everything changed on the eighth day following Julie's death. Holly had been waiting for, and at the same time, dreading, the arrival of one particular email. When she started up the office computer that morning, it was there waiting for her. It read:

'You are hereby given notification from the county coroner, that the post-mortem examinations of both Mrs Julie Ann Mason, and Master Oliver Martin Mason have been completed, and they are clear to be removed from the mortuary.'

"Tommy," Holly called, as the big man walked past the office, "it's here." No further explanation was necessary.

"Shit! Thanks Holly, I'll go over and see him now."

Tommy and George had spent many hours talking since Julie's death. At first, Tommy didn't say too much, he was purely there for George to talk at, shout at, cry on, and on one occasion, punch.

As the week passed however, the talking developed into two-way conversations, and with the help of a particularly fine single malt, Tommy encouraged George to talk about everything – the pain, broken dreams, Julie, Oliver, future plans lost forever, and more imminently, who would conduct their funerals, which is why, after briefing the team, Tommy was now in George's kitchen, telling him that Holly had received the Coroner's email.

The change in George was immediate. He had arranged and conducted thousands of funerals, as had his father before him, and each one was tailor made to suit the needs and wants of the person who had died, and their family. Now it was his turn, and everything, as always, had to be perfect.

"Send Charlie and Theo to the hospital please Tommy," George said, getting up from the kitchen table, rubbing his face, "I'm going to get cleaned up, then I'll be over."

"One step ahead of you, boss," Tommy replied, with a grin on his face, "they're already on their way."

"Good man!" George called back from halfway up the stairs.

CHAPTER 25

All of George's team pride themselves on the level of care they give to the people they look after. The fact that they are deceased, is irrelevant when it comes to the respect and dignity they deserve. Everyone in the team knows to treat the deceased person as if they were their loved one, which they do, or at least, they thought they did!

Charlie and Theo carefully placed the two stretchers next to each other in Mason's mortuary, and they looked the same as any other stretcher that had been there before. The deep red, corduroy covers, with the elasticated edging, covered each body, to allow for dignity during transportation. But, once the covers were removed, it would be a very different story. The words 'normal', 'usual', and 'standard' didn't apply here.

Charlie, lost in thought, jumped, as George approached him.

"Thank you, Charlie," he said, taking the young man's hand and giving it a firm shake, "thank you for bringing them home."

He then turned to Theo, and shook his hand too. "Thank you, Theo, I know it won't have been an easy thing to do, and you both will have taken the best of care, and it means the world to me."

Tommy entered the mortuary, and nodded his head to the two men, "Good job lads, now I think some alone time, eh?" He stood away from the door, so Charlie and Theo fully understood his meaning. Without a word, they both left.

Tommy knew the answer before he even spoke, but it was something that had to be said, "You don't have to do this you know? We can get them ready for . . . ." he stopped when George turned to look at him.

"You know better than that Tommy"

"Ay, boss, but I had to say it, just in case." Tommy turned around, and pulled out a green disposable apron from the dispenser, and a pair of extra-large nitrile gloves from the box. After donning his PPE, he turned back to George, who had already removed the stretcher covers.

The two men worked quickly and efficiently, neither having to say a word to the other, as they had been through this process together, countless times, but both men talked to Julie and Oliver, as they moved them both onto a single mortuary tray, so they could be together again.

George carefully and lovingly put moisturising cream on their hands and faces to protect from the cold of the fridges, and it was only then that Tommy noticed, for the first time ever, that George wasn't wearing gloves in the mortuary. These are his wife and son, he thought, so who could blame him?

After the formalities of measuring Julie, entering hers and Oliver's details in the mortuary register, and updating the name plate on the fridge door, George placed a small, blue, teddy bear with Oliver. They were both covered with a cotton sheet, and a plastic rose placed on top. They once again, appeared the same as everyone else in the Mason's mortuary, as the tray was slid into place, and the fridge door closed.

George turned to Tommy and gave the big Scotsman a hug. "Thank you, my friend, I wouldn't have been in a position to do this, if it wasn't for you."

"It was my sad privilege, George. An honour as always."

The two men separated, and Tommy took off his PPE and placed it in the contaminated waste bin. As both men washed their hands, George asked Tommy to gather the team in the tearoom in an hour. He wanted to address them all together, but had to make some calls first.

Tommy nodded, then went off to inform the team, and no doubt answer a few questions, while George remained in the mortuary.

He stood in front of the fridge door which now displayed Julie and Oliver's names.

"My beautiful Jules, and my gorgeous little man, Oli, I swear to you both, that whoever did this, will pay dearly. I shouldn't be seeing your names on this door. It's just not right. No matter what it takes, I will send them to hell. This is my oath!"

George kissed his fingers, then placed them on the cold metal of the door, and stood with his head bowed for a few seconds, before heading to his office, to start making arrangements.

An hour, and several phone calls later, George left his office, and made his way through the doors which separated the 'front of house' side of the business, with the 'staff only' restricted area. He noticed the smell of wood from the workshop as he walked past, and realised just how much he'd missed it. It made him smile. This business really was a part of him, and it ran through his blood.

There was no noise coming from the tearoom as he approached, not the usual banter or storytelling, and he wondered if Tommy had managed to get the team together, or maybe they had been called out on a coroner's transfer.

He entered the room, and almost lost his composure. The four members of his team were standing there waiting for him, and started to applaud as he entered the room. They all knew that George's world had been torn apart, and he had been lower than most people could imagine, and they wanted to show their unified support.

George laughed, then hugged each member of his team individually, thanking them for keeping him sane and for keeping the company going. He would never forget the dedication and support that each of them had shown.

"OK you lot," he said, as everyone settled down in their chairs around the table, "I asked Tommy to get you all together, so I could firstly, let you all know just how much you mean to me, but I guess we've just covered that, and secondly, I just wanted you to know that I will be conducted the funeral for Julie and Oliver, and they will be cremated together in the same coffin." George took a sip of the coffee that Tommy had handed him whilst talking, to allow the talking to settle down a bit.

"I didn't know that was possible." He heard Theo say, sounding surprised.

"Ay lad, it is for special reasons," Tommy replied, "I've only ever seen it once before, with twin baby girls, and that was a few years back now."

"That's right Tom," George added, "the Gregson sisters, Faith and Hope, that must be seven or eight years ago now, bless 'em. I've spoken with the crematorium, and they have given me their blessing, and because of the personal connection, I have also cleared it with the NAFD."

"They can't object can they boss?"

"I'd be surprised if they did Holly, but I thought it best to make them aware of my intentions, so there's no issue's further down the line. Now, I obviously don't have a date yet, but I do know that it's not going to be a fancy funeral, just something low-key and personal, although, given the nature of their deaths, there will be local press and police present, sorry Tommy, I know you have a special relationship with some of our boys in blue!"

Tommy gave George a big fake smile. "Oh joy!" he said.

"I have left a message for Graham Johns to get back to me, as I know Julie always liked the way he conducted his services, and I need to arrange for an over-sized coffin, so Julie can cuddle our boy forever." George's bottom lip and chin quivered as he said the last few words. Thinking something is always so much easier than saying them out loud.

He sniffed, then added, "Right, that's all. I'm going home for a bloody good drink, and I suggest you all do the same." With that, he put his cup on the table, and left the tearoom.

"Poor bugger" Charlie said, shaking his head, "you can't imagine the shit going through that man's head right now."

"I know," Holly replied, "You should have seen him in hospital that day, it was heart-breaking. Are you staying with him tonight Tom?"

"Ay Hols, I'm not gonna leave the poor bastard to drink that fine whisky by himself, what sort of a friend would I be? Now bugger off the lot of ye, and have a good weekend."

CHAPTER 26

George had never been too interested in computers as a child. He didn't have the games consoles or the high-tech toys that some of his friends would talk about. It wasn't that his parents couldn't afford such things, or that they wouldn't have bought them for him had he have asked. He just simply didn't have an interest. Most of his free time was spent in the coffin workshop when he was younger, and the lure of gaming and computers just seemed to pass him by.

Julie had helped getting the computers up and running, both at home and in the office. She seemed to have an innate understanding of computers and software, even if she'd never seen them before. George guessed that once you have a basic understanding, then you can adapt it to various software packages.

He could do with some of that knowledge now. He was sitting at the kitchen table, with a laptop open in front of him. He knew what he wanted, but had no idea how to find it. The pathways to a world of knowledge were at his fingertips, but he didn't have the map to show him the way.

George had seen TV programs, both fictional and factual, which made reference to the Deep Web and the Dark 'Net, but he was fairly certain they weren't places you could find purely by typing them into Google. He tried anyway, just in case. He found links to books, films, games, and TV shows, plus some YouTube links which looked promising.

After an hour of watching people talk about things, he had no understanding of, following links which led nowhere, and activating several pop-up adverts, George was becoming increasingly frustrated. He had heard terms such as VPN, .onion and Tor search engines, but as far as he was concerned, it was a different language.

George had been walking around his house, in a daze, for nearly a week, but now, finally, he had a plan. Not one that could have been devised by a sane man, but thanks to Dominic Watson, his sanity was in short supply at the moment. He just needed one key ingredient, and so far, it was proving very elusive. He could probably buy it through one of his chemical suppliers, but it was a restricted product, so would leave a clear and definite paper trail, hence his failed attempts to access the darker areas of the internet.

Having resigned himself to the fact that

his computer knowledge was woefully lacking, George, more out of annoyance than anything else, did exactly what Holly would have told him to do – he Googled it.

George typed 'How to buy chloroform in the UK'.

In less than a second, the search engine returned over a million results. Chemical companies, government pages, CoSHH data sheets, even details of a German rock band. Nothing of any use.

Then he saw it. Under the heading of 'Suggested Videos', was a video entitled 'Easy homemade chloroform'.

It was a different approach, and not one he'd even considered possible, but a few clicks later, and the final piece of the puzzle had fallen into place. George's plan was complete. He just needed a few simple ingredients.

Chloroform is used in industry as a solvent, but because of the effect the fumes have on the human brain, it is a restricted product. The nail varnish remover that George was just purchasing from his local chemist, and the bleach which he had bought earlier from a supermarket, were not. He'd used the self-service tils in both shops and paid cash. No reports, no paper trail, no suspicions raised.

George had watched several videos on how to make the chloroform, and even with his limited chemistry know-how, he was confident that, with some of the equipment he had in the old mortuary, he would be able to produce what he needed.

As soon as he arrived home, he placed the bottle of bleach in the freezer, and set about preparing the necessary equipment.

Although he was buzzing like an excited little boy at Christmas, he waited three hours before removing the chilled bleach from the freezer. Apparently, it had to be below -2 degrees, or the process would not work.

George had made detailed notes, taking key points from each video he watched, and he now followed them religiously.

George had returned home from his shopping trip just before 10.00, and now, less than twelve hours later, he was wrapping silver foil around a small brown bottle with a white screw cap, to help prevent the home-made chloroform inside, from degrading.

CHAPTER 27

olleen Buckingham had been a regular name in the local paper, since her disappearance ten weeks ago. She worked as a barmaid at 'The Farmer's Boy', a pub on the edge of town. It was a 17th century pub, with a colourful past. Stories of highwaymen, and having more than its fair share of resident hauntings, including the famous 'Grey Lady', kept historians busy in the local library's archives. The pub was now predominantly frequented by modern day horsemen, in the form of bikers, who had regular meets there, partly due to the pub being situated on a near dead-straight, 2-mile stretch of road. The sound of engines, were often heard screaming along 'Biker's Lane' as it was known locally.

Colleen had finished her shift early that day, just after 10pm, and as usual, had chosen to walk home, despite having several offers of lifts on the back of various bikes. Colleen liked the bikers, they were a good bunch of lads, but the motorbikes scared her, and she would never get on one.

She had two possible routes home, to choose from. The walk along Biker's Lane, down past the post office, and right into Halyard Road was the longer of the two options. On this particular day, Colleen had complained of having a headache, so had finished early, and chosen the shorter route, which took her along the chalk path surrounding Chantry Reservoir. She never made it home. She was reported missing after two days, when she never showed up for work.

Despite extensive searching of the pub, surrounding fields, and the reservoir, by the police, assisted by an army of leather-clad volunteers, Colleen was nowhere to be found.

Almost two months after she had gone missing, a man who had intended to spend a relaxing day fishing, saw something in the water, and hooked it out with his landing net. It was a brown leather bag, and it contained Colleen's phone and purse. Police diving teams, were once again, deployed to the reservoir, and cadaver dogs were brought in to search the surrounding area. On the second day of the search, Colleen's body was found, bent and twisted, inside the large, concrete pipe of a storm drain.

The post mortem, carried out by the County Coroner, determined that Colleen had suffered a massive brain haemorrhage. She had fallen down the incline into the reservoir, but was dead even before she entered the water. She was just 34.

CHAPTER 28

George and Julie had attended a Funeral Director's conference some years ago at a spa and health club, somewhere in Kent. The package included a weekend stay at the spa, with access to various treatments, and the hotel's restaurant. It wasn't really George's thing, but there would be several talks and demonstrations over the weekend, with no obligation to attend. Julie thought it would be a good idea to meet up with people from other funeral companies, so they could exchange ideas and views. Plus, of course, an Indian head massage and pedicure wouldn't go amiss either.

One of the speakers was a psychologist, a Dr Sophie Michaels, and her presentation was on the state of the human mind during times of extreme stress. She concluded that at the time when a person visits a funeral home to make arrangements for the funeral of a family member, their brain is so overloaded, that they will only hear 50% of what is said to them, and only comprehend 7% of that information.

George thought it was a fascinating statistic.

A fascinating statistic then, had become stark reality now. It had been nearly two weeks since Julie and Oliver arrived back home, and George was sitting in his office, staring blankly at the computer screen. He knew the numbers in the spreadsheet's columns meant something, but his brain just wouldn't focus long enough for him to make any sense of them.

George knew he'd had conversations with people, both personal and professional, but five minutes later, he had no idea what had been said, or who had said it.

He was a mess. An automaton, just going through the motions.

A knock on his door made him look up from the nonsense on his screen. Holly was standing there looking embarrassed to have disturbed him. "Sorry boss, I know you're busy, but there's a man here who says he wants to see you urgently."

"Sorry Holly, I'm really not up to seeing anyone right now, can you deal with it please?" George reached out for his cup of coffee, but it was cold. How long ago did he make that?

"I er, said you were busy, but he told me to say 'Tell Mr Mason that I've come to repay what I owe', does that make sense?"

Mr Mason? Only one person insisted on calling

him Mr Mason, despite various attempts by George for him to be less formal. George looked past Holly, and just as he'd guessed, saw Trigger standing in reception looking nervous.

"OK Holly thanks, show him into the arranging room and I'll make a couple of fresh cuppas and meet him in there." George wasn't in the mood or the right frame of mind to be meeting with anyone, but turning Trigger away felt wrong somehow, like kicking a puppy.

After a few minutes, George joined Trigger in the comfort of the arranging room, and handed him his heavily sugar-laden coffee.

"Please, sit down Trigger. Holly said something about a debt payment, but I'm not aware that you have an outstanding bill."

Trigger sat on the front edge of the couch, leaning forward with his elbows on his knees, staring intently at the cup he cradled in both hands. "I'm not here about money Mr Mason. You have always been very kind and generous when I've needed you, and I know you've always done right by me when it came to paying."

George wanted to say it was nothing, but Trigger was in full flow. He had clearly rehearsed what he wanted to say.

"It should never have happened, what happened to your good lady and your bubba Mr

Mason, and that's what I'm here to talk about."

George looked up from his coffee cup. The mention of Julie and Oliver focussing his attention.

"If people knew I was here talking, they would shut me up for good, but you're a good man Mr Mason, and you deserve to know. The law ain't found who did it, and they won't neither. They're in his pocket, and only look as far as the next handout."

"I'm sorry Trigger, but are you saying you know who is responsible for killing my wife and son?" George couldn't believe what he was hearing, or what he was seeing, as Trigger slowly nodded his head.

"I do Mr Mason, but if word gets out that it come from me, then you might as well measure me up for my coffin now."

Trigger knew he had come here to tell George everything he knew, or he'd just not have come at all, but now the time had arrived, he struggled to say it, knowing what fate would await him if certain people found out.

George jumped out of his seat as if he'd received an electric shock, "No-one will find out anything Trigger. Please, if you know anything, tell me, it has been my only thought."

"The young man who pulled the trigger is called Dominic Watson, but he's known as Nic. He's a gangster wannabe. The man who gave him the gun and the order to shoot, is called Hightop. He's the head of the Mad Hatters, and he's personally responsible for sending a lot of work your way, if you get my meaning."

Trigger rose from his seat, and handed George his now empty cup. "Thank you for the coffee, Mr Mason. I've got to be going now, as I've said what I came for, and I don't want to push my luck no more than is needed."

George's brain was still trying to catch up with the conversation. "But wait," George blurted out as Trigger reached the door, "where do I find these people?"

Trigger turned to face George. "Hightop isn't a man you find Mr Mason, he's a man who finds you, and God have mercy on you when he does. As for the kid, he just disappeared. There are people who knows where he is, but ain't none of 'em saying a word. If I were you though, I'd start with the owner at Julie's Gym, word is they are like family."

Trigger left the room, and the building, leaving George standing in the arranging room, shocked and confused. As he walked to the kitchen area with the dirty cups, he ran the whole conversation through his head for a second time, to try and garner any important information he'd missed first time.

He placed the cups in the sink just as something popped into his head. "Julie's gym? Julie never went to a gym!"

CHAPTER 29

Three days after the revolutionary meeting with Trigger, George had to go to the registry office. A family had brought the green registrar's certificate into the funeral home, as instructed by Marilyn, the registrar, thereby enabling the Funeral Director to proceed with a burial or cremation. For some inexplicable reason, and for only the second time that George could remember, Marilyn had forgotten to sign the certificate, rendering it useless.

After a quick call to her office, George drove into town, to get the mistake rectified. The office receptionist had warned George that there were emergency roadworks at the end of their street, due to a burst water pipe, so he would be best parking up in the old cinema car park, and walking from there.

George had spent many happy hours at the old cinema back in the day. He quietly reminisced as he walked from his car to the registry office. It was part of his childhood, and more. He and Julie often had dates there, followed by a pizza.

Sometimes they even bothered to watch the film they had paid to see, although not too often.

George had a guilty smile on his face as he approached the registry office. It was the first time he'd thought about Julie, and managed a smile since before he was last here, registered two deaths.

Marilyn was in the reception area when George entered. She greeted him sympathetically, just as George would have done. A well-practised routine. "Sorry about that George," she said, taking the green form from him, "I blame my baby brain."

George raised his eyebrows and checked himself before he spoke, "Baby brain? Your baby brain? Am I missing something?"

"Not me! Oh my God no, I'm 62, what would I want another baby for?" Marilyn raised both hands in mock shock as she spoke, "No, it's Laura, my daughter, she's expecting her third. I'm just using it as an excuse for being forgetful."

George took back the certificate, and left the two women standing in reception, chatting about babies, and the joys of being a grandparent.

There were two ways back to the old cinema. George could either go up the road, back the way he came, or walk down the road, to the pedestrianised walkway on the high street. It was a longer option, and looking back, George didn't know why he chose it. But he was forever glad he did.

It was about 200 yards to the pedestrianised area, and George barely looked up from the floor once. There were lots of people going about their normal lives, shopping, chatting, meeting up with friends, and George felt very distant from all of it. His life had stopped the day his family were killed. How is it possible that all these people around him are able to just carry on? How has it not affected them too?

A horn alerted George to the fact that he had walked the whole length of the pedestrianised area, and was now about to step into the road, in front of a delivery van. He didn't remember anything about the walk. He was there, then he was here, apparently without seeing or doing anything in between.

George stepped back quickly, and looked up at the sound of the horn. He couldn't believe what he was looking at. There, right in front of him, on the opposite side of the road, was a building, with a large sign. It consisted of just one word, and a word George knew intimately, but in a completely different context. 'Julie's'.

CHAPTER 30

I nternet searches, and George's limited powers of snooping around social media sites, had proven fairly useless for finding information about Julie's Gym. He knew the owner was called Francisco Juliano, but very little else. He would have to use old-school techniques to gather his information.

Over the next week, George walked or drove past the gym a total of twelve times. One time he had walked past just as Francisco was locking up, and practically walked into him. After stuttering a quick 'Evening!' he continued walking, before the old man could register his face. George walked past another two shopfronts before half turning and looking back. He saw the gym owner start to walk up a set of concrete steps that were nestled between the gym, and the Caribbean food store next door.

By the Friday, George knew that Francisco Juliano was a creature of habit. He opened the gym religiously at 5am, and locked up at 10pm on the dot. He lived above the gym, and George was pretty sure he lived alone. No wife, kids or pets.

George had to speak with him about Dominic Watson, and it had to be alone. The old Italian would never speak with him inside the gym, and George couldn't be seen to be showing an interest in his family's killer's whereabouts. His best bet would be to approach the old man as he closed up for the night. He might not know anything, but George had to be sure. Trigger had said that Dominic had gone away, and that, the two of them were like family. So, who better to ask where he was?

He would speak with Francisco Juliano tonight.

George once again parked his car in the old cinema carpark, and walked through the pedestrianised shopping area. He turned up the collar of his coat as protection against the rain which had been falling most of the evening. It made him feel like a spy on a clandestine meeting. It was five minutes to ten, but he knew there was no rush, a creature of habit is easy to entrap.

George could see the old man locking the front doors to the gym as he walked past the main shops across the road. He reached him, just as Francisco had his foot on the first step leading up to his flat.

"Excuse me," George said in a loud, direct voice, so as to be heard over the rain, "I'm wondering if you can help me?"

Francisco didn't step down from where he stood, but instead, stepped up. He didn't know if this man was simply lost, or if he was looking for trouble, so he wanted to make sure he had the height advantage.

"How can I help?" the old Italian replied, his voice, although clearly not as it once was, still sounded distinctly Mediterranean.

"Are you Francisco Juliano, the owner of Julie's Gym?"

"Who wants to know?"

George had rehearsed the scenario in his head several times, trying to find the best approach, so the old man would open up. After many false starts, he'd decided to simply be honest. Everything depended on how this man responded to what George had to say.

"Sorry, my name's George Mason, and I'm looking for a young man you might know. Dominic Watson?"

"Yes, I know Nic. Fastest hands I've seen in a long time, but I haven't seen him in weeks, sorry I can't help you." Francisco turned from George, and continued the assent to his flat.

"I'm sorry, but do you know where he is?" George called after the gym owner, "it is very important I contact him."

Francisco stopped on the stairs, but stayed with his back to George.

"As I said Mr Mason, I haven't seen him, and I don't know where he is. He has chosen to follow a path which will lead to no good. I can't help either of you, I'm sorry."

Ever since Trigger mentioned Dominic's name, and his connection to this gym, George had been like a kid waiting for Christmas Day. He had lived in despair and turmoil since his family were taken away from him, with no clue as to why. Now, finally, he was beginning to follow a trail which could lead to answers, and if George's plan worked, retribution.

Frustration boiled up inside George, and he leapt up the stairs, two as a time, and grabbed the old man's arm, spinning him around to face him.

"Look, I am desperate to find this Dominic person, and you are my only link to where he's hiding. If you know anything, I need you to tell me."

Francisco looked shocked at the sudden outburst, and pulled his arm from George's grasp.

"I'm no fool Mr Mason, I know who you are, and I've heard rumours about what happened," Francisco looked George square in the face as he spoke, "I am sorry about what has happening to your family, but no good will come from anything you are planning. I can't help you, so go away."

Francisco turned away from George and started up the stairs once more, but he had only taken a couple of steps before George was on him again, pushing the old man's back against the concrete side of the stairway.

"Can't help or won't help?" George shouted, his hands gripping the Italian's top and pushing him back, knocking the wind out of his lungs, "I need to find this man and no-one is going to get in my way."

George was desperate for answers, and he wasn't going to be blocked by this stubborn old man. Fuelled by adrenalin, he pulled Francisco towards him, then pushed him backwards against the wall again, to demonstrate his point, twice, three times, shouting at the gym owner as he did so, "Tell me what you know, tell me what you know!"

The old man didn't say another word, but instead, clutched at his chest, and slid vertically down the wall. George released his grip, and the old man slumped to a sitting position, still holding his chest, gasping for breath.

"Oh, you've got to be kidding me!" George shouted out, to no-one in particular. He crouched down next to Francisco, who was clearly having a heart attack, and felt his neck for a pulse. George felt two beats, then nothing. He leant towards the old man's mouth and listened, but there was silence. He had stopped breathing.

George was fully trained in CPR, but the situation was less than ideal. He would have to position Francisco so his feet were higher than his heart, which would be nearly impossible without the old man tumbling down the stairs into the street. It was then that an idea flashed into George's head. The one stumbling block he had left in his plan, was how to find Nic and administer the chloroform. And then what? Where would he be? Who would be there? What would he do next?

A much simpler solution had just presented itself, which answered all of those questions. If he couldn't get to Dominic Watson, he would let Dominic Watson come to him.

George stood up and calmly walked down the stairs, straightening his clothes as he went. He looked around once he reached the bottom, and making sure no-one was around, he stepped out, and crossed the road.

Forty minutes later, George was home, having a shower. He didn't know when the inevitable phone call would come in, but knew he'd have enough time to grab at least a few hours of much needed sleep.

CHAPTER 31

G eorge's phone rang just after 8am, just as he was leaving his house, to walk over to the office. The caller ID confirmed it to be the police control room.

Apparently, a gym user had been surprised when the doors to Julie's Gym were locked this morning when he arrived for his usual morning workout, just after 5am. He was even more surprised when he started up the stairs to the owner's flat, and found his lifeless body lying on the steps.

Although George knew exactly where the team were going, he dutifully took down the details as the police despatcher read them from her screen. George wrote down Francisco's name, address, and the police URN number, necessary to convey a deceased person, on behalf of the coroner.

The timing couldn't have been better. He walked across the yard and met Tommy just as he was arriving for work.

"Mornin' Tom", George said, greeting the big

Scotsman as he dismounted his bicycle, "jump in the ambo mate, we've got a call."

"Will do," Tommy replied, "I'll just put Susan away, then I'll be there."

George knew that Tommy had named his bike after an old girlfriend, but was always too afraid ask any further. He knew Tommy would tell him in the most minute and explicit detail, and there were some things he just didn't need to know.

George unlocked the ambulance, and opened the back, using the few minutes he had, to check they had all the equipment on-board. Gloves, body bag, wheeled stretcher, hand carry stretcher, wrist tags and coroner's forms. That should cover it. The ambulance was kitted out with far more equipment, including full cover-alls, heavy duty body bags, lifting equipment, torches, masks, boots, waders, high-viz jackets, and even hard hats, but for once, he knew exactly what they were going to be faced with once they arrived on scene, and the basics would be enough.

As always, Tommy drove. He and George were friends, and when on the ambulance, they were supposedly equal team mates, but Tommy could never bring himself to allow the boss to drive him around. It would be rude, somehow.

The roads into the centre of town were busy

at this time in the morning, but it still only took 20 minutes to arrive on scene. As always, George spoke with the police officer in charge to find out the situation, as Tommy proceeded with a quick dynamic risk assessment of the area, before gathering the equipment together.

George joined him at the rear of the ambulance.

"We have an elderly man, medium height, stocky build. Looks like a suspected heart attack, half way up the stairs. The ambo is close enough, so just a sheet, bag and the hand carry I think."

"Ay," replied the big man, "it looks a bit tricky on the stairs mind. There's a landing half way up, so we could lay the stretcher there, and carry him down to there in the bag."

Once the plan was agreed, the two men worked in relative silence. They knew what needed doing, and how best to do it. A quick look, or a subtle hand signal was all that was needed to communicate during the transfer onto the ambulance.

The two men placed the stretcher onto the ambulance, closed the rear doors, and gave a bow.

"Thanks Tom, the officer has confirmed there's no need for a police escort, so we can just go straight to the mortuary."

George and Tommy got into the cab of the ambulance, and as the Scotsman drove them to the hospital mortuary, George couldn't help but inwardly smile. What better way to cover your tracks at a crime scene, than to be the one removing the body? If the coroner did rule the death as suspicious, then any traces of his DNA found on, or around, the deceased, would automatically be discounted.

"That's a sly grin you got there, boss. Penny for them."

"Just thinking how much I love what we do Tommy. There really is no job like it."

CHAPTER 32

A few days later, at 4pm, George prepared the chapel in the same way he had done a thousand time1s before. The sides were dusted, the carpet hoovered, and the bin emptied. Everyone knew that the chapel was used daily by many different families, but George always liked it to appear as though each time was the first time in a new chapel. These things mattered.

With Tommy assisting him, George positioned the coffin in the chapel, so the foot end was facing the crucifix hanging on the wall. The coffin lid was removed and placed upright against the wall, so the polished name-plate could be clearly seen. After checking all details on the wrist tag, name plate, paperwork and doctor's forms were correct, George adjusted the position of the coffin slightly, making sure the wheels of the bier on which the coffin sat, were locked and turned inwards, so there was no risk of anyone tripping on them as they approached the coffin.

The frill which runs around the inside edge of

the coffin was laid over the side so no bare wood was visible, and as always, slight adjustments were made to the clothes of the person in the coffin, to ensure no creases or stray fluff or hair, would detract the visiting friend or family member from the reason they were there. To say goodbye to a loved one. Attention to detail is a major part of working within the funeral industry. A skill honed over many years, which George was just realising, could be used for devious as well as good reasons.

As always, before exiting the Chapel, George draped a full-length voile over the coffin, and dimmed the lights to a more comfortable level, not only helping to create a more calming atmosphere, but also to assist in making the deceased person more presentable.

George walked through the building towards the staff tearoom, passing through the workshop on his way. It was nearly the end of the day, and the team would either be finishing up a few small jobs, or winding down in the tearoom. This was something George actively encouraged in his team. Dealing with deceased people and grieving families can be very stressful, especially if the deceased person is young, or their death was an accident, murder or suicide. These things can take a toll on a person's mental health, and chatting to each other at the end of the day is a good way of letting off steam.

George could hear the banter, before he could even see the door leading to the tearoom. As usual Tommy was regaling stories of horrific coroner's removals he had previously been involved with, to anyone who would listen, but mainly for the benefit of Theo. Holly and Charlie had heard Tommy's stories multiple times, but they were always a source of amusement, if only to see what embellishment had been added since the last telling.

George stood in the open doorway with his arms crossed, casually leaning on the door frame, just as the Scotsman got to the part of his story where the two police officers on scene had to rush outside to be sick. Theo listened open mouthed as the rest of the team carried on with whatever they were doing. They each had their own stories, as everyone who works in this industry does, they just don't voice them as much as the resident story teller.

"Oh, it's two police officers now, is it?" George said with a chuckle, "No doubt it will be four police, two paramedics, and half of the Dragoon Guards before the year's out."

Charlie and Holly laughed. They both knew how Tommy liked to exaggerate a story, as if it wasn't gruesome enough to begin with. Theo looked like a rabbit in the headlights. He didn't know if the story was true or not, but didn't want to laugh and risk upsetting the big Scotsman.

"Ay, well there was a lot of people there being sick, right, left and centre, young Dory my lad, while we were getting on with our job, so anything's possible." Tommy replied with a smile on his face.

George clapped his hands together, "Right you lot, get off home. I've got a Chapel visit booked for 5.30, but there's no need for any of you to hang around."

A chair was scraped across the lino floor, and even before George had finished talking, Holly was walking past him, and with her customary "Night boss!", she was out the door. George laughed and shouted after her, "Was it something I said?"

"Go on you lot," George said, turning back to face the tearoom, "bugger off before I change my mind and find you all some work to do."

George returned to his office, and after ten minutes of various banging noises of lockers and doors, he was alone in the building. His visitor was due to arrive for the Chapel visit at 5.30, and most people arrive early to steady their nerves, so he had maybe twenty minutes to make sure everything was in place.

CHAPTER 33

The Chapel was prepared, and everything was ready in the old mortuary. The brown bottle, was with a handkerchief in his top righthand drawer. He knew it was there, but had to check one last time. Attention to detail was key. Sitting in his chair behind his desk, he opened the drawer. There, along with pens, scissors, a stapler, and assorted stationery, sat the small brown bottle with the white screw cap, wrapped in silver foil. George picked it up and gave it a gentle shake. He could feel the liquid slosh around inside, and couldn't help but smile. Everything rested on the contents of this seemingly innocuous bottle. Everything he had prepared would be for nothing without it, as he knew he would be unable to overpower his prey any other way.

George replaced the bottle next to the handkerchief and closed the drawer. As he did so, he found himself looking at the framed photo which took pride of place on his desk. A man, with his arm stretched forward towards the camera, clearly taking a selfie with his phone. Next to him is a woman with a baby in her arms. A happy photo, a happy place, a much happier time.

~~~~~~

George had an elderly aunt who had moved to Newchurch on the Isle of Wight, and when Oliver was six months old, they drove down to Lymington and caught the ferry over, so she could meet her great-nephew. George couldn't remember if Aunt Shelly was actually related to him or not, or if she was an old family friend who he was just brought up to call auntie, as was the way in his family. He guessed it was a generational thing.

After visiting for a few hours, and having lunch with Aunt Shelly, which of course included the obligatory corned beef and pickle sandwiches, which George had always associated with her since childhood, the old lady was showing signs of tiring, so they didn't stay for too long.

After driving around for a while, taking in the beautiful sights of the island, and with no particular agenda, George found himself driving down a very steep and winding road leading to the seaside town of Shanklin. He parked the car in the car park on the left, at the bottom of the hill, and they took Oliver across the road to the beach. George carried the sleeping child in his car seat, while Julie carried the rest of the baggage that all new parents have – changing bag, mat, nappies, various creams, bottles, wipes, and a first aid kit that would have put most hospitals to shame, which, since having Oliver, Julie insisted on taking everywhere 'just in case'.

Shanklin would forever remain a special place to the Masons, as it was Oliver's first visit to a beach. Little did they know at the time, but it would be his only visit too. The momentous occasion was lost on him though, as he stayed asleep in his seat for the majority of the time, but did wake up for a while, which is when George grabbed the opportunity to take the photo of the three of them, the sea in the background reflecting the bright afternoon sun.

A sharp noise brought George back to the here and now, and he realised he had picked up the photo frame and had been clutching it to his chest, trying to cuddle his family one last time. The noise again, sharp, familiar. Someone was tapping on the glass of the front door.

George kissed the photo of his wife and son sitting on a sunny beach without a care in the world, and carefully placed it back on his desk. Face down. As if this somehow protected them from seeing the man who had killed them, or maybe to protect them from witnessing the darkness that George was about to release. Darkness that he had been carrying with him since the day they were taken from him.

George stood up from his desk and walked out of his office, as he crossed the reception area, he could see a man standing outside, looking through the window. A look of relief on his face when he saw George approaching.

George unlocked the door and remained professional, despite his true feelings. "I'm sorry sir, we keep the front door locked out of hours, how may I help you?"

The man extended his arm to shake George's hand, "My name is Dominic Watson and I have an appointment to see Francisco Juliano".

A very important skill that anyone working in the funeral industry has to master, is the ability to hide your feelings and emotions, especially at very difficult moments. When lifting a loaded coffin onto shoulder, to carry from the hearse to the catafalque during a funeral, it should be done silently as a mark of respect. No mourners should have to hear a bearer groan or complain about the weight of a coffin. This is why George's team practise with a specially prepared, weighted coffin, especially when training new staff. Similarly, the sight, or more often, the overwhelming smell of transferring a deceased person with advanced decay during a coroner's removal, may be enough to send (according to Tommy), several people running for fresh air, but the team undertaking the transfer must never show any signs of revulsion, no matter what faces them. Any family member present at the time of transfer would find a negative reaction, insulting and disrespectful.

George had been in those situations, countless times, and had learned to remain stoic no matter what he was faced with, but now, shaking this man's hand, even his resolve was being tested. Dominic was a good few inches taller than George. Younger, fitter, and George could feel the imposing strength hinted at by the young man's grip.

As George shook hands, he wondered for the first time whether the contents of the little brown bottle with the white screw cap, would be enough.

Ending the handshake by using the same hand to gesture Dominic to step into the reception area, George closed and locked the front door. "Please step this way sir." George said, almost choking on the word 'sir' as he led his prey towards the arranging room.

Both men stood in the arranging room whilst George explained the process of the chapel visit. It was a speech he had given a thousand times before, so was able to go through the motions without having to concentrate.

While his mouth was telling Dominic about the cooler temperature and dimmed lights, and explaining about the doorbell on the table, his mind was calmly and methodically going through a check-list to make sure everything was in place. The back part of his brain that was working its way through each scenario, was happy that almost nothing had been left to chance. Everything that George could control was set and ready.

The front part of George's brain took over as he was coming to the end of his well-rehearsed speech, and he was fully alert as Dominic confirmed that everything was clear, and he had no questions.

"I will just go and make sure everything is in order, but I won't be a minute." George said in his best professional voice, calm and controlled. He knocked on the chapel door before entering, then closed it behind him. George adjusted the coffin veil so it only covered the bottom half of the deceased, and gave him a final look over to make sure he was as presentable as possible. Once happy, he exited the room, back to where Dominic was waiting.

Gesturing for the young man to follow, George walked back to the door which led from the arranging room to the chapel. After knocking gently on the door, George opened it and walked in. Dominic followed.

"Please take as much time as you like, and if there is anything you need, please don't hesitate to press the bell which will ring in my office."

With that, George left the chapel and closed the door behind him. Now to wait. How long that wait would be, depended on how emotionally attached Dominic was to his mentor. George guessed 10 minutes.

CHAPTER 34

Back in his office, George opened his desk drawer, and took out the small brown bottle with the white screw cap, and placed it next to the face down photo frame on his desk. He placed the handkerchief next to it, almost ceremonially. Like the priests he had seen so many times in church, preparing for Mass. George felt that the ritual of having the bottle near to his family photo was important, almost as if they were giving him their blessing.

George knew that he was at a crossroads, and at this point, nothing couldn't be undone. No-one had been hurt and no-one else was involved. He could just abandon his plan and walk away.

He also knew that he would never again be able to look at the photo of Julie and Oliver on that sunny beach in Shanklin. He may never have this opportunity again, and his demons may never rest. George knew that stopping now wasn't really an option and he was never seriously considering it, but surely every sane man reaches a point where they question their actions. Don't they?

The bell in his office rang gently, and George smiled as he checked his watch. Eight minutes, not bad!

After politely knocking on the door, George entered the chapel. Dominic half turned in his seat to face him, and held up an empty tissue box.

"I am so sorry sir; I didn't realise we had run out" George lied convincingly, "I will bring a new box immediately." and backed out of the chapel, closing the door as he went.

George's heart was beating so hard and fast, he could physically feel it inside his chest. This was it! The crucial moment had finally been reached after months of planning, and so far, it was all going according to plan.

Returning to his desk, he picked up the handkerchief and the little brown bottle, and loosened the white screw cap, unscrewing it as he walked back through the arranging room, picking up a new box of tissues from the table on the way.

George gave his customary gentle knock, then opened the door. He didn't say anything, just slid the new box of tissues onto the small table next to the chair, occupied by his family's killer.

CHAPTER 35

After the Funeral guy had left the room, Dominic just stood completely still for a minute. If he didn't look in the coffin, then he didn't have to believe any of this was real. This man was his friend and his mentor. He had chosen to be like a dad to Dominic during some pretty rough times, and that made him the closest thing to family he had ever known.

After taking a couple of extra deep breaths, Dominic lowered his gaze to look into the coffin. The man that lay before him wasn't Francisco. It took him a few seconds to realise just who or what he was looking at. Yes, it was the body of Francisco, but something was missing. He looked well-presented and at rest, but somehow also looked younger. There was no spark, no fire, no energy, and that is what made Francisco who he was. At that point, Dominic knew that the fiery spirit that lived inside this body had truly been released.

Feeling as though he had taken a blow to the stomach, he sat in the chair, and, for the first time in many years, wept. Not just a few tears, but a full-on cry, as though a floodgate had been opened. He sat with his head in his hands, leaning forward, so his tears simply fell to the floor. He reached over to the box on the table next to him, and pulled a tissue from the opening at the top. As he did so, the whole box lifted off the table, meaning only one thing. It was now empty.

"For fuck's sake, aren't these people supposed to check these things?" Without hesitation, he pressed his thumb on the button placed on the table.

After a knock, the chapel door opened. Dominic was annoyed and didn't want to speak, so just held the box up for the Funeral Director to see. He was clearly very embarrassed about such an oversight as he apologised to Dominic and left immediately.

Dominic remained in the chair, but turned back to face the coffin, and spoke to Francisco for the first time,

"Fucking idiot can't even get tissues right; you'll be lucky if you make it to your own funeral, with this bloke in charge, old man."

He heard the knock, and the door opened once more, then heard a new box of tissues being placed onto the table. He didn't pay much attention to the man who had just entered the room, partly because he wanted him to know that he was annoyed, and partly to hide his tear-stained face. He didn't like appearing vulnerable to anyone at any time. He gave George a half nod, more to dismiss him than anything else, and saw he had an awkward, embarrassed, expression. 'Weak' Dominic thought to himself. He never noticed that the FD was holding his breath.

CHAPTER 36

Growing up in the funeral industry meant George had spent years learning how to read people. He knew that, unlike a lot of people, Dominic wouldn't have brought any tissues with him. He was too macho to cry, so what would be the point? He also knew how to approach people in an almost subservient way, so as to never be the centre of attention. It was a skill to do your job without being noticed. A skill which George had learned well.

He entered the chapel and placed the tissue box on the table, stooping over to appear almost as if he were bowing, but actually hiding his hands. Dominic barely registered him as he entered the room, which was just as George wanted. As Dominic turned back to face the coffin, George quickly moved behind him and stood straight. He knew he had to act fast. His prey was faster, fitter, and a lot stronger, so the element of surprise was a must.

Dominic could sense George close behind him, but before he could register what was happening, George's left arm was around his neck, and something was pushed into his face.

George pushed the chloroform-soaked handkerchief into Dominic's face, making sure to cover both his nose and mouth. His left forearm was across Dominic's throat, and he gripped the upper right sleeve of his jacket as tightly as possible. As he quickly got his arms in position, he pushed down on Dominic's shoulders with all his weight to prevent him from standing.

At least, that had been the plan!

Dominic was on his feet with alarming speed, lifting George off the floor. He tried to buck George off his back by bending forward sharply at the waist, and throwing himself forward, and if it hadn't had been for the coffin restricting his movement, he would most likely have been successful in dislodging the FD.

Desperately strong hands grabbed at George's left arm, trying to yank it free, but George was finding strength that he never previously knew existed. Dominic stood upright, then launched them both backwards, battering George's back into the chapel wall. Once, twice. Although winded, he held on for all he was worth.

The explosive power, coupled with the initial surprise, had caused Dominic to take deep breaths in order to fill his lungs with oxygen, and it soon became apparent to George that his home-made chloroform was taking effect. Dominic tried feebly to grab the cloth from his face, but the chemical was doing its job, and doing it well. He took a step forward, then reversed George into the wall a third time, but there was no power, and it was more of a stumble.

George continued to hold on, with the handkerchief in place as they both tumbled to the floor, Dominic's legs no longer having the strength to hold them both up. Dominic tried feebly to throw his attacker to one side, but his muscles no longer had the strength, and the room was going dark. George loosened his grip, then repositioned himself so he could see Dominic's face, whilst still covering his nose and mouth. Once he was happy that the young man really was out for the count, George let go and rolled onto his back, gasping for air.

The whole attack lasted about a minute, start to finish, but to George it felt a lot longer. His body ached, caused in part by it being introduced to the chapel wall at high speed, but also by the amount of adrenalin that was surging through him. His shoulders and arms were buzzing, and he could barely lift them.

After five minutes trying to regain his breath and strength, George used the chair to push himself up from the chapel floor, and looked over at Dominic. This young man, now lying dormant and helpless at his feet, was responsible for taking his family from him. His one true Love. His son and heir. Dreams shattered. Plans destroyed. His world torn apart. Now was the time for retribution.

Moving a body is a very difficult thing. It's not like in the movies, where someone just picks up a body and throws it over their shoulder. A human body is a very heavy and cumbersome object to move. Only people working in the funeral industry truly understand the term 'dead weight'. Limb length, body position, weight distribution, and sometimes just sheer size, can make it an almost impossible task. Unless of course, you have specialised mechanical assistance. Pump activated hoists, electric scissor lifts, collapsible stretchers – all readily available in hospitals or to care home staff. Or, as in this case, a Funeral Directors!

There are two entrances to most funeral home chapels. A single door used by visitors, leading from an arranging room or lounge area, and a set of double doors, often hidden behind a curtain, leading from the chapel directly to the mortuary area, allowing easy access for the movement of coffins. George opened these doors, and wheeled in the mobile hoist he had positioned there earlier. It was the work of just a few minutes before Dominic's limp body was being lowered into an open body bag positioned on a mortuary tray. George removed the hoist's straps and zipped the bag closed, placing the chloroform-soaked handkerchief near Dominic's face, just in case he began to wake.

CHAPTER 37

Noise. No. Noise again. A voice. Quiet. A distant banging. A voice again. Shouting. Shouting something. A name. His name. Echoes. Sounds becoming clearer. The voice again, talking to him. Saying 'Don't move, Mr Watson'.

What had happened? Had he been in an accident? Where was he? A bright light made him scrunch up his face when he eventually felt able to open his eyes. He tried to shield his face, but his arms wouldn't move. Why couldn't he move his arms? What's going on?

"Don't move Mr Watson, if you do, you'll bleed out in a matter of minutes."

Dominic's eyes darted around the room. Everything was white and clinical. He could see metal trays and serious looking bottles. Was he in hospital? He couldn't remember what had happened or where he'd been. He felt very groggy, tired, and nauseous.

Something was put in front of his face, and he could see himself. His blurry vision slowly focused on the mirror, and he could see his head and chest. He felt naked and cold, and was still unable to move his arms. There was something near his neck. What was that?

"Did you hear what I said? Do not, under any circumstances, attempt to move!" The voice was coming from behind him. He was lying on his back on some sort of table, and someone was talking to him from above his head.

"Not that you are able to, but don't attempt to nod or shake your head, just answer me verbally. If you're not yet lucid enough for that, just blink hard twice to show me you've heard and understand."

Blink, blink.

"Good. Now please allow me to explain your current situation. As you can see in the mirror, you have a metal rod inserted into your carotid artery, to which a rubber tube is connected. I have sutured the incision closed to the best of my ability, but if you struggle, your artery will be ripped open, and you will bleed out. You will be dead inside two minutes. It is very important you understand the severity of what I am telling you. Do you understand?"

Dominic blinked twice again, and managed a gargled "'es".

"Excellent."

The mirror was removed and Dominic was once again staring at a stark white ceiling. It must be a hospital.

"To assist you in not moving, I have immobilised your head, by strapping it to the table,"

Dominic had seen this done in various TV shows to prevent someone from inadvertently injuring themself if they had a spinal injury. How did he end up in hospital? It must be serious. Had he been in a car accident? Why couldn't he remember?

The disjointed voice continued, "Your wrists and ankles are also strapped down, and I have taken the liberty of severing your Achilles and Distal Bicep tendons, just as a precaution. You will find that you are quite immobile. I used the contents of a syringe driver as a makeshift local anaesthetic as I don't want you to suffer any unnecessary pain. I hope it works OK for you."

Dominic's mind was suddenly very alert. Severed? What did he mean severed? On purpose? What the fuck is going on? He recognised hearing the voice before, but couldn't place it.

"Wha...wha," Dominic attempted, coughing and spluttering. "what the fuck is happening? Who are you? What the fuck have you done to me?"

"You don't know me Mr Watson, but I know you. In fact, I know almost everything about you. You have been, shall we say, the focus of my attention for a while now." George held up a silver chain, on which was hanging a St Christopher pendant. "You won't be needed this anymore either, you've only got one more journey to make, and I'll be looking over you all the way."

Dominic strained to move his head to the right, the couple of millimetres that his restraints allowed. "You're the funeral bloke! What the fuck are you doing to me? Get me outta here or I'll fucking kill you!"

"That Mr Watson, is simply not going to happen. Allow me to further explain your predicament." George moved further down the side of the table as he spoke, making it easier for Dominic to see him. "You are currently strapped to an embalming table, and quite unable to move. You are in a room that is very well insulated, and well away from anyone who may hear you. In fact, most people have forgotten that this room even exists. If somehow, you manage to break your bonds, you will find that your arms would be almost useless as your biceps are no longer connected to your forearms. If you managed to stand in an attempt to flee, you would find walking equally difficult and painful, as your calf muscles are no longer attached to your feet."

As George spoke, Dominic tested the strength of his restraints, but was unable to put any force behind his struggling. All his limbs felt cramped and as though someone were sitting on them.

George paused while Dominic wriggled around on the table, trying to break free. He stood there, observing for a while, and it brought back a memory of him as a young teen, with his best friend at the time, Chev Claridge. The two boys were spending the afternoon fishing at 'The Moat', a long lake which ran around the local farm. It had been a very quiet day, until Chev caught a decent sized carp. The boys got into such a state, trying to land the fish, that they knocked their tackle box into the water, and George trod on his compact camera, breaking the battery compartment. Once the fish was on the bank, the boys had to rescue their equipment from the water before they could disgorge the hook from the fish's mouth. All the while, the fish was flopping around on the bank, looking completely helpless.

George continued, "Also, as you are by now probably aware, you are feeling weak and light headed. Given your age, sex, and body mass, your vascular system should contain approximately

5.8 litres of blood. Currently however, thanks to the equipment I have at my disposal, your body is trying to function on just 4 litres."

Dominic looked down his body to see George standing next to, what looked like, a large, off-white food blender. The word 'Dodge' was clearly visible on the front. A tube entered the top of a large jar which sat on top, and whatever was in it, reminded him of medicine he used to take as a kid. His mum just called it 'the pink stuff'.

The funeral guy was right, Dominic felt fatigued. His body felt as though it was being pressed down into the table, and his head was spinning. "Look," even his own voice sounded quiet and distant. Was he dying? "I don't know who you are, or what the fuck you want with me, but you've got the wrong guy." Then, still refusing to accept the gravity of the situation, he added "I'm a fucking Mad Hatter, and you're going to get fucked up if you don't let me go!"

George leaned in, so the two of them were face to face. His voice very calm and controlled, "Oh, I know exactly who, and what you are Dominic, but there is nothing on this earth that you can threaten me with. Thanks to you, I have been to hell already, and now I'm back to settle the score."

Dominic had faced many fears in his time. The beatings he received from his father, street gangs claiming their turf, being stabbed in a pub fight, the loss of his sister. He had faced them all, but the way this man was talking, unsettled him. Not what he said, but the way he said it. So matter of fact, so studied. So finite.

The darkness that had sat at the edges of Dominic's vision, moved closer to the centre, and the last thing he heard was the funeral guy shouting "Don't you dare fucking die on me! Wake up, don't you . . ."

Blackness.

CHAPTER 38

G eorge was worried this might happen. The residual effects of the home-made chloroform, coupled with the body trying to function on a limited blood supply, had caused Dominic's brain to call time-out, and shut down. The young man was unconscious, but George couldn't risk him going into shock. That would be irreversible. Luckily, as always, George was prepared for every eventuality. The only saline he could find ahead of time, were bottles of eye wash, but close enough was good enough in this situation, and he picked up the large syringe he had prepared earlier.

The syringe was originally intended to be used for injecting embalming fluid directly into specific areas, such as the cheeks, lips, and forehead of the deceased, and occasionally, directly into the eye, and after having been in the old mortuary for so many years, George was pretty sure it was no longer sterile, and couldn't even say if it had been used or cleaned. But he did know that a dirty needle infection was the least of this man's worries. He inserted the needle into a vein in Dominic's arm, and slowly pushed down on the plunger.

It took George nearly half an hour to administer the whole 150ml syringe of saline. He watched the young man's face for signs of consciousness, and kept a check on his vitals throughout. Nearly an hour after passing out, Dominic started to wake.

"Hello again," George said in a chirpy, almost sing-song voice, "so nice to have you back. Sorry about that, I had to guess your weight and blood volume, and it looks like I took a little too much. Still, you're back now, so let's continue, shall we?"

Dominic drifted in out of consciousness for a few seconds, then opened his eyes. He didn't know where he was at first, but then it all came flooding back, when he realised, he couldn't move his head. The funeral guy! Something about his arms, he couldn't remember what. He could feel pain in his arms now, and his legs felt like they were on fire!

"I'll give you a few minutes to get yourself together," George said as he turned away, to face the equipment on the stand, "I've got a few bits to sort out here anyway."

"Look man, I have no idea what is going on, but this is fucked up. What did I ever do to you?" Dominic was trying desperately to sound defiant, but the cold, the pain, and the fear made it difficult for him to keep the strength in his voice, and even to him, it sounded weak and shaky.

George spun around quickly, and was leaning over Dominic, nose to nose with alarming speed. "What did you ever do to me?" George spat the words through gritted teeth.

He stood back up and returned to making adjustments to the equipment. "Allow me to tell you a little story, stop me if you've heard it before. It all begins with me having to run an errand. Nothing major, just had to visit a client to pick up some photos. Only I couldn't do it at the arranged time, as I was called out to work, so Julie, that's my wife, do you know her? I know you've seen her. Anyway, Julie said she'd run the errand for me, but she'd have to take Oliver with her. That's our son by the way. Great kid. I don't know if you've seen him or not, but that's by-the-by."

George had turned back to face the table, and was pacing around it, gesticulating with his arms as he told his story.

"Julie and Oliver were both in the car, heading home after running the errand, when, ... " George paused for a few seconds, then looked at Dominic quizzically, "do you know what happened then Mr Watson?"

Dominic's eyes were wide, and his mouth had fallen open while George talked. Wife and child? That's not right! He knew the end of George's story, but was afraid to hear it.

George saw the change in the young man's face. Realisation had indeed dawned. "I'll tell you what happened Mr Watson. You did! You happened. You happened to my wife, you happened to my son, and you happened to me!" George reached to the side, pulled over a white plastic chair and sat down next to the table, "and now Mr Watson, I'm going to sit here, and you are going to tell me what possible reason you could have had, for slaughtering my family."

Dominic's mind was racing. He knew nothing about a child. Is that why he had to disappear and be shut away? Even the Mad Hatters had lines they wouldn't cross. He didn't know!

When eventually Dominic found his voice, it came out in a broken whimper. "Shit, I'm sorry man, I had no idea. . . . I didn't know, I swear."

George raised his finger to his lips to shush the man quiet. "I'm not interested in what you did or didn't know, and I'm certainly not interested in your 'sorrys'. That's not why we're here. You have no right to say sorry, because you don't yet know what being sorry is, but you will, of that you can be sure. All I want to hear from you, is a plausible reason for why I can never hold my wife and son again."

Dominic knew that he was in serious trouble. He was completely at this man's mercy. Strapped down, crippled, and so incredibly weak. He had never felt so exposed and helpless. He had killed this man's family, yet there was no emotion, no anger, no resentment. This man was just like this room, stark, precise and clinical. Dominic surmised that it wasn't just this man's family he had taken from him, and there was nothing he could do to barter or reason his way out of this situation. Today is the day he would die!

After taking a couple of deep breaths to steady himself and to try and focus out the pain in his limbs, Dominic tried to explain how things had happened, but he was starting to panic now, and it all came out in a jumble, "It was for my sister man, that fucker killed her. I didn't know your boy was in the car. It was the final trail. I just needed to get to Hightop, that fucker owes me. It was all for Kelly. I'm sorry man, please don't kill me." All sense of bravado was now lost.

Nic, the street-smart member of the infamous Mad Hatter gang, was nothing more than a snivelling child. Weak and pathetic. George remained silent. The only sound in the room was Dominic crying, coughing, and trying desperately to get enough air into his lungs to oxygenate what little blood he had.

Dominic, lying on his back, bound to a marble mortuary table. George sitting in a chair to his side, with a thoughtful look on his face. An onlooker would be forgiven for thinking a family member were visiting a relative in hospital, or it was a scene from a very bizarre psychiatrist's office.

After Dominic's breathing had calmed enough, George broke the silence," If I am understanding you correctly, this Hightop person killed your sister, and you wanted revenge. To facilitate this revenge, you felt it necessary to join the very gang in which this person operates. How am I doing so far?"

"Hightop is untouchable man. He has his slabs of meat around him all the time. The only way to get to him is from the inside." Dominic was panicky and wanted to explain everything as quickly as possible, but his voice could only come out in short bursts, punctuated by having to gulp down precious air.

"That fucker shot my sister, and just sneered at her as she lay in the gutter. She was just in the wrong place at the wrong time, and got caught up in cross-fire, but he's the one who shot her, and the fucker just sneered." Dominic's voice trailed off through tears of pain as well as hopeless desperation.

"And the only way to achieve this goal was to slaughter my wife and son? Why?" No malice, no anger, just calm, genuine interest.

"It was just by chance, man."

Through coughs, choking, and having to stop for breath, it took Dominic nearly ten minutes to tell his story. George listening patiently and intently as he spoke of his hatred for Hightop, the pub fire, the beating in the club, and the meeting at the Kenyan Cafe.

"It was pure chance man. I pulled the eight of hearts from the deck. That's it. If it had been a different card, your family would still be here. I'm sorry man, I really am. I know what it's like to lose family and I..."

George stood up sharply, the back of his legs pushing the plastic chair across the floor, until it hit the far wall. Dominic stopped talking. Fear and cold making his body shake.

"I have worked in the funeral industry all my life," as he spoke, George slowly walked around the table towards the equipment on the side, "I have lost track of the number of times people have asked me the same questions, 'what's the worst thing you've seen?', 'do dead men get erections?', 'has anyone not actually been dead?', people always think they're the first to ask." George stood next to the equipment, and casually leant his elbow on the top of the glass jar, like a guy in film from the 50's leaning against a juke box, trying to impress a girl.

"But there's always been one question which I have often wondered about myself, and no-one has been able to provide an answer. What would it be like to embalm a living person?"

Dominic tried to say something, but his words just caught in his throat. Tears were streaming down his face, and he was shaking violently. Cold, fear, pain. His heart was pounding in his chest and echoing in his ears.

"Your driving force was to exact revenge on your sister's killer. You know how it feels to have that one singular thought in your head, all day and all night. You understand." George flicked a switch on the front of the machine, and a motor started whirring inside.

Pink liquid slowly pushed its way out of the jar, and along the tube towards Dominic's neck. George had cleaned and primed the tube with water while Dominic was unconscious, and as soon as the machine started up, Dominic screamed in anticipation as the water entered his artery ahead of the approaching pinkness.

"If what I've read is to be believed," George approached Dominic, raising his voice to be heard above the screams, "the embalming liquid will cause searing pain, like nothing you can imagine" he moved close to Dominic's face so he could witness the result of his retribution, "I said I never wanted to cause you any unnecessary pain, and that is true, but this pain is very necessary. It is the pain you gave me when you took away my family, and now, Mr Watson, I am giving it right back."

The pink embalming fluid reached the end of its journey, and entered Dominic's blood stream. The result was immediate, dramatic, and final.

As soon as the methanol and formalin mixture entered Dominic's artery, his body began convulsing. He could feel the liquid's progress through his bloodstream as it literally burned its way through the network of veins and capillaries. George stepped back, but continued to watch as Dominic's body bucked and leapt on the table, his limbs pulling viciously against the restraints. Dominic was screaming, but it wasn't a sound that George had ever heard before, and didn't think it was a noise a human should be capable of making. It was guttural, primal, and to George it was disturbingly beautiful.

George watched as the body in front of him bucked and heaved. One of the restraints gave way, and Dominic's right leg began flailing around, his foot flopping around pathetically without the support of the tendon. The leg gave more momentum to the wild bucking, and Dominic's body twisted around to the left, snapping his right arm above the elbow, as it was wrenched and pulled against the restraint.

Dominic was spitting blood from his mouth. His jaw was clenched so tight that George could hear his teeth cracking, and he had clearly bitten the end off of his tongue. George was fascinated watching the effects, as the embalming liquid coursed through Dominic's blood stream, and he was waiting anxiously for the inevitable moment when Dominic's heart would tear itself apart. A fitting end, considering he had done the same to George.

Once again, Dominic's body convulsed and twisted to the left. Tearing the tendons in his already broken arm, he turned almost completely over. The rubber tube delivering the pink liquid, pulled taught, and the metal rod pulled free from Dominic's neck, tearing his stitches in the process. The head restraint doing its job perfectly, meant the head had nowhere to turn, and with a sickening crunching and popping sound, Dominic Watson broke his own neck. His body flopping back to its starting point, flat on his back. The body hadn't settled before George leapt forward, trocar in hand.

George thrust the point of the trocar into

Dominic's abdomen, and upwards into his chest cavity. With a much-practised aim, the trocar punctured Dominic's barely beating heart. George stood back and watched a mixture of blood and pink embalming fluid leak out. The life literally drained out of Dominic, and pooled on his stomach, before cascading down his side, onto the marble table, where it joined the steady flow of blood streaming from the tear in Dominic's neck.

Dominic 'Nic' Watson died.

George wept. His legs gave way, and he fell to the mortuary floor. He wept and he sobbed and he wailed. Months of tension and pressure had built up within him and he'd had no way of activating the release valve. Until now. The person who had heartlessly executed his family, was now dead. More importantly, George had been given a reason why. It was a very shitty reason. Just by chance. A random card pulled from a deck, sealed their fate. It wasn't personal. In some ways that helped, but in others, it just added to the futility of their deaths.

George was drained. He had been running on pure adrenalin all evening. Now that was used up, his tanks were empty. He had a lot of work still to do before morning, but for now, he had no choice, but to give in to the tiredness that was consuming his body. Exhaustion claimed him, and he slept. The best sleep he'd had in a long while.

He awoke to a familiar whirring sound. Not a hoover, not a fan, but still something he recognised. He rubbed his eyes and face to wake himself, then realised the sound was the motor in the embalming machine. After the tube had been torn from Dominic's neck, the machine had continued to pump the remaining embalming liquid onto the floor, and was now whirring away, trying to expel the contents of an empty jar.

George reached up and gripped the edge of the embalming table. Using it to pull himself up, he flicked the switch on the front of the machine, and the whirring ceased. Turning to face Dominic's lifeless body, he said "Thank you Mr Watson for finally giving me an answer to the question. Now, it looks like we've made quite a mess. How about we get phase three underway?"

It was close to eleven o'clock. George had slept for a little over four hours. His body was telling him that he could do with several more, but his mind was already working through the jobs that needed completing before morning. There were several tasks that needed doing in a specific order, and the first one required a mop and bucket!

At two fifteen the next morning, George

collapsed into the welcoming comfort of his bed. The old mortuary room was spotlessly clean, the restraints, clothing, gloves, apron, body suit, and the little brown bottle with the white screw cap, were all disposed of, in the clinical waste bins. The only indicator that any of last night's events even took place, was an untagged body, in an unmarked body bag, lying on a tray in a fridge, in a room that most people had forgotten existed.

CHAPTER 39

T he official work day at Geo. Masons starts at 9am, but George's team are always in before then. Each staff member is paid from 8.30 to encourage them to come in and spend some social time together. Chatting about last night's TV, what they had for dinner, whatever their family got up to, just usual workmate banter. George knew that a close team is vitally important to a smoothly operated funeral. Each member of the team needs to know what has to be done, without a word being said, and close bonding is important. George usually used the time as an unofficial team brief, casually discussing the day ahead, whilst keeping the mood uplifted.

Today was no different. Tommy was the first in as normal, and had everyone's cups lined up, and teas and coffees poured, ready for each member to arrive. Just like normal.

Tommy handed George his cup of coffee as soon as he walked through the door, just like normal. Charlie and Theo were chatting away about some computer game as they entered the tearoom, just like normal. A minute later, George heard "Mornin' Boss" as Holly walked into the room. Just like normal.

Should it all be normal? Everything was normal for George, but everything had changed too. He had seen a countless number of deceased people over the years, but had never actually created one before. Should his mind allow him to carry on as normal? He suspected that Dominic's actions on that fateful day had taken away more than just his family. Something inside him had also died. Something was missing. The absence of which, had allowed him to conceive, believe, and achieve, Dominic's execution, and now, carry on as normal. He knew, that in itself, wasn't normal, and he hoped he could control it.

A hand gripped his shoulder. Its owner's Scottish voice breaking through his internal monologue. "Are ye alright big man?"

George realised that clearly, someone had spoken to him, but he hadn't heard them, as everyone in the tearoom was now looking at him.

"Yes, sorry, lost in my own thoughts for a minute there," George said, smiling broadly, "what did I miss?"

"Young Dory was asking how things are going

to go with today's funeral, what with the body bag an' all".

"Right, OK," George addressed the room, so everyone could hear, "as you all know, Colleen Buckingham was found in Chantry Reservoir, almost two months after she went missing on the way home from work. Water, time and wildlife have not been kind to her, which is why, since being released from the coroner, she has been sealed in a heavy-duty body bag. This bag is not to be opened. Take it from me, as harsh as it sounds, the reality is, you do not want the sight or smell, to be something that stays with you."

"We will of course, wear gloves as standard, when completing our final checks and sealing the coffin, and I will be asking for masks to be worn, even though the body bag will remain unopened. Once the coffin has been sealed, we can carry on just as we do for any other funeral." The team responded with nods, then carried on with their benign chatter.

"You know where I am if you need me," he said to an increasingly noisy room. He turned to Tommy and added, "Give me a shout when we're ready to seal Tom." He then left the room and went across to his office.

George sat at his desk, and once again looked at the framed photo of Jules and Oliver. The last job on his long list last night, was to stand the frame back up, and position it back where it belonged. His wife and son looked at him from Shanklin Beach once more. He wondered who they now saw – a murderer? An executioner? A man as evil as the one who had taken their lives? Or a husband and father who had been pushed beyond his breaking point, and had retaliated against someone hurting his family? George was comfortable with the new skin he was wearing, and he felt pretty sure his angels felt the same way, as they looked back at him from that perfect day.

~~~~~~

At 10.30, Tommy popped his head around the door to George's office. "Ready for closure when you are."

"OK Tom, I'll just finish this," George pointed his finger at the computer screen which displayed a spreadsheet detailing stock figures, "then I'll be there." George noted that Tommy had used the word 'closure' - how very apt.

George joined his team in the preparation room, and they all donned disposable face masks and gloves before entering the chapel. There, on a wheeled bier, was a coffin, with its lid resting on top. The nameplate on the lid showing Colleen Buckingham's name, age, and date of death, and as always, this was checked against the paperwork and identification tag, attached to the deceased. As the checks were carried out, Tommy explained to Theo, that the body bag wasn't to be opened, so the tag which would ordinarily be attached to the deceased person's left wrist, is looped through the metal rings on the two zips, effectively locking them shut. As was company policy, in such a situation, as FD, George had signed the tag to confirm that the details shown, were correct for the person inside.

Once all the details had been checked by three members of the team, including the FD and the hearse driver, the lid was placed back on to the coffin, and the six screws were tightened. Mrs Buckingham's coffin would now never be opened again. The next time the coffin screws would move, is when they fall to the floor of the cremator, as the coffin, and the body within, are transformed to ash.

CHAPTER 40

Victor Roberts had been the subject of various psychological studies as a child, because he had problems fitting in. When he was twelve, during a lunchtime in the school cafeteria, he had broken a girl's nose and cheekbone, because she had been ahead of him in the queue, and had taken the last cherry yogurt from the cooler. After she had sat down with her friends, he simply walked over, and hit her full in the face with a fire extinguisher, before calmly taking the yogurt from her tray, and placing it on his own.

When asked later, why he had resorted to extreme violence in response to such a trivial matter, he simply replied, "She wouldn't have given it to me if I'd asked, so I took it".

Different doctors, psychologists, and therapists blamed his actions, on him having come from a broken home, society, the alcohol and drug abuse by his mum whilst pregnant, and even the fact he was never breast fed. Whatever the so-called experts disagreed about, the one thing they all agreed on, was that young Master Roberts had an anti-social personality disorder. Even then, they couldn't decide whether he was a sociopath, psychopath, or had narcissistic personality disorder. Over time, the one label that seemed to be used more than others was 'high functioning sociopath, bordering on psychopathy'.

Victor moved schools and institutions often throughout his adolescence, never staying anywhere longer than six months. Despite this, he had a voracious appetite for learning, and would quickly gain an unfavourable reputation among the teaching staff, for correcting them if their facts were not accurate.

His contempt for his teachers and fellow students meant that he often found himself in trouble or ostracised, but it never fazed him, as he always knew he was both superior, and detached from everyone else around him. He rarely got upset or mad, but on the occasions he did, his response was always very decisive, and usually brutally violent.

Much had changed for Victor in the twenty years since the incident with the fire extinguisher in the cafeteria. He had discovered that his ability to be completely detached from those around him, had given him opportunities that others missed, and he had taken full advantage of them. He had excelled in his chosen career, and had established an enviable reputation, both for intelligence and ruthlessness.

Now, as the current leader of the notorious Mad Hatters, Victor 'Hightop' Roberts wasn't angry or mad, but he was frustrated. Dominic Watson had disappeared, apparently without a trace, which caused potentially harmful issues on various levels.

Hightop was recruiting Nic into the Mad Hatters, as the kid had potential, so if his disappearance was the result of actions taken by a rival gang, then repercussions would follow. If Nic had taken it upon himself to disappear, then word would circulate that Hightop was incompetent for not being in control of his men, especially a new recruit.

No rival gang was claiming responsibility, so if Nic had been taken out by someone else, who? A new gang in town, looking to muscle in on his territory? No reports had been flagged up from the various police officers on the Hatter's books, so it was unlikely, but surely no individual person had the skills or resources necessary to make someone simply disappear, so if he was dead, where was the body?

Hightop didn't like being frustrated. It upset him. Which meant no-one was safe!

CHAPTER 41

George and his team knew that Colleen's funeral would be a big affair. Floral tributes had started arriving the day before, and florist's vans were still arriving, up to an hour before departure time. Loading the coffin had taken longer than normal simply due to the large number of tributes to display inside. Bouquets, wreaths, single and double ended sprays. Too many to fit in the back of the hearse with the coffin, so a few of the larger tributes had to be tied to the flower rails on the hearse's roof. At the very rear of the hearse, by the head of the coffin, Tommy carefully placed the 3d floral picture of a motorbike, complete with Harley motifs.

Colleen didn't have any family, apart from her Mum who lived in a home for people living with dementia, but her extended family was large, and loud. Very loud!

Dozens of bikers lined the twelve-mile route to the crematorium, which, naturally, included driving along 'Biker's Lane'. George paging the hearse past the pub where Colleen worked.

As the hearse passed the mounted mourners, the bike's engines were revved and the horns were sounded. Once passed, each biker joined the cortège forming behind the hearse. By the time they reached the crematorium, there were over forty motorbikes in procession behind the hearse. It was the longest, and by far, the noisiest cortège George had ever known.

The local press was waiting at the crematorium, but thankfully, they kept a respectful distance. Being faced with several dozen, leather-clad, bearded, tattooed, and emotional bikers, will have that effect on people, even press photographers looking to fill their precious column inches.

The service went well, and was very emotional, as they often are when a young person has died before their time. George's team were present, but unnecessary – it was made very clear at the start of the funeral arrangement, that coffin bearers would not be needed. The coffin wasn't carried in to chapel on shoulder, in the traditional manner, but was raised up, and passed forward down the central aisle, from biker to biker. Dozens of leather jackets creaking, as arms were held aloft. The coffin looked like a rock star, crowd surfing over their fans. Reverend Hirst even wore a black leather jacket, with the Holy cross displayed in studs on the back, as a mark of respect.

Once the curtains had surrounded the coffin, signalling the end of the service, everyone left the chapel to Europe's 'The Final Countdown', and regrouped outside, in the flower court. George lost count of the number of hands he shook, and 'thank-you's' he received, as he made his way back to the hearse, where Tommy was standing diligently by the driver's door. The rest of the team had driven to the crematorium, and had now returned back, in the pool car, as there is not enough room for a full crew, as well as the FD, in the hearse. Besides, every spare inch of space was needed in the hearse, to accommodate the huge number of flowers that surrounded the coffin.

George nodded to Tommy as he approached the hearse, and the Scotsman opened his door, got in, and started the engine. George got in to the passenger seat, and, as Tommy pulled away, heading back to base, he said, "That was something to see, eh?"

"It sure was my friend," George said, letting out a large breath of relief, "it all went to plan, but I just want to be gone, before all those bikes start up again. My ears are still ringing."

Tommy laughed, and the two of them drove back to base without another word, just as they had done for years. Just like normal.

CHAPTER 42

T he next day, just like normal, Tommy was in the tearoom before anyone else, and had timed the pouring of the drinks, to perfection.
"Good morning young Dory," Tommy said, as Theo entered, "your brew is ready when you are."

"Thanks Tommy," he said, picking up his cup from the side as he walked past, "did you see any of the game yesterday?"

"You know I don't have time for watching twenty-two millionaires chasing an inflated pig's bladder around a field. Stop watching that rubbish, it will make you soft."

"Right Tommy, and watching rugby makes you hard, does it?" Theo replied with a laugh.

Tommy had noticed a change in the young lad since his day in the mortuary with George. He was a bit more confident in himself, and had even started to return banter when Tommy ribbed him. Theo had been involved in an embalming, and hadn't fainted or thrown up! He had passed his own personal rite of passage, and it showed. Tommy would never let the lad openly know it, but he was proud that the kid was building his confidence, and starting to realise that maybe he could do this job after all.

Charlie was next to arrive, to be greeted with a "Mornin' Charlie-boy!" from the big Scotsman.

"Morning my good man," Charlie replied in a mock posh accent, "a pint of the usual, if you would be so kind."

"So sorry guvna" Tommy answered, playing along, "the usual is orf this morning, all we've got is tea."

"Then tea it shall be, but I will be having words with the management!"

Charlie sat at the table, next to Theo, who was smiling at the Python-esque skit the two men just played out.

George walked along the corridor towards the tearoom. He was tired, and felt bad about what he had to do next. He had a great team and they trusted him, but it had to be done.

Before he reached the door, he heard "Mornin' Boss, are you well?" from behind him. He didn't need to turn around.

"Morning Holly. Yes, I'm well. Are you well?"

"I am well." Neither of them knew why or

when the ritual started, but they greeting each other in the same manner every morning. It is strange how some things stick.

Both George and Holly collected their coffees from Tommy, and everyone said their hello's and good morning's.

Once the four members of his team had taken their seats, George held up the piece of paper he had carried from his office.

"OK guys, I just have a couple of things to say this morning. Firstly, I've received an email from Mrs Herbert regarding the funeral for her late husband last week. It's quite long, and I won't read it all out, but it will be left on the table, should anyone wish to read it themselves." The four of them exchanged puzzled looks and shrugs, each trying to think if anything had been out of line on the particular funeral.

George continued, "The one part I wanted to read to you all, says, 'Thank you all for helping to make a sad occasion more bearable, and for all the professionalism and dignity shown, especially the young lady who drove the limousine. It was so nice to see a lady undertaker, and she was so thoughtful and caring.'"

Holly's face turned pink, as the guys cheered and banged the table. Cries of "Well done Holly", "Speech, speech", and "Young lady? Yeah right!"

echoed around the room.

Charlie instantly regretted saying the last one as Holly's fist connected with his arm.

George was always happy to see the banter between his team members. It helped to forge good working relationships, but it also made what he was about to say, even harder.

"Alright you lot, settle down! This next bit's important, as it affects us all. I've had a mandate come through from the NAFD." he turned the page around, to show the team an official looking letter, "It states that in order for Funeral Directors associated with the NAFD to comply with recently updated guidelines regarding GDPR, the Association is, from this date, implementing the mandate, that only one person must be present at the time of a coffin being sealed, and that person must be the Funeral Director carrying out the funeral."

Tommy, Holly, Charlie, and even Theo, all started talking at once. It sounded like a drunken squabble outside a kebab shop, as each team member began firing off questions, and vocalising their surprise and disbelief.

George stood silently in the doorway for five minutes until the commotion had settled.

"I hear what you're all saying, and this is as much of a surprise to me, as it is to you.

I have emailed the Secretary of the NAFD for confirmation and clarification of this new rule, but until we hear otherwise, we have to abide by what it says."

Again, the questions came thick and fast. George patted his hands in the air with the universally recognised sign of 'settle down'. He felt bad about lying to his team, and creating the fake document, and if he could have thought of another way that didn't include this deception, he'd have jumped at it.

"I don't understand where the NAFD are going with this, but for now at least, we don't have a choice. Why it makes a difference to data protection when we all see the personal details of the deceased person whilst in our care, I have no idea. We just need to be seen to be complying with the rules, even the ones we don't understand."

The standing rule that a coffin must only be closed in the presence of at least three people, including the FD and hearse driver, made perfect sense to everyone. It helped to eliminate errors, such as a mis-spelled name plate, or spotting a ring that should have been removed, and alleviated the possibility of suspicion, should a family choose to contest whether the deceased person was wearing a specific item of jewellery when the coffin was closed. This new rule made no sense, and seemed detrimental to the funeral industry as a whole.

George placated his team by saying that the rules associated with both the NAFD and the new, high-profile buzzword of the GDPR, rarely made sense, and knowing the NAFD, they would reverse the decision shortly anyway.

George left his team debating the new policy as they drank their brews, and headed back to his office. Slumping backwards into his chair, he looked once again at Julie and Oliver, on the sunny beach in Shanklin.

"Why is it, that I've been responsible for two men losing their lives, but lying to my team feels like the worst thing I've done?" George looked at his family's ever-smiling faces for an answer, he knew they could never give him.

CHAPTER 43

T ommy and a delivery driver were unloading supplies from the back of a van. Bottles of chemicals and boxes of equipment used in the mortuary.

"Dory, gissa hand here son!" Tommy shouted across the yard as Theo arrived for work.

Theo quickened his pace, and put his bag down, next to the large double gates which lead to the workshop. Usually locked and bolted, but open now, so they could bring in the delivery.

With the three men working in a chain, the goods were off the van in no time. The driver passed them to Theo, who in turn passed them to Tommy, who stacked them just inside the doors, so they could be counted, and checked against the invoice.

Once he had obtained a signature, the driver got back in his van, and drove out of the yard, narrowly missing two men who were just walking in.

Tommy and Theo were busy ferrying the boxes from the doorway to the mortuary, when the two men approached.

"Morning gents," the shorter of the two men said in a loud and clear voice, "is Mr George Mason available please, we'd like a quick word."

Tommy put down the box he had just started to lift, and stood up. The man who had spoken was in his late forties, about 5' 8" and was clearly no stranger to the gym. The second man was in his mid-twenties, and much taller. He recognised who the men were straight away, but asked the question anyway.

"Ay, and who wants to know?"

"My name is Detective Sargeant Tony Burton, and this is my colleague Detective Kai Gardener, and we would like to speak with your boss if he's around?" Both men held up their identification cards, as DS Burton introduced them.

Tommy didn't need to see their ID. He knew they were police as soon as he saw them. There is just something about a plain clothes copper. No matter how they dress, they might as well just still be wearing uniform. It was that obvious.

"Dory, can you find Mr Mason please, while I show these two gentlemen to the arranging room."

Theo replied "Yes Tommy" and ran off towards the office.

A few minutes later, George entered the arranging room to find Tommy standing by the door, watching the two policemen, like a guard dog watching a potential intruder.

"Thanks Tom," George said, placing a hand on the big Scotsman's shoulder, "I'll take it from here." George turned to the officers, as Tommy left the room.

"I'm sorry for Tommy, he has something of a chequered past, and has had one or two brushes with the law, shall we say? But that was all a long time ago, how can I help you gents?"

DS Burton made the introductions, and each man leant forward and shook hands with George. He in turn gestured for the men to sit down, and the three of them sat at the table.

"We are investigating the disappearance of a Mr Dominic Watson, and some of his acquaintances said that he may have visited your premises."

It had been three days since George had taken care of Mr Watson. He knew a visit from the police was inevitable, in fact, he would have worried had they not wanted to speak with him. That may have meant that the Mad Hatters were looking for him instead. George didn't doubt that Detectives Burton and Gardener would report back to Hightop before filing their official report, but he would rather not be face to face with the gang leader if he could help it. Not yet anyway!

"Dominic Watson? Yes, I remember him. He came to visit his friend in the chapel on Monday, Mr Francisco Juliano. It's his funeral tomorrow. You say he's disappeared?"

"Yes sir," DS Burton replied with just the slightest tone in his voice. Suspicion maybe? "what time did Mr Watson arrive and leave Mr Mason?"

"We keep records of all chapel visits, so I can find out for definite if you'd like, but his appointment was half five, and he was here just under an hour in total I believe."

"Did anyone else see him arrive or leave?" Detective Gardener asked, as he wrote notes in his book.

"Not as far as I know. My team had left for the night, and it was just me here."

"Did Mr Watson appear upset or distracted while he was here?"

"This is a funeral home Detective Gardener. I would be surprised if someone coming to visit a friend in the chapel, wasn't upset and distracted."

DS Burton, a little embarrassed by his colleague's last question, took charge again. "So, are you saying Mr Mason, that you are unaware of Mr Watson's whereabouts?"

"I can honestly say, hand on heart, that I have no idea where Mr Watson is, Detective Sargeant."

DS Burton reached into his pocket, and retrieved a business card. "If you should think of anything that you feel may help us with our enquiry, please get in touch."

Both officers shook George's hand again as they left, and George returned to his office. He sat in his chair and looked at the photo on his desk.

"Well, it's true," he said to his wife and son as they looked at him from the beach, "I don't know where Mr Watson is right now. But I'm guessing it's somewhere very hot!"

CHAPTER 44

The back room of the Kenyan Cafe was not currently a good place to be, and several members of the Mad Hatters were wishing they were anywhere else right now, but Hightop had called a meeting, so here is where they were.

The air was thick with smoke and misery. They knew what the meeting was about, but no-one had any definitive answers, and they were all hoping that they wouldn't be the one in Hightop's sights when he arrived. Various theories were being discussed, some louder and more animated than others.

"It's got to be the Cooks Boys, they've been itching to make their mark in this area."

"No chance. Those bitches wouldn't dare try anything. The little pussy couldn't take the heat, and ran away, it's as simple as that."

"I dunno man, why go through with the shooting if you ain't got the balls?"

"It ain't nothin' to do with . . . ."

But the views of the last gang member went unheard, as he, and the rest of the people in the room fell silent as the door opened and Hightop walked in followed by his usual entourage.

"Where is Dominic Watson?" A simple question, asked in a calm and direct way, aimed at everyone in the room.

No-one said a word.

Hightop turned to one of his bodyguards who had escorted him into the room, "Did I just say that out loud Sam, or did I just think it?"

"Out loud Guv" came the rumbling reply.

"Yeah, that's what I thought, only no-one appears to have heard me. I'll try again." Hightop cleared his throat to emphasise his point, "Where, and I really would like an answer this time, is Dominic Watson?"

Everyone in the room looked around at everyone else, secretly praying that they didn't have to be the one to report back, that they had nothing to report back.

Finally, one of the gang, a tall, red-haired man, with a scar running across his nose, broke the silence. "We don't yet know boss."

"Aah, finally, someone found their voice, thank you Scratch for having the manners to reply to me."

Scratch took a deep breath, and stepped back, all too happy to become lost in the crowd again. The spotlight of Hightop's gaze was too intense for him.

"So, no-one has anything to report?" Hightop removed his coat and took his seat as he spoke. "No word on the street, no official police report, no bar room whispers, and nothing being flagged up by our rivals! What does that tell us?"

Head shakes. Shrugs. Silence.

One of the junior members saw an opportunity to impress, and wondered why no-one else was speaking up, "He must have done a runner boss!"

Hightop spun around in his chair and fixed his gaze on the gang member with an opinion.

"Is that so? He done a runner boss," Hightop mimicked, "so what you are implying is that I am so naïve, so ill-informed, and so incompetent, that a member of my gang could just walk away without so much as a trace, and I wouldn't know where they'd gone, is that it?"

The junior member appeared frozen to the spot, and he could feel himself start to shake, especially when he saw those people nearest to him, taking steps to physically, as well as symbolically, distance themselves from him.

"N-no boss, I wasn't saying that, I just. . ." Hightop stopped him mid-sentence by lazily raising his hand.

"As foolish as this man's words are, it would appear, in the absence of any other evidence, that he may speak the truth. Mr Watson has indeed managed to evade me once before, however, I know it to not be the case."

Hightop placed both hands on the table in front of him, and interlaced his fingers, as he often did when deep in thought.

"As part of his third trial, Dominic Watson shot and killed a mother and her son. He was then removed from the area, and hidden away until the heat died down. Following the unexpected death of a man he held in high esteem, he managed to evade his watcher, and make his way back to town, to visit his friend before the funeral."

The people in the room listened intently as Hightop continued to list the facts.

"The funeral home where Nic's friend was residing, belongs to a George Mason. The woman shot and killed by Mr Watson during his trial, was called Julie Mason, wife of one George Mason, and the 10-month-old child was Oliver Mason, and was indeed, the son of the very same, George Mason, Funeral Director!"

Despite themselves, the people in the room couldn't help but express their surprise. They all starting talking at once, and the noise rose sharply.

Hightop silenced the room immediately by banging his fist on the table, knocking over a cup as he did so. The sound of the coffee spilling onto the floor was the only other sound as he spoke.

"So, gentlemen, please allow me to ask another question – who is going to tell me something about Mr George Mason?"

CHAPTER 45

Being a Funeral Director means that you see some pretty horrific things, especially when involved with coroner's transfers, and you soon get used to seeing blood and broken bones. George had seen it all, from road traffic accidents, suicides and murders, to reclusive hoarders who have died in their flats, and not been missed for weeks, sometimes months. Once discovered, their bodies are quite literally alive with maggots.

He had seen them all many times, and built up an immunity to the natural reaction facing most people in that situation – to be sick!

This was different. This was something new. He was in the clean and sterile surroundings of the old mortuary. The same room where he had cleansed the world of his family's murderer, but nothing felt clean about the task ahead of him.

The first part had been easy. He had removed the unmarked body bag from the fridge, and had transferred the deceased onto his mortuary table. As with all post-mortem cases, the first task is to cut along the coroner's stitches, from the throat to the pubic bone, reopening the chest and stomach cavities.

The coroner has to cut through a person's ribs and remove their rib cage and sternum, in order to gain access to the protected organs beneath, the heart and lungs. Once the post-mortem is complete, this is loosely placed back in position before the cavities are sutured closed. George lifted the chest plate out of position, and laid it on the table. This gave him the access he needed to remove the bright yellow clinical waste bag from inside the body.

It is a little-known fact, that each person who has had a post-mortem, will have a clinical waste bag in their stomach, or more to the point, where their stomach used to be. Post mortems are brutal. In order for the coroner to ascertain precisely how a person died, they need to examine every part of that person.

All internal organs will be removed and, if necessary, dissected. They will be removed, weighed and examined. Samples will be taken for testing and viewing under a microscope. The heart, liver, lungs, spleen, intestines, kidneys, and stomach are removed. The person's throat and tongue are removed and examined in the same way, and finally, the back quarter of the skull is cut away, and the brain is also removed, weighed, examined, and dissected for analysis.

Once the coroner has finished examining the organs, they are then collected together, in a bright yellow clinical waste bag, and placed into the deceased person's chest/stomach cavity, before they are sutured closed.

George placed the bag into the drainage sink, and used a pair of scissors to snip off one of the bottom corners. Stomach contents, blood, and other bodily fluids drained from the bag, and disappeared down the large plug hole. The smell made even George cough beneath his mask.

Until this point, George had remained unusually quiet. His usual banter had deserted him, and for once, he was lost for words.

He moved to the head-end of the mortuary table, and spoke to the deceased person for the first time.

"I am so very sorry that you got caught up in this whole mess, Colleen. You had already been through so much, and didn't need to be a part of this too. If the timings were different, and I could have avoided using you in this way, then I would have."

George softly stroked Colleen's hair as he spoke to her, as if somehow trying to pacify her and keep her calm, although he made sure to avoid the loose section at the rear of her skull.

"Dominic Watson was a bad man Colleen, you know that. He justified doing what he did, by saying it was to exact revenge for Hightop killing his sister. I understand his reasons, and even sympathise with him, but he made a very big mistake when he involved my family in his plans. He had to go, and I had to be rid of him as quickly as possible. I am sorry that all of your biker friends carried a murderer into chapel, and not you, but no-one will ever know."

George continued talking to Colleen as he gathered together some of the medical equipment he would need.

"We both know that you're no longer in there, and all that is left is an empty shell that once carried you around. Your heart and mind are no longer in your body, and your soul was released the day you died."

George wasn't sure if he was trying to comfort Colleen, or himself. To continue with what needed to be done, he had to depersonalise the body in front of him as much as possible. He had to convince himself that the essence of the person was no longer here, just an empty husk. A redundant machine that needed to be dismantled.

It had taken just over five hours to complete

the task. Removing Colleen's head had been easy enough physically. The lack of throat, tongue and brain made the skull very light, and easy to manoeuvre, but George had to cover her face, in order to get the job done. Once the head was removed, and wrapped in several layers of cling film, the rest of the operation was relatively simple.

When he'd finished, George had a total of nineteen, neatly wrapped parcels, bundled together in a body bag, on a stainless-steel mortuary tray. Most of Colleen's internal organs had been sliced into manageable pieces, and flushed down the sluice, but George had wrapped her heart and brain together in cling film, as he felt that was more appropriate than ending up being flushed into the drainage system.

George had a plan for the disposal of seventeen of the packages, but the other two would be more difficult and present a high level of risk.

He pulled the zip closed on the body bag, and pushed the large metal tray back into the fridge. He was physically and emotionally drained, and he took, what felt like, his first real breath of the evening. He closed the fridge door, pushed his back against it, and slowly slid to the floor. There, slumped on the mortuary floor, in front of the old fridges, George wept for his soul.

CHAPTER 46

G

eorge closed the mortuary door behind him. "Well Mr Juliano," he said to the coffin, "we meet again sir."

George reached over, and lifted the lid from the coffin, to reveal Francisco laying face up, with his eyes closed and his hands interlaced on his stomach. He was dressed in a simple royal blue gown, and he looked very peaceful. A stark contrast to the last time he and George had talked on the steps to his flat. Francisco had no family. The cost of the funeral was being met by funds raised by the members of his gym, and of course, they had chosen to carry the coffin. No self-respecting gym rat is going to stand by and watch someone else lift a heavy object. Where's the glory in that?

"I'm sorry that we meet in such funereal circumstances, but you should be contented knowing that your passing served my purposes very well, and for that, I thank you." George checked the identification tags, paperwork, and coffin nameplate while he talked to the recumbent gym owner.

"When we first met, I remember you telling me that our mutual friend, Nic Watson had the fastest hands you'd seen for a long time," as he spoke, George reached down to one of the mortuary's stainless-steel cupboards, and unlocked the doors, "so I thought you would appreciate these as a parting gift," George placed two packages by Francisco's feet, each about a foot long, and bound in cling film. "Unfortunately, they're not his, and these hands were used to pulling pints, not punches, but I'm sure you can appreciate the symbolism."

George positioned the lid back on top of the coffin, and inserted the six bolts into the pre-drilled holes. The tops of the bolts were cube shaped, which he tightened with the aid of a special spanner he always kept in his pocket. The coffin was now sealed forever, and Mr Francisco Juliano would be cremated along with the first two of George's special packages. Seventeen to go!

George opened the mortuary door, and the team came in and escorted the coffin to the back of the hearse, to begin the loading procedure while he made his way to his office.

Sitting in his chair, behind his desk, George picked up the photo of his family once more, and chatted to them as if they were in the room with him.

"Hi Jules, hi Oli, how are you both today? Enjoying the sunshine as always, eh? You know what's happening today, so I don't need to explain it to you, and no, I'm not proud of what has to happen, but you know there is no other way." he sat back in his chair and held the photo frame to his chest, "I miss you both so much it hurts, and I'm having to take each day as it comes. I've got to see this through to the end, but once it's over, we can see each other again."

George jumped at the sound of someone knocking on the door frame of his office door.

"Sorry to disturb you George, but the hearse is all ready, and Holly and Dory have gone ahead in the pool car. They've taken the orders of service with them. Are you alright big man?"

"What? Er, yes, thanks Tommy," George stammered, "I'll be out in a minute." he added, placing the framed photo back on his desk.

Tommy nodded, and walked back to the garage area, where George joined him and Charlie, to inspect the hearse before departing. As always, the vehicle was spotlessly clean, and there were no finger marks on the acres of glass that made up the rear of the vehicle. The coffin was loaded symmetrically, both side to side, and front to back, and the floral tribute, in this case, a three-dimensional dumbbell made from chrysanthemums spray painted black, was placed on top of the coffin, just below the name plate.

Tommy stood next to the driver's door, awaiting George's instruction to get in and start the engine, while Charlie was ready to open the double doors so the hearse could drive out to the yard.

"Thank you, gentlemen."

Tommy got in, and started the engine, and Charlie pulled open the doors. Once the hearse had pulled past, he closed them again, and took up his position in the hearse, sitting behind Tommy. George stood in front of the hearse, and donned his top hat. He gave a small nod to Tommy, before turning around, and paging the vehicle out onto the road to begin its journey to the crematorium.

The mood, as always, was sombre inside the hearse. Professional courtesy means that all banter and joking stops once the team are on a funeral, but George felt as though there was something else. Tommy appeared uncharacteristically preoccupied, even to the point of clipping a curb when negotiating a roundabout. He made a mental note to have a chat with the big Scotsman sometime, to make sure he was OK.

The rest of the funeral service went without a hitch. The coffin was carried into the chapel by four of Julie's regulars, to the sound of Survivor's 'Eye Of The Tiger' playing on the sound system. Corny, but appropriate.

Malcolm Burrows, the celebrant leading the service, did a good job of telling the story of Francisco's life, both before, and since, coming to England. Francisco had shared many stories with the people training at his gym, usually to inspire them to focus and work hard to achieve their goals, so Malcolm had managed to obtain a lot of material, with which to produce a fitting eulogy.

Once the service had finished, and the congregation was out in the flower court, George couldn't help but smile when the coffin bearers were telling other gym rats how heavy the coffin felt on their shoulders as they walked. Carrying a coffin is a learned skill, and not all about brute strength. If the bearers all step in time, then the coffin stays still and the movement is smooth. If, as in this case, the bearers ignore the instructions given to them by the hearse driver, because clearly, they know how to lift heavy objects, then the hard underneath of the coffin will bounce slightly all the way down the aisle to the catafalque. George knew they would have bruised shoulders for days.

As always, George stood at a respectful distance from the deceased's friends and family, quietly observing, without making them feel pressured that they have to head off to the reception as soon as possible. The crematorium was always busy and had a tight schedule, but George always tried to eliminate any urgency. He didn't want anyone to feel as though the funeral service was a production line, no matter how close to the truth that may be.

The mourners were mainly people from the gym, but there were a couple of other shop keepers and business owners, who knew Francisco from the high street, as well as the occasional unknown person, who always seemed to appear when there was as funeral to attend.

Aside from hearing about the huge effort it took to carry the coffin, the chat was the same as George had heard a thousand times before, 'nice flowers', 'lovely service', 'very fitting music'. But then, it was as if a wave had spread across the crowd. One person had overheard a name being mentioned, then had questioned it as well, then others were pondering the same. Like an out-of-control wildfire, everyone's conversations changed to be the same topic – where was Nic

Watson, Francisco was like a father to him?

George listened intently, whilst maintaining his thousand-yard stare to give the impression he was not interested. While he slowly scanned the people before him, trying to pick out snippets of guesses and theories as to where he might be, two men caught his eye. They were dressed in dark suits, like most people attending a funeral, and they were wearing dark glasses, which again, isn't uncommon. What stood out for George though, was the fact that they were standing apart from the other attendees. They weren't talking to each other, and no-one was interested in approaching them to talk either, and George got the intense impression that these two gentlemen were staring directly at him!

CHAPTER 47

G eorge had been very careful with the pace at which he was disposing of the packages, containing Colleen Buckingham's body parts. It had been just under three weeks since her coffin, containing the body of Nic Watson, was carried over-head by various chapters of motorbike clubs, and he had so far, managed to dispose of eleven of the nineteen cling film wrapped parcels.

He was particularly pleased with managing to dispose of Colleen's head and pelvic area, thanks to a homeless man who had been found dead in a shallow ditch behind the library. The coroner had performed a post-mortem and ruled that the man died of Hepatitis C. He was therefore considered contagious, and sealed in a body bag. It was the work of just a few minutes for George to open the bag, and hide the large packages inside. The man had no family and no money, so, as a matter of public health, it was the responsibility of the council to provide the means of his funeral, which would mean he would be buried in a pauper's grave.

George knew that Colleen's skull and pelvis would have to be disposed of in a different way to the other seventeen packages. Their size and density would mean that they would survive the heat of the cremation, at least enough to raise suspicion when the attendant raked the ashes from the cremator, into the ashes pan. Large bones such as these need further processing in a cremulator, which ruled this out as the chosen method of disposal.

Burial is a riskier means of disposal, as the packages will always remain in the coffin, unlike cremation, which will completely destroy all evidence, but for just these two packages, there was no other way. The chances of this infectious, homeless man being the subject of an exhumation order was extremely slim, especially as he had already been examined by the coroner, so George knew it was a golden opportunity, he couldn't afford to miss.

George's criteria for selecting which coffins would include a little something extra, was simple enough. It had to be a cremation, obviously, and the family had to have either already visited their loved one in the chapel of rest, or chosen not to have anyone attend the chapel at all. He estimated that all eight remaining packages would be nothing but ash within two weeks. All he had to do was remain calm, keep following the same formula, and stick to the plan.

The unfortunate fact about any plan, is that it is often rigid, slow to adapt, and has to conform to a strict set of rules, otherwise it falls apart. Even the most meticulous plan can be derailed by the smallest of anomalies.

George would soon discover that his plan had an anomaly, but it wasn't small. In fact, it was 6' 2" and Scottish!

It had felt like a very long week, but finally it was Friday. The team were tired, and everyone was looking forward to recharging over the weekend. George could have been mistaken, but again, he had the feeling that something was bothering Tommy. The big man wasn't being his usual self – no exaggerated stories, no funny quips, and he even caught Theo off guard by calling him his real name! It was actually a relief to George, when Tommy approached him and asked for a chat in private.

There was less than an hour to go of the working week, so George went to the tearoom, and told everyone else to bugger off, and enjoy the weekend, thanking them for their hard work during a tough week. Needless to say, he didn't get any arguments, and no-one needed telling twice.

"Where would you like to chat Tommy," George asked, moving his arm like a game-show hostess showing off the star prize, "here, or in my office?"

"Here is good," Tommy replied, "in fact I need to get something from my locker anyway."

He turned around, and stepped over to the bank of metal lockers, taking up the far wall of the tearoom. As he opened his locker, he heard George pull out a chair and sit down.

"So, what's up Tommy? I've sensed an uneasiness a few times this week. Is there something I can help with?"

Tommy turned back to face George, and took the two steps needed to cover the distance between them.

"Oh ay, there have been a few things on my mind this week, but before we discuss them, I'm just going to leave this here." Tommy placed the object he had taken from his locker, onto the tearoom table. It was a package, about four inches across, twelve inches long, and wrapped in cling film.

CHAPTER 48

George stared at the package, as if he could make it disappear purely by willpower. Tommy watched his face, not saying a word.

"What's that Tommy, and where did you get it?" George's voice was trembling as he spoke.

Tommy, without saying a word, sat down opposite George, and slowly started to remove the cling film from the package.

Like two grand-master champions, examining a chess board, neither man spoke, and the tension was palpable. Tommy continued to unwrap the package in front of him.

Finally, Tommy broke the silence, "I've known you since you were a wee bairn, George. In fact, now that your dear ma and pa are no longer here, God rest their souls, there's not a man alive who has known you longer than I have." George watched transfixed, as the layers of cling film were diminishing from around the package as the Scotsman spoke.

"So, before we get down to discussing what has been bothering me this week, I just want to know one thing," Tommy had timed it to perfection. The last wrap of cling film fell away from the contents of the package just as he delivered his punch-line, "would you like some of this?"

George had been nervously fidgeting in his seat, and couldn't take his eyes off of the object that now sat on the table between the two men. It was a foot long, meatball sub with melted cheese.

"I knew we'd be staying late, so grabbed something to eat, you can have half if you wish, eyes bigger than my belly." Tommy watched George's look of horror, as he revealed the package's contents. He had sweat on his brow, and had started to inch his chair backwards with his feet.

"It's a fucking sandwich!" George blurted out, as if to convince himself of what he was seeing.

"Yes George," Tommy said, leaning towards him, "it's a fucking sandwich. But the question isn't what it is, it's what did you expect it to be?"

George stared at the sandwich with his mouth open. His heart was racing, and his brain was going haywire trying to think of every scenario at once.

Did Tommy know? Yes, of course he knew, he

didn't just come here to share his lunch!

How much did he know? Enough definitely, too much probably.

What now? Confess? Deny? Accuse?

What did Tommy want? Money? The truth? Answers?

How was this possible?

Tommy watched George's face as he just sat there, staring. As if hearing George's last question, Tommy broke the silence.

"So young Dory asks me the other day, 'How have things changed since you've worked here Tommy?', so I tell him about the way we make coffins has changed, as we used to make the whole thing from scratch, not just fit them out to suit. I tell him about new technology making it easier for us to lift and transport the deceased, and how mortuary equipment has evolved over time. Then I says to him, about seeing some of the old stuff." George stopped staring at the sandwich, and looked at Tommy as he spoke.

"We go to the old mortuary. He didn't even know it existed, but then it's only really the old timers like us who remember it I suppose. The strange thing was, when I opened the door, do you know what I saw? George? Any idea?"

George didn't know what to say. Everything he had planned had just crashed in the most dramatic fashion. He just stared blankly at the

Scotsman, unable to speak or even move his head.

"I'll tell you, shall I?" Tommy continued, "Nothing. Just a clean mortuary. It looked clean and it smelled clean, which of course, is just how a working mortuary should be. Except this mortuary hadn't been used for at least six years that I know of, so why did it smell so clean? The kid didn't notice anything was out of order, so I showed him the old equipment, including the outdated embalming machine, which I must say, also appeared very clean considering it hadn't been used in so long."

George continued to keep his gaze focused on Tommy, as the big man rose from his seat and stepped over to the kitchen area, to flick the kettle on. He always loves to tell a story. He loves the flair and tension, but for once, no embellishment was necessary. This was as real and as horrific as it could get.

"After giving the kid the penny tour, he returned to the workshop, but I stayed to have a look around. Coffee?" Tommy rhetorically asked, looking back over his shoulder.

Tommy prepared two cups of coffee, without waiting for an answer, and continued with his monologue, "Naturally, with my interest piqued, I had a look in the fridges, which by the way, Dory didn't spot were turned on, and I'm pretty sure you know what I found."

The high-pitched sound of the teaspoon hitting the sides of the mugs as Tommy stirred the drinks, seemed to fill the room, as neither man said a word.

"Actually," Tommy said, turning around and placing both coffees on the table, "before I go any further, do you know what else I found strange this week? No?" The storytelling Scotsman sat back down opposite George, and took a sip from his cup.

"I had just dropped off some paperwork at the crem, and I bumped into Tony Hearn, you know, the FD from Pinetrees? Anyway, we chatted about various things for a minute, then I asked him what he thought of the new NAFD ruling about only the FD closing the coffin. Well, he looked at me like I'd just grown another head or something. He said he'd heard no such thing, and the idea was laughable. Weird, eh?" To allow for dramatic pause, Tommy drank some coffee before continuing.

"I just told him that I must have heard it wrong and got mixed up. It did make me wonder though, why would the NAFD send out new legislation, but not to all Funeral Directors? It doesn't make sense, unless of course, there was no such legislation, and it was simply fabricated by someone. But to what end?"

Tommy pushed George's coffee cup across the table towards him. George didn't know if it were a friendly gesture, or if his opponent was positioning his Queen for checkmate.

"So, tell me George, what, or more to the point who, did I find in the old fridge?"

George looked down at the cup in front of him. The tiny bubbles in the middle were still spinning around where the coffee had been stirred. He felt the same way, helplessly spinning around, just seconds away from popping!

George didn't know what to say, how to say it, or where to start. As he looked up at Tommy, a tear ran down his cheek, and he said, so quietly that it was almost inaudible, "The barmaid."

CHAPTER 49

I t took a further two cups of coffee, and nearly an hour for George to explain to Tommy, how and why the barmaid from the Farmer's Boy pub was neatly dissected and wrapped in cling film, in the old mortuary fridges.

He had known the big Scotsman all his life, so didn't hold back on any details. He owed him that much at least. Dominic Watson and his trials to join the Mad Hatters in order to revenge his sister's death, which he blamed on the ruthless Hightop. Confronting Francisco Juliano, then using him to lure Nic out of hiding. Using the old mortuary to exact his own revenge on the person who took away his world. Seizing the opportunity of Colleen's sealed body bag to dispose of Nic. Fabricating the NAFD ruling to allow him the time and secrecy he needed, to gradually dispose of the packages stored in the old fridge.

As George talked, Tommy listened, not saying a word. He noted how George's voice almost trailed off to a whisper when describing how he had cut up Colleen's body, but was animated and passionate throughout describing the torturous pain Nic Watson endured before dying.

"So, there it is," George said, afraid to look up from the coffee cup sitting on the table in front of him, "now you know it all."

Tommy didn't reply or react for a few minutes. The silence in the room was deafening, and George didn't know what to expect next.

Tommy's reaction, when it came, certainly took George by surprise. The big man stood up, and turned around towards the kettle. He placed both hands on the counter, bent forward, and started to laugh.

After a full minute of laughing, Tommy turned around, wiping tears from his eyes to find a very confused George staring at him.

"You mean to tell me that the little snot-nosed kid who I taught how to tie their shoes, has managed to do all that on his own? Impressive I must say!" Tommy stepped back to the table, and sat down in his chair again, "I just have one question."

"Really", George replied, rather bemused, "I've just explained to you how I have been at least partly responsible for the death of two people, and the mutilation and illegal disposal of a third, and you have just one question?"

George's mind was spinning in all directions at once. He had just confessed to his truly horrific, although in his head, totally justifiable, crimes, and the last thing he expected to be met with, was laughter. Although he was definitely not in the right position to take the moral high-ground, he took umbrage at Tommy's reaction, and couldn't hide the tone in his reply.

"What one question could you possibly have?"

Tommy calmly looked his boss in the eye, and simply said "Why didn't you ask for my help?"

"Wait, what?" George spluttered. He had been expecting anger, disgust, and disappointment, not an offer of help.

"Your wee laddy and his mammy didn't deserve what happened to them, but that nasty piece of work did, and you delivered the only sort of justice possible. I just wish I could have helped."

George still wasn't sure he was hearing this right.

"In fact," Tommy continued, "I'd have kept the bastard around for a few days, and really made him pay. That's always been your biggest flaw young George, you're too kind."

Now it was George's turn to laugh. "I've just

described to you how I strapped a man to a mortuary table, and embalmed him while he still alive, and you say I'm too kind? I'm not sure Mr Watson would agree with you."

"That wee cunt signed his own death certificate as soon as he pulled his trigger on your family," Tommy reached across and placed his hand on George's shoulder to reassure him, "what man wouldn't have done the same as you?"

George knew that Tommy had something of a shady past, but didn't know to what lengths. His father had spoken to him about always allowing Tommy to take days off work at very short notice, and George had continued to extend the privilege without really understanding why. As a kid, he was aware of a problem with some street punks vandalising the local cemetery, and Tommy had, in his dad's words, 'resolved the issue', but clearly the shade of Tommy's past was a little darker than he had anticipated.

George was still feeling shell-shocked from Tommy's reaction to what, George thought, would be the most devastating words to ever leave his mouth.

"So, what now Tommy? Where do we go from here?"

"It must have been quite some burden carrying

this on your own boss, but that stops now. I understand why you lied to the team, and if I know anything about you, I know that must have been a tough thing to do."

George nodded sadly, "You've no idea Tom."

"Then you need to undo that particular mess right away." Tommy got up from his chair, and walked over to his locker, retrieving his phone. "Tell the guys that the NAFD have revoked the ruling, and things are to revert back to how they should be, and I'll take care of the rest of the packages in the fridge."

"Fuck me Tommy," George said, shaking his head in disbelief of what had just happened, "you never fail to surprise, do you know that?"

CHAPTER 50

T ommy spotted them first. He was in the yard, cleaning the limousine with Charlie when the car went slowly past for the second time.

From the courtyard, it is possible to look out onto the road, through the archway originally used by teams of horses pulling the coaches. From where Tommy stood, the aperture of the opening meant that there was only the briefest glimpse of any car that passed, and if the driver of the black Audi had driven past normally, then it wouldn't have registered in Tommy's brain, but two slow passes were significant and deliberate.

Maybe they were lost and looking for an address. Maybe not.

"That was weird Tom," Charlie said, standing up from wiping the front bumper of the limousine, "did you see the way those blokes were looking in?"

"I did young Charlie-boy," he replied, throwing

his cloth into the plastic bin marked 'dirty only', and walking towards the archway leading out onto the road, "do me a favour will ye? Stay here."

Charlie watched as Tommy walked down the driveway to the arch. He saw the big Scotsman look around, then change direction as he crossed over the road. Then Tommy did something that, in the four years he had known him, Charlie had never seen him do before – he unbuttoned his cuffs, and rolled up his sleeves.

"Tea up, you two," Theo shouted, as he walked out of the garage, into the courtyard, carrying two cups, "you alright Charlie? What's up?"

"What? Er, yeah. Do us a favour Theo, can you ask George to come out here? I think something's wrong. Tommy just rolled up his sleeves."

Theo, failing to understand the significance, quipped "About bloody time he did some work. Where is he?"

Charlie turned to face the young lad, and repeated his request with more emphasis.

"Alright Charlie," Theo said, putting the cups down on the empty cable drum that the guys used as a make-shift table, "but I don't see what the big deal is."

Theo wandered back into the garage, then through into the workshop, where George was sitting at the bench, engraving a name plate.

"Hey boss," Theo said once the engraving machine had whirred to a stop, "what's the big deal about Tommy rolling up his sleeves?"

George gave a little laugh as he replied, "I wondered when you'd notice," he said, turning around in the chair, "the truth is, I don't actually know. I've known Tommy all my life, and in all that time, I've only seen him with bare arms once. I was a kid back then, so I don't remember the circumstances, but it's something of a running joke with the lads now."

George stood up, and removed the name plate from the engraver as he spoke. "Some people have guessed that his arms are scarred, but no doubt, if that were the case, he'd have a fanciful story as to how it happened. Some have guessed that he's got some embarrassing tattoos, which I think is closer to the truth, and one person who used to work here, even suggested that Tommy worked as a drag act at the weekends, so his arms were smoothly shaved, mind you, he never said it to Tommy's face! Why do you ask?"

"It's just that Charlie seemed really worked up about him rolling up his sleeves just now, out in the courtyard."

"What?" George said, alarmed, "Why didn't you say sooner?" He dropped the nameplate onto the table, and ran outside. Just as Tommy was walking back towards them, his sleeves rolled back down, and his cuffs fastened.

"Everything alright Tom?" George asked, as the big man walked past them.

"Oh ay," he replied nonchalantly, walking over to the cable drum, "this my brew?"

George knew that Tommy had secrets. He remembered his dad telling him in private, that there was a lot more to Tommy than people saw, and if they were very unfortunate, they would find out just how much more there was. He also said that there weren't many truly dangerous people in the world, but Tommy may well be one of them. It all seemed like bravado to George at the time, but the more he got to know the big Scotsman as an adult, the more he wondered exactly what it was his dad knew.

CHAPTER 51

T ommy knew there would be repercussions from Dominic disappearing, and that it wouldn't take a genius to consider George as having had something to do with it.

Since discovering Colleen's body parts in the old mortuary fridge, and confronting George about just how they got there, he had been watching and waiting for someone to make a move, and here they were, two pawns come to keep a watch, or snoop around and report back to their boss.

Tommy walked through the archway, and spotted the black Audi parked up on the other side of the road. He crossed over, and hoping that they were old-school, not 'wet behind the ears' rookies, he undid his shirt cuffs, and rolled up his sleeves. That action alone, could be seen as a threat - a man readying himself for a fight, but Tommy did it to prevent a fight, not start one, although, if his message were misunderstood, he would be fine with that too.

The man behind the steering wheel was Danny Drummond, better known as Drummer. Not because of his surname, but because he actually was a drummer, and he once killed a man with a drumstick, when he was being disruptive in a pub where he was jamming with some friends. The guy was drunk, obnoxious, and very vocal about the barmaid's assets, and the fact that she'd probably slept with half the men in the pub. Whether that were true or not, isn't recorded, but unfortunately for the man, the person she happened to be sleeping with at the time, was Danny the drummer.

Danny followed the man into the toilets, and while he was trying to hold himself up at the urinals, while pissing on the floor, Danny approached from behind, and stuck half the length of the drumstick in the man's right ear. He was dead before he landed in his own piss puddle.

Drummer had been a Mad Hatter for over fifteen years, which meant he had seen a lot of things, and been involved in a lot of situations. It also meant, he was now considered to be one of 'the old boys', and as such, his duties included babysitting the younger guys until they knew the score. Test their loyalty, teach them the hidden rules, and generally put them through their paces to assess whether they were still worthy of being part of the crew. He was well respected by his fellow Hatters, and was one of the few people Hightop trusted.

His passenger was known as Rusty, on account of his bright, ginger hair. Drummer didn't know his real name, nor did he care, he just knew that the kid had messed up on a recent job for the Hatters, so Hightop wanted him assessed. He was in his late twenties, a bit scrawny, and just never shut up! If Drummer had to hear about the 'sweet thing' he was banging, one more time, he would probably just shoot the kid and have done with it.

"Who's this crazy fool, prepping for a barny?" Rusty said out loud, to no-one in particular.

Tommy approached the passenger side of the car, and tapped on the window, which silently lowered until it was fully open.

"Y'alright gents?" Tommy placed both hands at the bottom of the open window, leaning on the door, with his fingers inside the car. You seem lost."

"What's it to you bitch? Get off our car!"

Tommy gave Rusty a cursory look, then turned his attention to Drummer, "Your lady friend here seems to have a bit of a problem with a concerned citizen asking if you need help, so I'll ask you instead, is there anything you need help with?"

"Who the fuck are you calling a. . ." Tommy's hand moved too quick for the young man to react. With his elbow as the fulcrum point, Tommy quickly snapped the back of his fist into the man's nose, forcing his head backwards into the headrest.

Drummer was a little surprised, but didn't react. Whoever this man was, he was clearly very confident in his abilities, plus he was on the other side of the car to him. Besides, he couldn't blame anyone for wanting to bust the impertinent kid's nose.

Rusty cupped his hands over his nose, and bent forward, his eyes streaming, "What the fuck!" blood spitting from his mouth as he spoke.

Tommy had placed his hands back on the car door, but changed his hand position slightly. Instead of having his fingers on the inside of the car, he had moved his hands around, so that his thumbs were inside. This displayed the inside of his forearms to the driver.

"I do like to help people," Tommy said, calmly addressing the more senior person in the driving seat, "but if I can't, then I've always got friends I can call on to assist."

Drummer looked at this strange Scotsman as if he were crazy. It took some balls to even approach their car, let alone violate and dominate the situation so effortlessly. As he was contemplating his next move, he noticed the man rotate his forearm, until it was fully facing him. His next move suddenly became very clear.

"I see from your face, that we fully understand each other, am I right?"

"Er, yeah," stammered Drummer.

"That's good," replied Tommy with a big grin on his face, "I was hoping we could come to an agreement without this getting messy."

"What the fuck! You busted my fucking nose! I'm gonna fuckin' kill you, bitch" Rusty shouted through his cupped hands.

"Shut the fuck up Rusty!" Drummer shouted at his passenger.

"Ay Rusty, do be quiet while the grown-ups are talking." Tommy added. "Now, I will say this slowly, so there can be no misunderstanding. The Masons have been very good to me over the years. They gave me a chance when no-one else would, and they helped me when I needed it the most. Now, the one thing I want you to take back to whoever sent you, is that the Masons, and everyone associated with them, are my family, and as such, fall under my protection. Is that clear?"

"They're your family, got it." Drummer responded nervously.

"Good," Tommy said, pushing himself up, off the car, "now run along, I think I've got a brew waiting."

Drummer pressed a button on the arm rest of his door, and the window closed. "Shit!" he shouted, banging his hands on the steering wheel in front of him, "Shit, shit shit!"

He checked his mirrors, partly to check for traffic, but also to make sure the Scotsman was still walking away, then put the car in gear, and drove forward.

"What the fuck are you doing Drummer?" Rusty asked, pulling his hand away from his nose, and checking for blood, "that bloke needs sorting."

"Oh right, and who's going to do that Rusty, you? Look at ya, sitting there, dripping blood all over the upholstery. Just shut it OK? If I hear another word out of you before we get back, it won't just be your nose that's fucked, got it?"

Rusty was very confused about what was going on, but he knew better than to argue with Drummer when he was this worked up.

Drummer hit the steering wheel again, "Shit!

Hightop will not be happy about this."

CHAPTER 52

H ightop was sitting in a green leather, wing backed chair, in his private office, in the back room of the Kenyan Cafe, like an old refined gentleman, savouring the aroma and euphoria of one of his many vices. Thankfully, for those in the adjoining room, unlike some of his pleasures, this particular one did not involve inflicted cruel and exceptional pain, just to record the reaction.

Hightop's mind didn't work in the same way as most of the people around him, and he saw solutions to problems that most people couldn't even imagine were possible. Big problems however, needed serious thought, and for that, he demanded silence. One of the first lessons Drummer taught any new person joining the Mad Hatters, was to never interrupt Hightop when he was smoking a cigar. That was his indicator that he was not to be disturbed, no matter what.

Which was why, it was something of a surprise to him, to be rudely disturbed as he was enjoying the solitude of a Montecristo No.2, from his favourite tobacconist, James J. Fox of London.

The first thing that happened, when the commotion started in the alleyway, downstairs, was for two of Hightop's closest bodyguards to run upstairs, and enter his office, forming a defensive barrier between him and whatever was causing the noise.

The second thing to happen, was for the door to burst open, and for Rusty to land in a heap on the floor, holding his ear, and shouting obscenities!

"Who's fucking side are you on, Drummer?" He shouted, as the older man entered the room, "You let that sweaty get away with busting my fucking nose, and now you're turning on me too!"

Drummer ignored the cries from the floor, and approached the stairs leading up to Hightop's office. Hearing Drummer's voice, Hightop gave the command, and the two guards stood aside, following their boss downstairs.

"Sorry for the intrusion Hightop," Drummer said, then noticing the cigar, added, "especially at a time like this. Something's come up, which you need to know."

"Please continue Drummer, and I am hoping what you have to tell me, will explain why I have a whinging Rusty bleeding on my floor."

"'Cos the chicken-shit prick bloody hit me, that's why" Rusty shouted from the floor behind Drummer.

Hightop waved his hand at Drummer, and the big man stepped aside, slowly shaking his head at Rusty's outburst.

"Rusty," Hightop began, walking towards the young man on the floor, "am I to understand that you have some sort of a grievance towards Drummer?"

"What? Yeah, too bloody right I do, that fu . . . ."

Hightop's foot landed squarely on Rusty's chest as he stomped the man to the ground. Rusty curled into the fetal position, holding his chest, and coughing to try and catch his breath.

"Please don't shout out obscenities when addressing me, I consider that to be terribly rude" Hightop explained in a calm and composed voice.

He extended his hand in a friendly, helpful gesture, "Now, take my hand and stand up, and we will attempt communicating properly."

Still curled up in pain, but too afraid not to accept the offer, Rusty gingerly reached up and placed his hand in Hightop's.

Hightop's grip was like a steel trap, and Rusty

cried out as the leader of the Mad Hatters squeezed his knuckles together. Hightop sucked hard on his cigar, until the end glowed bright orange. He then took the cigar from his lips, with his other hand, and stubbed it out on the back of Rusty's hand. The intense pain was immediate and unforgiving.

"You completely ruined that 'cristo for me, so it only seems right that you finish it." He twisted the cigar into the crying man's hand as he spoke, whilst maintaining his vice-like grip.

"Now stand up," he said, yanking Rusty's arm upwards, so he had no choice but to follow, "and we can discuss this properly."

"That's better," Hightop said, still completely composed, "now, anyone who has a grievance with a member of my gang, should bring it to me, and we can discuss the matter in a calm and gentlemanly fashion," he released his grip on Rusty's hand, who immediately cradled it to his still hurting chest, "so I repeat my question from earlier; am I to believe that you have a grievance towards Drummer?"

"Yeah, I mean, yes," Rusty stammered, too scared to talk, but too scared not to, "not only did he let the Scottish tosser walk away after he busted my nose, but then he punched me in the side of the head, and threw me through the door."

"I see," Hightop replied, turning his back on the whimpering man, "and what do you have to say in reply Drummer?"

"I'll reply to the second point first if I may," Hightop gave a slight nod of the head, so Drummer continued, "I punched the little prick because he simply doesn't know when to shut up. He thinks he knows everything about everything, but in fact knows very little of anything, and what he does know, he simply doesn't shut up about."

"Point taken," Hightop replied, "I can see where you would have an issue with that, but what about the nose-breaking Scotsman? Rusty says you allowed this man to punch him in the face, then simply walk away, is this correct?"

"It is, and this again shows Rusty's lack of observation, knowledge, and no doubt, respect. That Scottish tosser, as Rusty so eloquently put it, just happens to be a Talisman."

The atmosphere in the room changed as soon as the word was said. Even Hightop's tone dramatically changed. Gone was the court room banter delivery of the past few minutes, replaced with a much more serious inflection.

"Are you sure, Drummer?

"Yes, positive. There was no mistaking the

scarring on his forearm, it was definitely the Talisman's Helm of Awe. I've only ever seen this version once before, but it's not something you forget. He's definitely a Talisman boss."

All thoughts of Rusty now wiped from his mind, Hightop returned upstairs, entered his office, and dismissed his two bodyguards.

"This complicates matters." Sitting in his high-backed leather chair, he opened his Scritto Venezia humidor, and took out another Montecristo No.2.

CHAPTER 53

D rummer walked over to the percolator, and poured himself a large black coffee, before sitting at the table. The rest of the room gathered around him, as he drew a symbol on a napkin. Six tridents arranged in a circle, facing outwards, like the spokes of a wheel.

The half a dozen people in the room leaned in to better see the drawing.

"Are you seriously saying that this Scots bloke, whoever he is, is an actual Talisman?" One of the onlookers asked, "I thought they were just a legend."

"A myth to remind us that there's always someone more ruthless and deadly than us you mean? That no matter how bad-ass we are, we will never be the top dogs? It's true that they have become a thing of legend, and if you're lucky, that's how they'll stay, but trust me, they are very real." Drummer tapped the pen on the napkin. "This is called The Helm of Awe, and is a symbol of protection. It symbolises that anyone under a

Talisman's protection has nothing to fear."

Rusty sat himself down in a chair opposite Drummer, still nursing his burnt hand, "Who are these Talisman people? I've never heard of them. What, are they a rival gang or something?"

"A gang of sorts, well, at least, that's how they started out" explained Drummer, "but definitely not a rival. If a Talisman has an issue with you, then you are quite simply a dead man, and there wouldn't be a damn thing anyone could do about it."

"Bullshit," Rusty exclaimed, "if someone came looking for a Mad Hatter, then he'd find all of us, and some serious shit!"

"A Talisman would quite happily go through all of us, to get to the one man they were looking for," Drummer explained, looking up at the petulant Rusty, "there are hundreds, possibly thousands of Talisman members, no-one knows for sure. They are more of a secret society than a gang, with enormous wealth and endless resources. There are rumours that some are in high-ranking military positions, police, bankers, even government, to ensure they are untouchable, as well as everyday people, leading everyday lives. Until of course, they get the call. No Talisman outranks another, no matter what job they do. They are fiercely loyal, and if one Talisman has a problem with you, then they all do, which is what makes them so dangerous, because no-one knows who they are."

"We do," said Rusty, "we know that the Scotsman is a Talisman. So, if they're so secret, how comes he showed you this tattoo thing?"

"Probably because, thanks to Nic Watson, he is too pre-occupied with helping his friend cope with the loss of his wife and child, and prepare for their funeral. Warning us off like that was a simpler and quicker option than having to dispose of two bodies and our car."

Rusty snorted a laugh, "Yeah right! Ain't no-one doing that to us, that's bollocks!"

Rusty ducked to the side, as Drummer's empty coffee cup, flew across the table, and caught him on the shoulder.

"What the fuck, Drummer?"

"You really are an insolent prick, Rusty. All you've done is bitch about your busted nose, but you've no idea just how lucky you are, that's all you got. Not many people piss of a Talisman and live to tell the tale, so I would seriously watch your arse from now on, because if he puts the call out on you, then you're as good as dead. There's fuck all anyone can do about it, and I for one, don't want to be near you and end up as collateral damage because you're a gobby cunt."

"Alright man, chill out for fuck's sake, I get it, they're serious news."

Hightop was standing at the bottom of the stairs, listening to the boys argue. He cleared his throat to get everyone's attention, which of course, he immediately got.

"I have given this matter some serious thought," he said, "and I've made a few phone calls to spread the word that a Talisman is now involved with the Nic Watson issue. That should calm the waters with our rival associates when they hear of my next move. I have spoken with Mr George Mason, and asked for a meeting, once his wife and son's funerals have taken place, and he has, of course, accepted."

CHAPTER 54

George opened his eyes, and stared at his phone sitting on the bedside table. The alarm was getting louder the longer he left it, the repeating tune now impossible to ignore. The phone now started vibrating. He didn't know it did that. He'd never let an alarm ring for so long. Slowly, the phone vibrated its way across the surface of the table, steadily working its way towards the edge. Just as it seemed the phone was destined to fall, unceremoniously, onto the bedroom floor, George reached out, and caught it as it started to topple off the side.

"Alright!" he said, swiping the alarm symbol off the face of his phone, "I'm up already!"

George lay back on his bed, looking up at the ceiling. He knew this day had been steadily approaching, but he still couldn't believe it was finally here. Would the day be cancelled if he didn't get up? If he left it alone, maybe it would leave him alone, and he wouldn't have to try and make it through the ordeal of the next 24 hours. Did all his clients feel this way on the morning of their loved one's funeral?

George got up, and headed for the bathroom, knowing he would never find answers to his questions. He ran his shower a couple of notches hotter than he normally liked, on the setting that Julie always used. He didn't know why. Maybe he was trying to connect with her somehow. Stupid he knew, but he felt as though he just needed to for some reason. It didn't last long, after suffering the heat for about a minute, he re-adjusted the temperature dial to his usual setting – how could she stand it that hot?

After his shower, George threw on a pair of joggers and a t-shirt, and made his way to the kitchen. He wasn't going to risk getting his breakfast on his suit. Not today of all days! He filled the water reservoir on the coffee machine, and got two cups ready while the water trickled through the filter. Right on cue, there was a knock on the kitchen door, and it opened without waiting for an answer.

"Mornin' boss, are ye alright?"

"Good morning Tommy, did you hear the click of the coffee machine or what? Come in mate, it's just about ready."

Tommy entered the kitchen, and closed the door behind him.

"How are ye feeling this morning? Doing

alright, eh?" Tommy asked tentatively.

"A bit numb to tell you the truth Tom. It's almost likc I'm not actually here, if that makes sense?" George passed Tommy his cup of coffee, and signalled for the big man to join him at the table.

"That it does," Tommy replied, sitting in a chair opposite George, "it's like you're battling with yourself to see who you're going to be today."

George gave Tommy a quizzical look over the top of his coffee cup as he drank.

"I'm serious," the big Scot continued, "are you attending this funeral as a Funeral Director, or as a man who has lost his wife and child? You have attended thousands of funerals over the years, but none like this. Your usual professional stoicism has got to be put to one side, to allow your emotions out. You know better than most, that's what funerals are for."

"Bloody hell Tommy, don't go all 'Sophie Michaels' on me."

"Just proving that I do listen when you tell us about psycho mumbo-jumbo clap-trap." Tommy said, raising his coffee cup in a triumphant salute.

"I hear what you're saying though Tom, and

you're right. I always tell my clients how important it is not to bottle up their emotions at a funeral. It is an important part of the healing process. I just didn't realise it applied even more to me, than it does to most people."

"Ay. I know we've discussed it before, and I think I know the answer, but if you want me to conduct, so you can attend purely as a husband and father, I would be honoured."

"Thanks Tom," George said, getting up and putting his empty cup in the sink, "I really appreciate it, and I know you would do us proud, but it's something I need to do.

"Of course," Tommy stood up and placed his empty cup in the sink, next to George's, "but if you change your mind, just give me a shout. I'm going back over to get the guys prepped, and besides," Tommy paused, and raised his hand to his ear, "ah yes, I think Charlie just put the kettle on."

George held out his hand, and Tommy shook it.

"Thank you, Tommy. I don't know how I'd have managed any of this without you. I probably owe you thanks for more than I know, and I'm guessing, more than I want to know too. Thank you, for everything."

Tommy simply gave a humble little nod, and said "My privilege George" before leaving the house, and crossing the yard to join the rest of the team.

CHAPTER 55

Tommy was right, George had arranged and officiated on literally thousands of funerals over the years, and he had developed certain likes and dislikes when it came to funeral services.

Funerals, just like the life the of the person being celebrated and remembered, are individual and unique, and something desirable to one person, may be abhorrent to someone else. To some people, planning and arranging the funeral is all part of the grieving process, and they find it to be cathartic. Sorting out photos, finding favourite music or hymns, and arranging for tributes to include favourite flowers, all help to make them feel as though they are creating something special for their loved one.

Other people however, use a funeral service as a show-piece to display their wealth, under the guise of 'nothing is too much' for their loved one. Multiple limousines, a horse-drawn hearse, an expensive, American style casket, dove release, a photographer, and hundreds, sometimes, thousands of pounds worth of floral tributes.

George, of course, could plan and produce any kind of funeral he wanted. He had the money, and the contacts, and the carriage-master had already been in touch to offer his team of horses and a hearse carriage for free. But working at a funeral home, means you are part of a team, and George wanted his team involved at all stages. He didn't want his wife and son's coffin being driven to the crematorium by anyone other than Tommy. It was unthinkable, and Julie would never have forgiven him.

A simple service was all that was required. A nicely made coffin, oversized to accommodate both of its occupants, but nothing expensive or fancy. A nice, double ended floral spray to adorn the top of the coffin, yellow and pink roses, with individual tribute cards from each member of the team. Several celebrants, ministers, and humanists had of course, offered their services for free. George had observed hundreds of various celebrants give funeral services over the years, so to be the one chosen by someone with so much experience, was a big feather in their cap, it also ensured them future work from George, of course! George had accepted Graham Johns' offer, as George had always liked the way he memorised and delivered the poems with feeling, and not just read them out from the order of service.

The service was booked for 1.30pm in the Willow Chapel of the local crematorium, and would feature a live webcast, so those people who were unable to travel, could still attend, albeit virtually.

George made his way over to the tearoom to join the rest of the team at 10.30, after changing his mind about his choice of tie for the third time, and his shoes, once. The team, as a whole, had a brew together, and chatted about happier times with Julie and Oliver. They were a close-knit team, and were all feeling various degrees of loss, as well as feeling it radiate from their boss.

At midday, George gathered everyone together in the mortuary, so they could all be a part of sealing the coffin for the last time. Even though, they all knew who was in the coffin, they still played it by the book, and checked all the identification tags and paperwork. The blue teddy that George had initially placed with Oliver, was still with him in the coffin, as well as a photograph, identical to the one in pride of place on his desk, which George had placed in Julie's hands. Before the coffin lid was screwed into place, George removed the bear, and replaced it with an identical one.

"My Oli has been sleeping with this one since he came back home," George explained to the team, "and I've been sleeping with the other.

Now it's time to swap." George felt Tommy's big hand squeeze his shoulder as he made the exchange, and he heard Holly begin to cry.

Once the lid was in place, and the screws tightened, the team placed the floral tribute on top, and loaded the coffin onto the hearse. They still had nearly forty minutes before they had to leave, so to inject some normality and morale into the situation, Charlie went to the tearoom, and put the kettle on!

George retired to his office, to prepare himself, both mentally and physically, for the funeral, just as he had done so many times before. He changed into his frock coat, and brushed his top-hat with the clothes brush, even if it didn't need it. He then looked over to the umbrella stand, containing the antique ebony walking cane, topped with the silver globe.

The cane symbolised everything wholesome, honest, decent, and upstanding, that his father and grandfather had embodied. By his actions, George had tarnished the Mason name, and that is something he would never be able to change.

George jumped as the cane rose from the umbrella stand, and he was so deep in thought, that it took him a second to realise that Tommy had picked it up, and was now standing in the doorway, weighing it in his hands.

"Sorry Tom, I didn't see you there."

"Ay, I gathered that, after I spoke to you, but you didn't hear."

"Yeah, sorry, I was miles away." George said quickly, his heart still racing from the shock.

"Penny for your thoughts there, boss." Tommy inquired, slowly spinning the cane like a baton.

"Just trying to sort things out with my conscience I guess," George said, taking his seat behind his desk, "what I did, I did for my family," George picked up the framed photo, "but by doing so, I ruined my family name."

"I see," Tommy said, entering the room, and placing the cane on George's desk, "well it is true that family is very important, especially with an established and respected name like Mason," Tommy took off his jacket, and placed it on the back of the chair nearest him. "but you can't accuse yourself of ruining something, if you don't fully understand it to begin with."

"It's my family Tommy, of course I understand it. My grandfather started this business, then it was handed to me through my father. They were both well-respected men, who believed in honesty and valued family above all else."

"Ay, that is true," Tommy said, undoing the

cuff of his shirt, "but that doesn't mean you know everything." Tommy rolled up his sleeve, uncovering the scarification of the Helm of Awe design. George put down the photo, and leaned forward in his chair, so he could see more clearly.

"Not every family is held together with blood. Some are bonded by something even stronger. An oath, a code, a way of life. We see families here every week, arguing, bickering, and fighting over money, possessions, or status. Blood ties these people together, but nothing else." Tommy turned his forearm around more, so George could see the full detail of the symbol, cut into his skin. "I am part of a global family that a lot of people say doesn't exist. I am a Talisman, and I am bound by oath, to protect any other member of my family, fighting side by side if necessary, whatever it takes. Do you understand?"

George was frowning, but nodded his head. "So, you're like some sort of secret society, with strong beliefs and undying loyalty, who are willing to kill if necessary, to protect your beliefs? So that's why you never show your arms! But what does this have to do with me?"

"You went all-out for your family George. Despite your previous beliefs that you would never wish to harm anyone, when that evil fuck murdered your family, it awoke something inside you that meant nothing on this planet was going to get in your way. Nothing was going to stop you from hunting down the man who took your family from you, and wiping him from the face of the earth."

George sat back in his seat, flustered. "But that makes me no better than him! Dominic Watson destroyed my life, but is that justification for what I did? It's not the right way. It's not the Mason way!"

Tommy stood up, rolled down his shirt sleeve, and fastened the cuff. He smiled at George, as he picked his coat up from the back of the chair, before walking towards the door. "Doing whatever it takes to protect the honour of your family, isn't the Mason way eh? Fighting for what's right, no matter what form that fight may take, isn't the Mason way eh? Being ruthlessly loyal to your family, and facing any challenge head-on, isn't the Mason way, eh? Tommy stopped in the doorway, and turned to face George.

"Before you can decide whether you've blackened the family name, you really need to understand the actions of the people who came before you, so you have some perspective." George was still puzzled by what Tommy was saying, but his next question really took him by surprise. "Before you decide anything young George, ask yourself this: did you ever see your father with his sleeves rolled up?"

George was lost for words as Tommy left the office. His father was a Talisman? How was that even possible? Of course, he'd seen his dad's arms! Hadn't he? He wore a suit at work of course, so they were always covered then, but surely there must have been some time? His dad never owned a t-shirt, but George always assumed that was a generational thing. Even after his father's death, George didn't see his bare arms, as Tommy had prepared and dressed him, before he was placed in his coffin.

"Bloody hell!" George exclaimed to an empty room.

He picked up the cane from his desk, and used it to push himself out of his chair. Maybe he was the right person to proudly wield the cane, and the Mason name, after all.

CHAPTER 56

T here are many secret signals and gestures between an established partnership of Funeral Director and hearse driver, which allows them to communicate during the course of the funeral, without the family being aware. Subtle looks, or hidden hand gestures from the Director can convey that the team are to either leave the flowers on the coffin or take them out to the flower court, for instance, or simply that they are to quietly approach the Director for further instruction.

A hidden observer, knowing where to look, and what to look for, would have spotted a very subtle nod of the head as George walked past Tommy to get to the front of the hearse, and was that a knowing wink, or just a slight twitch?

Tommy stood, respectfully, next to the driver's door, awaiting instruction from George, that he was ready to page the hearse out of the yard, and Holly, Charlie, and Theo did the same by the limousine. George looked at them, and felt very proud that he had such a great team to work with, as well as supporting him personally.

"Thank you, team!" George exclaimed, as he placed his hat on his head. All members of the team entered their vehicles at the same time, and George waited for Tommy to make eye contact, which was the signal that he was ready. George gave a small bow to the front of the hearse, then turned and began walking towards the main road. The hearse followed closely behind, and the limousine tucked in behind the hearse.

George stood at the exit to Mason's yard, looking for a suitable gap in the traffic. His right hand held the ebony cane, and his left hand was held behind his back, with his hand spread wide, palm facing Tommy. A clear indication that he was to wait. A delivery van stopped in the road, blocking all vehicles behind him. George nodded thanks to the driver, closed his left fist, and walked forward. Tommy kept a respectful three feet gap between George and the front of the hearse, and Holly did the same between the hearse and the front of the limousine. A well-practised cortège moving in harmony.

The road on which Mason's Funeral Directors is located, is a fairly busy, main road, so George didn't like to hold up the traffic for too long. His usual page lasted about a minute, and took him a couple of hundred yards down the road, to where a large willow tree grew on the village green. On this occasion however, he walked twice as far. It only seemed right, as there were two people in the coffin.

After paging as far as he felt was necessary, George stepped to the side of the road, and removed his hat, holding it upright in his left hand, looking as he were about to throw it like a frisbee. Tommy drove up to where George stood, and stopped the hearse precisely so the rear wheels were in front of his feet. This meant that when George bowed, before entering the vehicle, he was in line with the head of the person, or in this case, people, in the coffin.

After bowing, George got in to the passenger seat of the hearse, and Tommy continued on the route he had driven countless times before.

"Thank you for the illuminating chat Tommy," George picked imaginary fluff from his hat as he spoke, "it was quite an eye opener."

"Not a problem boss," Tommy stopped at a red traffic light, and turned to face George, "Julie and young Oliver would be very proud of the way you handled the situation, and don't you ever doubt it. So would your dad"

George smiled as the hearse pulled away from the lights. He wasn't sure if Tommy was giving him encouragement, or a command, but he was just glad to have the big Scotsman beside him regardless.

The rest of the journey to the crematorium was the same as any other, people stopped their cars on roundabouts to allow the funeral to pass, old men doffed their caps and bowed their heads out of respect, and several people crossed themselves at the sight of the coffin.

Eventually, Tommy drove the hearse through the main gates of the crematorium. There is a winding road, through a wooded area, before turning right, then a straight road to the chapel entrance. The usual place for the hearse to stop, for the FD to start paging, is just as they exit the wooded area, once the chapel entrance is in sight. Tommy brought the hearse to a halt as soon as Holly's limousine had turned off to follow the road leading to the car park.

"A longer page might be called for here too, I think boss."

"That's a good suggestion Tommy, thank you."

George exited the hearse, walked to the front, donned his hat and bowed, then turned, and paged the vehicle along the tree lined road.

As George walked, he could see glimpses of the straight road in front of the chapel entrance, but he couldn't see the chapel building, as there were people in the way. As soon as he cleared the trees, and turned the corner, George understood why Tommy insisted on a longer walk. Both sides of the 150-metre road were lined with Funeral Directors, funeral operatives, crematorium staff, and celebrants. George couldn't believe it. As he walked proudly down the centre of the road, all the Funeral Directors removed their hats, and everyone bowed as the coffin passed them. Overwhelming pride, sadness, happiness, and humility meant that George's cheeks were wet with tears by the time he reached the entrance to the building.

Tommy positioned the hearse, so the rear of the hearse was in line with the chapel doors, as George once again, removed his hat and bowed to the coffin. Charlie, Holly, and Theo, who had made their way from the limousine parking area, to the chapel entrance, while George was paging the hearse, bowed in unison with George.

"You bastard!" George jokingly said to Tommy as he exited the driver's seat, and walked to the rear of the hearse.

"Me?" Tommy replied, feigning innocence as he opened the rear of the hearse, "I've no idea what you mean boss. Anyway, it was Holly's idea."

Tommy opened the back of the hearse, and the team proceeded to perform their duties without need for further instruction. Orders of service were laid out on seats, and photos of

Julie holding Oliver, were placed on easels at the front of the chapel. George placed his hat and cane on the passenger seat of the hearse, then joined Graham Johns, to make final checks with the chapel attendant that they had the correct running order for the music.

With everything ready, George went back outside to welcome the family and friends who were waiting for the service to begin.

"Ladies and Gentlemen, firstly, I would like to thank you all for joining me here today. I know some of you have travelled quite a distance, and it is very much appreciated. Secondly, can I ask, before we go into the chapel, that everyone checks that their mobile phones are switched off, or turned to silent? Thank you."

George waited for the usual few minutes for bags to be opened, phones fumbled with, and replaced. As always, there was someone who didn't know how to turn their sounds off, and as always, there were two or three people getting in a muddle, trying to help them all at the same time.

"OK ladies and gentlemen," George announced once the noise had again settled, "will you please follow me into the chapel."

As George turned towards the chapel, and led the congregation through the doors, the chapel attendant pressed a discrete button on the wall. Prompted by the buzzer sounding in her room, the organist started the play Julie's favourite hymn, as chosen by George, 'And Did Those Feet In Ancient Times' while the congregation found their seats.

George couldn't help but smile when he heard the soulful sound of the pipe organ. Julie wasn't particularly religious, and he doubted if she even knew the real title of the piece of music, but after seeing the England rugby team sing 'Jerusalem' during a Six Nations tournament at Twickenham, it instantly became a firm favourite.

George walked to the catafalque, then turned to face his friends and family, who were, as George had seen many times, following tradition, and filling the chapel seats from the back of the room first.

"There are plenty of seats at the front still," George announced, opening his arms wide to indicate the empty benches, "and please use both sides of the chapel."

Once everyone was settled in their seats, George walked back up the aisle to join his team who were dutifully waiting at the back of the hearse. Four bearers, standing in a square, facing each other – being the shortest, Theo and Holly were nearest the hearse, whilst Charlie and

Tommy stood a couple of feet away, in readiness to receive the heavier, head-end of the coffin.

George stood at the head of the gathering, looking through the tunnel of bearers, directly at the head-end of the coffin, as he heard the chapel's sound system play the haunting beginning of 'The Sound Of Silence' by Disturbed.

"OK guys," George said softly to his team, "before we go in, I'd just like to take advantage of the fact that none of you will talk whilst in formation, to tell you how proud I am of you all." As expected, no-one moved and no-one said a word, but glances and raised eyebrows were shared between the team, as George continued. "This has been a tough time for us all, and you have been a credit to your profession, to me, and to yourselves."

George's voice broke as he spoke, and his bottom lip was quivering with raw emotion. Every member of the team had tears on their cheeks, but did their best to maintain dignity and composure.

"My entire world collapsed around me when I lost Julie and Oli, and I would never have survived it, if it hadn't been for the support, I received from you four." George wiped his eyes, and took a deep breath, "Come on George," he said to himself, "pull yourself together man."

George turned his head towards the chapel entrance, to hear David Draiman singing 'narrow streets of cobblestone'. Still plenty of time.

"I know the emotional weight of this coffin will far surpass the physical weight, as you carry it down the aisle. Each one of you is an extended member of our family, and I know, if Jules had a choice, she wouldn't want to have been carried by anybody else."

Despite their best efforts, each team member was now sniffing, blowing air out of puffed cheeks, or sobbing.

"In respect of what I've just said, once we have carried in, and I dismiss you from your duties, instead of leaving through the bearer's exit at the side, as usual, I want you all to take a seat on the reserved front pew, so we can all sit together as a family. I have spoken with Tony at Pinetrees, and his team will take care of the flowers, and will return the hearse back to base."

It was too much for George to expect his team to remain composed in such circumstances, and Tommy was the first to break. He stepped forward, and embraced George in a hug. That was all the encouragement the others needed, and George now stood, fully enveloped by his team, hugging him and sobbing.

There is a breaking point in every funeral.

Emotions are high, and everyone is carrying around so much tension and grief, that it has to erupt at some point. For some, it is crying during a poem, or a particular piece of music, for others, it may be released with laughter through a funny eulogy. Whatever the trigger, or how it is expressed, it is thought to be a key part of the funeral process, and it may be the whole purpose of the service – to unite people, through sharing a communal release of emotion.

This was their release. George and his team of extended family members, stood together at the rear of the hearse, united in an emotional, yet private, display of affection, support, and family unity.

'silence like a cancer grows' played out of the chapel's speakers, and George knew he had just under a minute before reaching the key part of the song.

"Thank you, guys." George said, wiping his eyes, as the four members of his team retook their positions, and composed themselves for the task ahead, eyes were wiped, noses were blown, and necks, shoulders, and arms were shaken to release the tension.

"We have all carried at this chapel hundreds of times, so we know what's what, and where. When the song gets to the bit about 'neon God', that's our cue to begin. A nice steady carry, and with any luck, the timing should be spot on.

'and the people bowed and prayed' "OK, here we go."

'to the neon God they made' "Thank you team" George instructed, as he walked between the members of his team, to start drawing the coffin from the back of the hearse. As the coffin reached them, each team member placed their hands underneath, and fed it back until all five people were supporting the weight. The team now moved as one, stepping away from the hearse to clear the overhanging tailgate, before lifting the coffin onto their shoulders on George's command.

Some Funeral Directors like to lead the coffin into the chapel, from the front, but this never sat comfortably with George. He felt that the deceased person should be the priority, not the Director, after all, the person in the coffin is the reason everyone was there. Also, the safety of the deceased person was the Funeral Director's main concern at all times, so how could he ensure that, if he had his back to the coffin, especially during the most precarious part of its journey, being carried five feet off the ground, balancing on the shoulders of four or six people, particularly if family have requested to carry into the chapel.

After a brief pause, George gave the command, "Thank you team", and each bearer stepped off with their left leg, and proceeded to carry the coffin into the building, in perfect step.

"Can the congregation please stand!" Graham announced, as the bearers entered the inner doors of the chapel itself.

Every step the team took was measured and precise. The coffin, with its precious cargo, remained steady and straight, as if it were travelling on a set of rails, such was the determined professionalism of the team.

Twenty seconds after entering the chapel, the team reached the catafalque, and stopped, perfectly still, with the coffin resting on their shoulders, until George gave the instruction to lower.

George raised his hands, and placed them under the head-end of the coffin to help the team smoothly lower into hand. "Thank you, team!"

The much-practised manoeuvre was performed to perfection, and the coffin was lowered, so the foot-end met the rollers set into the top of the catafalque. The process was a mirror-image of the team removing the coffin from the hearse, and as George pushed the coffin gently over the catafalque's rollers, the team stepped forward, either side of the raised dais, keeping their positions relative to the coffin.

The timing couldn't have been better. The four

bearers stood in formation, facing the coffin, but watching George out the corner of their eyes. After a pause, to match the beat of the music, George bowed to the coffin, and the rest of his team bowed with him. Perfect symmetry, precisely executed.

George and his team, as one person, returned to their upright positions, and once again, George gave the instruction, "Thank you team. With military precision, each member of the team turned to face the congregation, and filed past George. As instructed, instead of exiting the chapel through the bearer's door, Tommy, Charlie, Theo, and Holly made their way to the front pew. As they did this, George took a final bow, just as the last note of 'The Sound Of Silence' rang out. After standing back up, George placed a hand on the coffin, and said a private prayer, before taking a step back, then turning, and taking his seat in the front pew.

George heard Graham begin the service in his customary way, "Good afternoon family and friends, my name is Graham Johns. I am a member of the Association Of Independent Celebrants, and it is my honour to have been asked to conduct this funeral service for Julie and Oliver Mason."

Poems were read, stories were shared, and Graham's eulogy, created from various stories and memories from friends and family, made members of the congregation, laugh and cry in equal amounts – the perfect combination.

Much of what was said, washed over George. He had attended thousands of funerals, but had never entertained the thought that one day, he would be attending this particular one. He knew the service was going on around him, but his mind wasn't really in attendance.

He had chosen Leonard Cohen's 'Hallelujah' as the piece of music, played for quiet reflection, in the middle of the service. He had heard the piece several times at funerals, and had chosen the 'Pentatonix' version, as the pure a cappella style really lends itself well to the raw emotive power of the song.

George lent forward in his seat as the song began, and sobbed with his head in his hands. By the time the quintet had reached the crescendo, there wasn't a dry eye in the chapel. Graham Johns had to wait for a couple of minutes after the music had ended, for people to compose themselves, before he could continue.

The service ended in the usual way, with the blessing and commitment, followed by the Lord's Prayer, and a poem. Graham had chosen Mary Elizabeth Frye's 'Do not stand at my grave and weep', which, of course, he had memorised, and read with passion.

As arranged, during his reading, George stood and walked to the front of the chapel, facing the catafalque. His team, following a subtle hand gesture from George, joined him, standing behind him in perfect formation, for the closing of the curtains.

Once they were in place, Graham pressed a button on his lectern, and the inner voile curtain began to close from either side of the coffin laden catafalque. As the two curtains met in the middle, the light directly above the coffin dimmed, and the main, purple velvet curtains moved along their track, until they too, surrounded the coffin. As the gap between the curtains grew closer, George and his team, as one, gave a final bow.

Graham Johns had finished the poem, and Stuart, the chapel attendant, seeing George stand straight again, made his way along the right wall of the chapel, to open the doors leading to the flower court, pressing a button on a remote, held in his hand, as he did so.

Israel Kamakawiwo'ole's famous ukulele version of 'Somewhere over the rainbow' played over the chapel's sound system, and signalled the end of the service. George left the chapel, and closely followed by his four-person entourage, led the congregation out to the flower court, where, as agreed, the team from Pinetrees had laid out the flowers and cards from well-wishers.

George never understood why families spent so much time in the flower court. Yes, it was a nice place to finally take a breath following an emotional service, and there were always some people who weren't going to the reception venue, but after ten minutes of shaking hands, and thanking people for attending, he was itching to head off to the Craigwen Hotel, where he knew, a very special 30-year-old would be waiting for him.

George looked over the heads of the people currently telling him just how sorry they were, and straight away, made eye contact with Holly - 'eye's on FD mode' as always! He nodded his head, and she knew it was time to fetch the limousine.

CHAPTER 57

The Craigwen Hotel is a country-house style hotel, with fitness and leisure facilities, and is the flagship for a high-end chain of exclusive hotels. The impressive, and stylish white building complex, boasts a Michelin star restaurant, gym, swimming pool, spa, and sauna, but that's not the reason George had chosen The Craigwen as the venue for the reception.

Hotel, restaurant, and pub managers, know the value of staying on the right side of a Funeral Director. They have the power to send a lot of business their way, when clients ask for recommendations for reception venues. Madeline Whiting was no exception. At just twenty-seven, Maddie was young to be in charge of such a prestigious hotel, but with her charm, business sense, and an almost supernatural power to be liked by almost everyone who met her, she had proven herself more than up to the task.

George and Julie had enjoyed several meals,

with complimentary bottles of wine, at the Craigwen, and over time, the three of them had become friends. The use of the hotel for the reception, was of course, like the wine, complimentary. However, it was something that Maddie had introduced George and Julie to, after one of their meals, that was the main reason Craigwen was his hotel of choice.

Aside from the main bar used by most patrons of the restaurant, there was a smaller, more private bar, for the more discerning clientele. Soft, brown leather sofas, an open wood fire, and shelves of books, gave the whiskey bar the feel of a gentleman's club from the past. Tasteful artwork, and framed black and white photographs adorned the walls, evidence of yet more of Maddie's talents.

It was in this bar, that George now sat with his team. The five of them, sitting on three sofas, placed in a U shape, around a glass topped, oak coffee table. On the table were five, heavy, led crystal glasses, a jug of water, and a wooden box, decorated with brass corners.

"Lady, and gents," George began, speaking softly, as if on hallowed ground, "welcome to Craigwen's whisky bar. They have over two hundred different varieties of whisky here, but there is one very special one, I would like to introduce you to."

George shuffled forward on the sofa, and opened the wooden box. Inside, on the left, was a red leather book, held in place with ribbon, and on the right, was a panel, in matching red leather, embossed with the Glenfiddich emblem. George pulled a tab on the panel, and it opened to reveal a compartment housing a bottle of whisky. "This is a thirty-year old bottle of Glenfiddich single malt whisky, probably one of the finest whiskies ever produced, and it costs over £400 a bottle."

Holly and Theo let out audible gasps, Charlie shuffled in his seat, and looked at Tommy. Tommy raised his eyebrows in awe.

"I can't think of a more fitting way to toast, not only my wife and son, but also the best team of friends a man could wish for."

George lifted the bottle from the box, and twisted the bottle open. The cap 'click-clicked' as the seal broke. George paused to breath in the aroma, before pouring a healthy measure into all five glasses. He then did the same with the water jug, just adding a small amount to each glass.

George handed a glass to each member of his team, and held his own high, in the time-honoured tradition of announcing a toast.

"Some people have great family," he began, "and others have great friends. I am fortunate to have had both." He looked around at the four faces, watching him intently. "This is a toast to my amazing Jules, and my beautiful boy, Oli." George's resolve once again abandoned him, his voice breaking as he said his son's name. "To lost family!" he announced, holding his glass up, before putting it to his mouth, and taking a large sip.

The four friends raised their glasses, "To lost family!" they said as one.

"The best way to see light," George raised his glass again, as he spoke, "is to be in darkness, and I have certainly found some light while in my darkest moments." He paused to look at each person sat in front of him. "To new found family!" he said, before again, taking a sip from his glass.

"New found family!" returned the chorus.

"Before we go any further, I would just like to make one more toast, if you'll indulge me." Thinking the toasts were over, the four friends had started chatting, but settled down again as George spoke. "For reasons which will remain unsaid, I would just like to propose a toast to Colleen Buckingham, former barmaid of the Farmer's Boy Pub. Colleen!" George swigged the remaining contents of his glass, and savoured the burning sensation on his tongue for a few seconds, before swallowing.

Although three of the gathered friends were slightly bemused behind the reasoning for the toast, all four of them repeated her name and sipped their whisky.

In the days and weeks that followed, on various occasions, Tommy was quizzed by all three of his colleagues, as to the reason behind George toasting Colleen. He, of course, pleaded ignorance every time.

CHAPTER 58

T he rest of the evening at the hotel, as far as George was aware, passed without a problem. After spending the quality time with his friends in the whisky bar, the rest of the evening was taken up with performing his duties as the chief mourner. Shaking hands with people he barely knew, being hugged by distant relatives, and listening to people wax lyrical about how wonderful Julie was, which of course, she was, but people didn't really know what they were saying, they were just talking for the sake of it. Normal. Mundane. Nothing to report.

The same couldn't be said about everyone's evening however.

Rusty had been humiliated by Tommy, belittled by Drummer, and spurned and burned by Hightop. He had to find a way to re-establish his position within the gang's hierarchy, and he would use anything he could find, to gain an advantage. Everyone knew that the Funeral Director had something to do with Nic's disappearance, but Hightop was refusing to retaliate, because of the nose-busting Talisman. Hightop had made the wrong decision in Rusty's eyes, and it was a sign of weakness that couldn't be ignored.

Wearing the dark grey suit, white shirt, and dark tie, that had been provided to him, by his social worker to wear at his last probation hearing, Rusty blended into the background, surrounded by dozens of people in similar attire.

No-one else within the Mad Hatters could be trusted to stand against Hightop, for fear of reprisal, but Rusty knew plenty of people outside of the gang, who would only be too happy to help him. Two 'eight balls' and a promise that their help wouldn't be forgotten when he was eventually gang leader, had meant that Rusty wasn't alone at the reception party. The two guys weren't loyal, trustworthy, or particularly smart, but were tough and capable, which was perfect for a one-off job such as this.

The plan, as Rusty had explained to the hired goons, two days previously, as they sat in the dimly-lit backroom of The Crawling Ivy pub, was to get George alone, preferably outside, in the hotel's grounds, and gut him like a fish. The retaliation had to be decisive, and messy. A message had to be sent to people both inside and outside of the Mad Hatters, that it was time he was taken seriously. With this one move,

Rusty would not only open the eyes of those who doubted him, but would weaken Hightop's position, leaving him vulnerable to attack, both from without and within. It was time for a change.

Rusty would approach George at the reception, and tell him that he had important information regarding exactly how his wife and son died, and that there was more to it than he knew. Saying that he needs to speak with him in private, Rusty would lure the unsuspecting Funeral Director outside, where they could grab him, and get him somewhere quiet, so Rusty could exact revenge and so begin his meteoric rise through the ranks.

After casually circling the room once, Rusty could see no sign of any of the funeral staff. The ground floor of the Craigwen Hotel had lots of off-shoots and corridors, inglenooks, and secluded rooms, but he couldn't have missed five people, all dressed in mourning suits, with grey striped trousers. His two associates stood near the tables of buffet food, casually helping themselves to prawn vol-au-vents and beef sandwiches, whilst watching for Rusty's signal.

Rusty stood with his back against the bar, holding a glass of the free wine, so he could observe the room without appearing obvious. It was then that he saw the door which led to the whisky bar, tucked away, near the side of the bar. He placed his glass on the counter, and excused his way through a small group of mourners, so he could check out the room which was previously hidden to him. Before he reached the door, five people, all wearing mourning suits filed out, into the main bar area. Among them were his target, and the bastard Talisman.

As soon as George made an appearance, he was surrounded by well-wishers, all vying for his attention. He looked like a celebrity being hounded by the paparazzi. People were shaking his hand, hugging him, and offering to fetch him a drink. Clearly, Rusty wouldn't be getting near to him for a while, so he stepped back to watch from a distance.

"I need something to help soak up that whisky," Charlie exclaimed, making his way to the buffet tables. Holly and Theo following closely behind, "there'd better be some mini sausages."

"You three make a start, and I'll join ye in a minute," Tommy called after them, "I just need to drain the dragon first."

Rusty watched as Tommy broke away from the crowd, and headed down a narrow corridor to the toilets. Looking over to the buffet table, he gestured for his accomplices to join him.

"Change of plan," he talked fast, partly because

of limited time, and partly through excitement, "George is too tied up for me to get anywhere near him, so I'm going to take out the Scots cunt instead. I'll follow him into the toilets, and have a little chat with our so-called tough friend, while you wait outside. If you don't hear anything after one minute, then come in and we'll take the bastard out."

The three of them made their way, single-file down the narrow corridor, and the two men stood either side of the toilet door, while Rusty pushed it open and went in.

Apart from Rusty and Tommy, the bathroom was otherwise empty. A row of four toilet cubicles ran along the left wall, opposite four hand basins on the right, the wall above them, fully covered by a large mirror. Tommy stood with his back to Rusty, utilising one of the five urinals fitted to the end wall.

Rusty took a couple of steps into the room, but stopped when Tommy turned away from the urinal, zipping up his trousers as he did so. As Tommy turned towards the basins, he saw Rusty standing there, and a brief smile appeared on his face. He approached the basin, and proceeded to wash his hands.

"Do you remember me, you Scottish cunt?" Rusty spat the words at the man nonchalantly washing his hands.

Without stopping what he was doing, Tommy calmly turned his head, and pretended to see Rusty for the first time. "Oh ay, you do look a little familiar. Didn't you used to have a nose that worked?" Tommy chuckled as he turned back to face the mirror, as if Rusty didn't exist.

"Keep laughing old man," Rusty reached his hand behind his back, and pulled a flick-knife from his waistband. The sound of the blade snapping open, echoed around the empty bathroom, "let's see how much you laugh when I fuck your face up with a nice Chelsea Smile!"

Tommy sighed loudly as he shook the excess water from his hands, then stepped over to the paper towel dispenser. He pulled out two sheets, and turned to face Rusty, as he dried his hands.

"I busted your nose without even blinking an eye, so are you sure you want to do this, wee man?" Rusty lifted his arm, so the point of the knife was pointing directly at Tommy.

"Oh ay, you've got your little toothpick, but that still doesn't tip the balance in your favour, if you get my meaning."

Just then, Tommy saw the bathroom door open, and two men entered. They stood behind, and to either side of Rusty. Big men. Tough men. Men who looked like they were very handy in a fight.

"Oh, I see!" Tommy nodded his head slowly as he threw the wet paper towel into the bin. "I'm at the funeral of some people I loved dearly, and I really don't think this is the time nor place. I would much rather you just turn around and fuck off, so I'll ask you one last time," as Tommy spoke, he leant his back against the wall, crossed his legs, and folded his arms, adopting the least defensive posture he could, "are you sure you want to do this, wee man?"

Rusty smiled when he heard the bathroom door open and close behind him, and he could sense a man standing either side of him, just out of his vision. He couldn't believe the audacity of the man in front of him. Out-manned and unarmed, but still trying to out-psyche him, by acting like he's not afraid that he's just about to get totally fucked over.

"Take a look around old man, because this is the last room you'll ever see," the adrenalin was pumping in Rusty's veins as he prepared to launch his attack, "rather a fitting place for a piece of shit to die!" he shouted, taking a step forward.

"True enough I suppose," the big Scotsman replied, then paused for just a second before adding, "thank you boys!"

Rusty would never know how he died. He

would never know how his two associates died either. All he knew, was that one second, he was transferring his weight onto his right leg, ready to lunge forward, and the next second, the bathroom floor appeared to be rushing up to meet his face, and an immense, and very sudden pressure was applied to the back of his neck.

Tommy slowly unfolded his arms, and stepped off from the wall. "What a dumb twat," he said to the Talisman who was lifting his boot off of Rusty's neck, "I gave him the option of walking away."

"Yeah, his two boyfriends outside the door were no smarter Tom. You get back to the reception, we'll take care of the rubbish."

CHAPTER 59

L ife had pretty much returned to normal in the two weeks following the Mason family funeral, or as normal as it could be for George, as he was trying his best to figure out just how his life would work without Julie and Oli.

Charlie and Holly had returned to the crematorium the day after the funeral, and collected the floral tributes, which they delivered to Ashwell House care home, which specialises in caring for people living with dementia. Mason's Funeral Directors were (unfortunately for some) well known to the staff at the home, and it was only fitting that the floral tributes be used in activities for the residents, designed to keep their minds and hands active.

George and the team had arranged, prepared, and conducted funerals just as before, and everyone was finding their own way of dealing with the loss that was felt every day.

On the third Monday following his family's funeral, George took a call, which reminded him that things were indeed, far from normal.

As Tommy passed his office, George called out to him, "Tommy, can I have a word?"

"Sure boss, what's up?"

"Step in and shut the door mate."

Tommy did as he was asked, then sat in the chair, facing George at his desk.

"I've had another phone call from this Hightop character," George explained, almost spitting out the name, as if the word itself tasted bitter, "he wants to meet with me this Friday, to discuss, as he puts it, our future plans, which will benefit us both."

"I see," Tommy replied, "and I take it you're not exactly happy about the proposal?"

"That my friend, is the understatement of the year. I've taken care of the scum who killed my family, but this wanker gave him the order, and the means to do it." George stood up sharply, and paced around his office like a frustrated animal, mumbling incoherently to himself. He then turned to face Tommy again, "How can I allow this shit-for-brains arsehole to walk around, apparently without a care in the world, knowing that he's ultimately responsible for their deaths?" George gesticulated towards the framed photo on his desk.

George sat back down in his chair, "I wouldn't normally ask this Tommy, but I don 't know how else to approach this situation. You have connections to certain people. People who are capable of dealing with problems like this Hightop piece-of-shit. Can you not have a word, give an order, make a phone-call, or whatever it is you do?"

Tommy sat quietly for a few seconds before answering. "George, you are far more than just my boss. You, like your father before you, are like family to me, and other than yourself, no-one wants revenge for what this scum did to Julie and Oliver, more than I do. However, the Talismen aren't a bunch of mercenaries, who just swoop in and wipe out people we don't like. We have sworn an oath to be protectors, not avengers, no matter how justified it would be."

George leant back in his chair, looking up at the ceiling, with his hands rubbing his face.

"I was afraid you would say something like that, but there has to be something that can be done. This Hightop wants to make me some sort of an offer, and from what I've heard, if I say no, then I might as well just set fire to my office myself, because it will equate to the same thing. I'm not making a deal with the cunt who ordered my family dead, but I'm not going to live in fear, surrounding myself with Talismen, either."

"That's very interesting," Tommy said, rising from his seat, "you might be on to something there."

"On to something? What do you mean?"

"I'll need to make some calls, and I'll need tomorrow off work if that's ok, and, oh yeah, I'll need the use of your car." Tommy spoke quickly, as his brain was formulating a high-speed plan, and he was fighting to keep up.

"Yes, of course." George agreed, although not quite sure to what.

"He wants to meet on Friday you said? Did he say where?"

"He said he would come here, once we'd closed."

"OK," said Tommy, staring into the distance, as if reading the plan on a screen behind George, "you'll need to tell him that you want a different meeting place, somewhere neutral for both parties. I'll tell you where, once I've made some calls."

With that, Tommy walked out of the office, just pausing long enough to retrieve a set of car keys from the key safe, hanging on the office wall.

George had no idea what Tommy had in mind,

but had a suspicion that it wouldn't be long before he found out.

CHAPTER 60

T he ringing phone woke George from a restless doze. Working in the funeral industry for so long, George was used to grabbing sleep as and when he could, and he had once again, fallen asleep on the couch in front of the TV, dreaming of the idyllic day on the beach in Shanklin. Instinctively, he picked up his pen and pad, before picking up the phone, ready to take down the details from the police control room.

The phone's display showed the time as being 10.18pm, but the number on the screen wasn't that of the control room, it was Tommy. It had been about thirty-six hours since Tommy and George had last spoken, in his office, and George was keen to learn of his plan.

George tentatively answered his phone, "Hi Tommy."

"Hello George, don't say anything, just listen to what I'm going to say, and trust me."

George was surprised by Tommy's tone and

instructions, but he did trust him, and knew there must be a good reason for the call.

After a brief silence, which confirmed George's compliance, Tommy continued. "There is a new restaurant on the high street, near the library, called 'Ridgeways'. You need to be there at 11.30. Dress smart. You don't need to bring anything, other than an open mind"

With that, the call finished, and George sat, looking at his phone, wondering what Tommy had in mind. With a little over an hour to get ready, George went upstairs to grab a shower and get ready.

~~~~~~

George drove to the high street in the pool car, and parked in the car park behind the restaurant. The clock on the car's dash showed 11.22pm. The front of the restaurant was dark, and looked to be closed when he drove past, but there were several cars in the car park, including his own.

George had no idea what to expect as he walked to the front of the restaurant. There were still no signs that it was open, but he tried the door, just in case. It was locked. Not knowing what else to do, George waited patiently, to see if Tommy would show.

At precisely 11.30pm, the doors to Ridgeways were unlocked, and pushed open. Tommy beckoned George to enter, and smiled at him as he approached. "Trust me." he whispered to George, as he first tied a blindfold over George's eyes, then placed a hood over his head.

In complete darkness, and with his hearing muffled by the hood, George was led inside. 'This can't be real, surely', he thought to himself.

CHAPTER 61

A n unfamiliar voice spoke, with authority, as the hood was removed from George's head, "George Mason, you have been brought forward to stand in front of the Council of the Talisman. The purpose of this gathering is to ascertain whether you have the character, desire, and will, to be considered for inclusion within the folds of our institution, and whether you can be judged as worthy, honest, and trustworthy, in order to keep safe, the secrets that will be entrusted to you."

'Shit,' George thought, 'this really is happening.'

The disjointed voice continued, "Like most people you meet, you are currently in the dark as to the real workings of the world. Your blindfold represents your inability to see the internal workings of the great machine, that moves continuously, unseen by those who wish not to see, yet are forever influenced by its actions."

"Who brings this man forward, to face the

Council?"

"I do, Council-Leader, Arnold Thomas Rogers".

George was relieved to hear Tommy's voice, and was surprised to discover that Tommy was standing beside him.

"Thank you, Arnold, and do you vouch for this man's character, and find him to be trustworthy of the secrets he will be party to, should he be accepted within the fold?"

"I do Council-Leader, on my oath."

"Very well. I see that you have petitioned the Council, and have included detailed information regarding Mr Mason's extort, should it be necessary to invoke the third action."

"I have Council-Leader, complete, just, and true."

George listened intently to what was being asked, and the responses given. He was still shocked that he was being considered for induction as a Talisman, and the magnitude of the occasion was not lost on him.

The Council-Leader, again, turned his attention to George, "Mr George Mason, you have been proposed for recommendation as a Talisman, by a Talisman, and it is on his oath that you are now judged. Before you are led from the darkness, into the light, you must first understand the gravity of the question I will soon ask. There are five levels of intervention, should the Council deem them necessary, and you are bound by your oath to abide by them."

George became aware of movement around him, as people stood from their seats. He could feel that he was standing within an enclosed circle.

A voice behind him, made him jump, "Action One. You will be brought before the Council to explain yourself."

"Action Two." A different voice, off to George's right side. "Your proposer will be brought before the Council to put forward your case."

Another voice, this time, from the opposite point on the circle. "Action Three. The information provided by your proposer, detailing your extort, shall be used by the Council, in any way they deem necessary."

The next voice came, as George had predicted, from behind his left ear. "Action Four. The information detailed in your proposer's extort shall be used by the Council, in any way they deem necessary."

Finally, the fifth voice, was again, directly in front of George. "Action Five. Termination of both parties."

"The Talismen are an ancient order of protectors, Mr Mason," the Council-Leader explained, "and we take our duties and responsibilities very seriously indeed. Should you ever be found to be mis-using the secrets of the order, or to be conducting yourself in a manner which would endanger the order's reputation or moral code, then the Council shall invoke one of the five actions just explained to you. Both yourself, and Mr Rogers, as your proposer, are responsible for your actions, and likewise, for any actions imposed against you."

The people surrounding George retook their seats, and once the noise subsided, the Council-Leader proceeded.

"Mr George Mason, up until this point, none of the secrets of the Talismen have been revealed to you, and you are no more aware of the identity of our members, than you were before you entered this room. Before answering this next question, you must fully understand the commitment you will be making. A Talisman swears an oath to come to the aid of another, no matter the situation or circumstance, and the permanent mark of the Talisman shall not be exposed, unless, as a form of identification to another, or as part of the protection of a righteous other. Do you understand and agree to the terms, as I have described them to you?"

George's mouth felt very dry, but he managed to stutter out his reply, "Yes, I, I do."

"Arnold, as George's proposer, will you please remove his blindfold?"

George felt Tommy move behind him and undo the knot holding the blindfold in place.

George had to blink a couple of times to get his eyes accustomed to the light, but once they were, he could see that he was indeed, standing within a circle of twelve people, an even mix of men and women. The man who had been identified as the Council-Leader, was standing directly in front of George. He stepped forward, and held out his hand, which George shook.

"Welcome to the light, George." he said.

There was a short round of applause from the assembled circle of people, and George felt himself smile. Probably for the first time since he lost his family.

Tommy turned to George, and shook his hand.
"We need to leave this room for a short while, so the second part of the ceremony can be set up," he explained, "so come this way."

Tommy led George to the cloakroom area of the restaurant, where they were alone.

"Tomorrow morning, you need to call this

Hightop person, and tell him you want to meet at a location of your choosing, so you can be sure that it is neutral and safe. If he's as desperate to meet with you as I think, then he'll agree, even if he refuses at first, just to save face."

George listened intently as Tommy spoke. "OK," he agreed, "so where do I choose?"

"Here," Tommy confirmed, "Friday at 8. He won't come alone, but that won't be a problem."

George nodded to show that he understood, although he clearly didn't understand as much as the man in front of him.

"So, how are you feeling George?" Tommy asked.

"A bit light headed to tell the truth. I can't believe this is all real. Am I really going to be a Talisman?"

"You've always been a Talisman George," Tommy explained, "a Talisman isn't who you are, who you are, is a Talisman."

Tommy chuckled at the confused look on George's face, so explained further.

"You are a just man, who has beliefs and honour. You have tried to live an honest life, and you have shown that you will do anything to protect your core beliefs."

George considered what Tommy was saying.

"The extort that the Council-Leader mentioned, I presume that is referring to Nic Watson?"

"The Council knows something about every Talisman, something that will guarantee the secrets will remain just that. The information will never be used to cause harm, unless the person causes harm to the honour and sanctity of the Talismen."

"And if I were to go rogue and reveal the secrets, then the Council would exact revenge on you, as well as me?"

"Yes," Tommy replied, "just as they would with my proposer, if I were to dishonour the beliefs."

George thought for a minute, before adding, "I just have two questions. The first being, what happens next?"

"You will need to change out of your clothes, and wear this," Tommy opened up a large briefcase, and pulled out a sleeveless, sackcloth garment, "each Talisman is marked with the Helm of Awe design. It symbolises both that you belong to the global family of the Talismen, and as such, are protected by whatever means necessary, and also, that you are a protector, of those in need, of each other, and of the secrets that will be explained in due time. What is your second question?"

George laughed as he spoke, "How the hell did I not know your first name is Arnold?"

CHAPTER 62

The restaurant looked similar when George was led back in, but now there was a strange looking chair in the middle of the circle. The large oak, high-backed chair wouldn't have looked out of place being used as a throne. Symbols and runes were carved on the back, and the seat was covered in a purple velvet. Beside it, sat an ordinary swivel stool, which looked child-sized in comparison, and a metal trolley, which would have looked more at home in his mortuary.

The arm-rest on one side of the chair, was angled out at 45 degrees, and had two large brown leather straps, with metal buckles. It was an impressive and imposing piece of furniture, and as he walked closer, George couldn't help but look to see if there were cables attached to the chair, as it reminded him strongly of the electric chair he had seen in a documentary about serial killer, Ted Bundy.

"George Mason," the Council-Leader's voice brought George back to the here and now, "through testimony of your proposer, which is strengthened by yourself being the son of a Talisman, the Council have confirmed that your inclusion is justified. You have been accordingly prepared and attired with the ceremonial waistcoat, so you are indeed ready to receive the honoured mark of the Talisman, the Helm of Awe."

Tommy helped his boss to sit back in the foreboding chair. His right arm was strapped to the armrest, with his palm and forearm facing upper-most.

The Council-Leader and Tommy, stood directly in front of George. "It is customary that I ask the new initiate whether they would like for a pain-relieving ointment to be applied to their skin before the mark is applied."

George could see Tommy staring at him, gently, but intentionally shaking his head, as if trying to convey a very important message.

"No thank you, Council-Leader", George answered, although he knew that secretly would have liked to have given a different answer.

"That's probably just as well," replied the Council-Leader, "the initiate's ability to endure pain, in order to achieve their ultimate goal, is the true mark of a Talisman. Plus, we don't actually have any, but tradition states I have to ask the question."

The Council-Leader turned his back to George, and addressed the room. "The initiate has been proven to be a worthy bearer of the mark of a Talisman. He is properly attired, and has been correctly prepared to receive the mark," the gathered audience, murmured their collective agreement and approval, "may the Scribe please step forward?"

A man, who until now, had remained unseen by George, stepped into the circle of people. He too was wearing a hessian vest, as well as a pair of black latex gloves. He sat on the stool, next to George's outstretched arm, and removed the cloth which was covering his equipment on the trolley. George could see various scalpels, tweezers, and other cutting tools, and felt the colour drain from his cheeks.

The Scribe adjusted his stool, before picking up one of the scalpels. "I'm not going to lie to you," he said in a soft Welsh accent, "this is going to hurt like a bitch!"

CHAPTER 63

George barely slept that night. His brain was replaying the events of the evening. Was it real? Is he really a Talisman now? He imagined his father going through the same ritual, and wondered what the Council knew about his own dad, that he didn't. What was his extort?

George's head wasn't the only reason he couldn't sleep. Whichever way he lay, something was putting pressure on his right arm. He had taken strong painkillers as soon as he was home, and although they had taken the edge off the pain, his skin was intensely sensitive.

It was nearly 4am before George's head hit his pillow, and he'd been tossing and turning for nearly an hour. Faced with the obvious fact that sleep just wasn't going to happen, he got up and made a pot of strong coffee. Something told him, that it was going to be a long day!

George waited until 10 o'clock, and he in his office, before dialling the number that Hightop had called him from. He was tired, despite the high level of caffeine now in his system, and his arm hurt with every movement. The wound was wrapped in cling-film, and his arm was uncomfortable and sweaty, as well as stinging constantly. The call was answered on the second ring, and he tried to compose himself, to convince Hightop of a venue change, without his pain distracting him.

"Speak!"

The gruff voice on the phone was impatient and sounded irritable, as if the owner had been disturbed from an important task, to answer the phone.

"This is George Mason," the person on the other end of the phone, didn't offer a reply, so George continued, "I have a meeting arranged with Hightop, but I would like to suggest a change of location."

"Wait!"

Telephone etiquette was clearly not a prerequisite for membership into the Mad Hatters, and George allowed himself a smile as he imagined Hightop's henchmen attending a telephone workshop seminar, to learn how to project a smile over the phone.

George's request had obviously caught Hightop's attention, as the next voice on the phone, was his.

"Good morning George. I understand from my colleague, that you would like a change of venue for our meeting. Can I ask why this is so?"

"I just think that somewhere more public would be a better choice, until we get to know each other better I mean."

"Are you saying you don't trust me enough to be alone with me?"

George could spot a leading question a mile off, and avoided the obvious answer that Hightop was fishing for, that George was in any way afraid of him. That would give Hightop the upper hand in any subsequent situation.

"Not at all. I'm just thinking that neither of us know the other well enough to be alone with them. Your Dominic Watson made the mistake of underestimating someone, and trusting them, and that didn't work out too well for him. I wouldn't want either of us to make the same error of judgement."

George smiled when he heard Hightop stifle a gasp, at him virtually admitting to being responsible for Dominic's disappearance.

"Very wise I'm sure," Hightop replied, his voice lacking just a touch of its usual confidence, "do you have anywhere in mind?"

George saw movement out of the corner of his eye, as Hightop was speaking, and he looked out of his office window, to see Tommy chatting to someone in the yard. He couldn't see the person's face, but recognised him from the way he moved.

"George?" Hightop's voice, drew his attention back to the call.

"Where? Er, actually yes. There is a rather high-class restaurant, recently opened in town, Ridgeways, do you know it?"

"I know of it, yes." Hightop answered, a little unconvincingly.

"I won't ever be able to eat there with Julie, but I hear the food is exceptional. I hate dining alone in restaurants, so how about we meet there on Friday, instead of here? A much more friendly environment, than a funeral home, for two professionals to meet, don't you think?"

"I think I understand where you're coming from George. OK, I will meet you there at 8pm on Friday, oh, and George?"

"Yes, Hightop?"

"Leave the Scotsman at home."

George smiled as he ended the call, and turned to face Tommy, who had entered the office while he was on the phone.

"Any luck, boss?"

"He's agreed to meet at the restaurant. D'you know Tommy, for some strange reason, I get the impression that our Mr Hightop isn't a fan of yours."

Tommy pretended to be hurt by the revelation, "Oh no! However will I sleep at night?" he laughed.

George laughed at Tommy's reply, then, in a more considered tone, added, "Are you sure this is the right thing to do Tom? You know he won't be alone, right?"

"Don't you worry boss," the big Scotsman replied, "the one thing he will definitely be, is alone, I can guarantee you of that."

George absent-mindedly rubbed his arm as he spoke, "Was that Trigger I saw you with just now?"

"The very same," Tommy replied with a smile, "he brought me this." Tommy placed a shoe box on George's desk.

"What is it?" George asked, perplexed.

Tommy opened the lid, and showed George what was inside, "Just a little something for dessert." he explained.

~~~~~~

Hightop handed the phone back to his reluctant receptionist, and told him to send Drummer up to see him.

A few minutes later, there was a knock on Hightop's door, and he beckoned Drummer to enter.

"Drummer, Ridgeways restaurant, do you know it?"

"Er, yeah, I've seen it. Down the main road, by O'Reilly's"

"Is it one of ours?"

"No boss, it used to be the Golden Tamarin, run by the Joshua Gang, but it's been empty for a few years."

"It looks like it's re-opened under new management," Hightop said, with a hint of disapproval in his voice, "so we need to pay them a visit sometime anyway, but for now, I want you to do a sweep, before I meet with the Funeral Director tomorrow night."

"No problem. Layout, finances, and background checks? I'll make some calls, then go and check it out first-hand."

"Thanks Drummer." Hightop opened the

humidor on his desk, and took out a Montecristo No.2. "Oh, and Drummer!"

"Boss?"

"Take someone with you, but keep it discreet."

"Will do."

Drummer closed the office door behind him, and went downstairs to find Pug. If there was something that needed doing, no questions asked, and Hightop wanted to know it would be done right, first time, he would call on Drummer. He was his right-hand man.

Pug was the right-hand man's, right-hand man, and Drummer found him front of house, in the Kenyan Café, cradling a half-finished cappuccino.

"You up for a little drive Pug?" Drummer asked, knowing full well what the answer would be.

"Just say the word 'D'," Pug replied in his nasally voice, "where are we off to?" Pug's voice, and his nick-name, were the result of his nose being broken too many times, for even him, to remember.

"Just a little recce work on the Q.T" Drummer explained, "and it's a posh place, so behave yourself."

"You mean no guns?"

Yes, Pug, I mean no guns. What is it with you and guns?"

"I dunno, I guess we just have an understanding."

"You need counselling," Drummer joked with his friend, "come on, drink up, we don't have long, and we'll need to change first."

CHAPTER 64

Just after 11pm, a dark grey Jaguar F-Pace, with blacked-out privacy windows, parked outside the entrance to Ridgeways restaurant. Two serious looking men, wearing dark suits, and even darker glasses, white shirts, red ties, and communication ear-pieces, exited the vehicle, and entered the building.

Evan, the concierge, met and greeted the men. A lot of the clientele at the restaurant used close protection bodyguards, so he wasn't fazed by the men as they approached his desk in reception.

"Good evening gentlemen, do you have a reservation to dine?"

"Our client was here earlier this evening," Drummer exclaimed, removing his glasses as he spoke, "and believes he may have left his phone here, maybe in the bathroom."

"Oh, I see," said Evan, feigning surprise, "I shall ask one of my staff to take a look for you."

"Actually, if it is ok with you, we would like

to take a look for ourselves, our client's phone contains sensitive information, and the fewer people who come in to contact with it, the better. I'm sure you understand?"

"But of course, we here at Ridgeways, fully appreciate and protect our diner's privacy and confidentiality, so please feel free to look around, but please do not disturb any of our clientele."

"Thank you for your co-operation," said Pug, as the two men walked past Evan, into the main room of the restaurant, "don't worry, we will be discrete."

Once the two men were out of sight, Evan took his mobile phone from his pocket, and called a saved contact. The phone was answered on the second ring.

"There are two here now," Evan told the recipient of the call, "just snooping around. . . . .no, badly disguised as bodyguards. . . . yes, no problem."

Evan ended the call after his contact had thanked him for the information, in his broad Scottish accent.

Five minutes later, the two men re-emerged, and walked straight through reception to the main doors.

"Any luck gentlemen?" Evan called after them.

"False alarm," Pug replied, "our client just called us from his phone, it wasn't lost after all."

Drummer and Pug returned to Hightop's office, to report their findings.

"It looks like a proper nice place boss, all silver service and smart waiters. There's even a guy playing a piano."

"Really Pug? How illuminating, thank you." Hightop knew that Pug was loyal, and he tolerated him to a point, for Drummer's benefit, but there was just something about the man that unsettled him. Maybe it was that he reminded Hightop of the old-school image of gangsters: guns, broken noses, and strong cockney accents, or maybe it was simply the fact that Pug's voice grated on him.

Drummer sensed Hightop's less than enthusiastic reply, and stepped in to offer further information. "The main entrance is on the high street, which leads into a reception area. From there, a large doorway leads to the restaurant area itself, and the kitchens are off to the side. Fire exits are at the back, near the bathrooms, and lead out to the car park which is at the rear."

"Thank you, Drummer. Any concerns?"

"No boss, it all checks out. Tony ran a police check, and nothing flagged up. The place has been open about six months now, and seems to be doing well. The food looked really good, a bit fancy for my liking, but definitely a top-class gaff."

"OK, thank you boys," said Hightop, dismissing the two of them with a wave of his hand, "get some rest Drummer, I want you with me tomorrow when I have my meeting."

Drummer nodded his understanding, and, unknown to him, left Hightop's office for the very last time.

CHAPTER 65

Drummer drove the Jag to Ridgeways, and pulled up outside the main entrance at 7.55pm. Unusually, Hightop sat in the passenger seat, but only because the rear seats were taken up by the imposing figure of Deano, the rhino-sized slab of beef.

"Take the car 'round back Drummer, check out the car park, then meet us inside."

"Will do boss." Drummer confirmed, as the two men exited the car. The suspension visibly lifting as Deano's bulk shifted from his seat.

As the two men crossed the path, the doorman standing in front of the restaurant, opened the doors. "Good evening gentlemen," he said, touching the peak of his cap, "welcome to Ridgeways."

Inside the reception area, Evan looked up from his computer screen, and welcomed the two men. "Good evening gents, do you have a reservation this evening?"

"I am here to meet with Mr Mason," replied Hightop, "and my associate would like a table for one, preferably with a bench seat."

"Table for two, in the name of Mason," Evan confirmed, checking his computer screen, "yes sir. Please follow me through, and I will take you to your table. Mr Mason arrived just a few minutes ago." He then looked at the massive man standing behind the smartly dressed gentleman. "If you'd just like to wait here for a few minutes, I will have a booth prepared for you."

Deano looked to his boss for confirmation, then remained in reception after Hightop nodded his approval.

Hightop looked around the restaurant, as he followed the concierge to the table. The restaurant was clearly popular. Nearly all thirty tables were occupied with diners enjoying their meals. Mostly couples, engaged in private discussions, but there were a few groups of four and six – most likely businessmen and women, looking to impress their clients with fine dining on company expense accounts.

The mirror-lined walls, reflected the soft mood lighting back into the room, which, coupled with the cream and ivory décor and linen, gave the restaurant an impression of warmth and elegance. The ambience was further enhanced by a pianist, playing softly in the centre of the room.

George stood as the two men approached the table.

"Good evening," he said, "please." gesturing with his hand for the man to take his seat.

"Would you like a drink before you order, sir?" asked Evan, helping Hightop with his chair.

"Whisky Mac" replied Hightop without looking at the concierge.

The two men sat opposite each other, neither one breaking the silence, each quietly weighing up the other.

A waiter arrived, with a silver tray, on which sat a drink's glass.

"Whisky Mac sir?"

Hightop nodded at the waiter, who placed the glass in front of him.

"Also sir, the concierge has asked me to tell you that your associate has been seated at table 12." The waiter pointed to a table just over the seated man's left shoulder, three rows back.

Hightop nodded once more, again too arrogant to bring himself to speak to staff. He looked over his shoulder to see Deano squeezed into a semi-circular booth, the glasses and cutlery in front of him, looking as though they belonged in a doll's house in comparison to him.

~~~~~~~~~~

Drummer drove the Jag to the rear of the building, and did a lap around the car park. He wasn't expecting to find anything out of the ordinary, but it was a standard security measure. Satisfied that there was no risk, he parked the car in a space, and turned off the engine.

Before Drummer could release his seat belt, and open the driver's door, there was a knock on his window, which startled him, as he hadn't seen anyone approach the vehicle. He pressed the button and lowered the driver's window. "What's the fucking idea?"

"Hello again Daniel." replied the man standing beside the car. He bent forward, so he was at the same level as the man sitting in the car. Not that Drummer needed to see his face to know who he was, there was no mistaking the Scottish accent.

"Your boss has asked me to deliver a message to you," as Tommy spoke, Drummer realised that he had called him by his first name, which meant he probably knew a lot more about him, "he said that there's no need for you to wait for him, so just take the car back to the Kenyan Café, and he'll catch up with you sometime."

"You know I can't do that. Unless Hightop gives me further instructions himself, then I need to meet him inside."

"Your boss won't be leaving here in anything other than pieces, so your services won't be needed for the rest of the evening."

Drummer quickly considered the situation, and soon realised that he was short on options. Disappointing, and abandoning his boss, wasn't something that would easily be forgiven, and the chances are, he wouldn't live long enough to rebuild Hightop's trust. On the other hand, the Talisman standing at his door, was more of an immediate threat, and would need to be neutralised before he could make his way into the restaurant.

Before he could decide which of the shit options to take, another man appeared immediately in front of the car, carrying a baseball bat over his shoulder. Drummer caught movement in his rear-view mirror, and saw a third person standing there too. Instinctively, he looked to the left, and wasn't surprised to see that all sides of his car were now being guarded by a Talisman.

"It would appear that you have left me few options," he said without looking at Tommy, "but if I disobey my boss, then you might as well kill me now, because the result will be the same. One word from Hightop and Deano will snap me like a dry twig."

"The absolute unit that he walked in with?" Tommy laughed, "Don't you worry about him, he's already being taken care of."

Drummer sat in the driver's seat, with both hands gripping the steering wheel. His mind trying to calculate the scenario with the best chances of him surviving.

"So, what now?" Drummer asked, resigning himself to resolving the most immediate threat.

"Your boss' actions have decided his fate, so it's only fair that you get the same opportunity. Leave now, and you get to go home in this lovely looking motor, or stay and remain loyal to this prick, and go home in a body bag."

Drummer nodded his head, and started the car's engine. "If you're going to kill him," Drummer said, turning to face Tommy, "do me a favour, and make sure you do it properly, otherwise you're digging my grave."

Tommy stood up and signalled for the other men to step away from the car, as it started to pull out of the parking space, "Don't you worry about that Danny-Boy," he said, with a large smile on his face, "young Victor doesn't know what's coming, but I promise you, it will be most righteous."

CHAPTER 66

George ended the pissing contest, by speaking first. "Thank you for agreeing to a change of venue at short notice," a gracious 'don't mention it' nod from Hightop, "I just felt these were nicer surroundings than my workplace."

"And who knows what fate may await a person at such an ominous location?" Hightop said with a sly grin, clearly referring to Dominic's disappearance.

George ignored the inference, and continued regardless, "So what is it you would like to discuss with me?"

Hightop smiled, "Patience George, there's no need to rush our conversation. Let's enjoy our meal and get to know each other a while."

The waiter brought over the menus, and a wine list, and informed the two gents of the chef's specials for the evening.

Hightop ordered ballotine of duck liver,

with damson and pistachio for starters, with a main course of Buckhurst Park roe deer, with pear, chestnut, and juniper. George's order consisted of Argyle smoked salmon with soda bread and crème fraiche, and 28 day matured, Bannockburn rib eye steak, cooked medium-rare, with a Bordelaise sauce.

Hightop handed the wine list to the waiter, and ordered a bottle of 1975 Gaja Barbera Sori Vagnona.

"Very good sir." the waiter replied, taking the folders and leaving the gentlemen alone.

Hightop sipped his drink, the clanking ice being the only noise between the two men, until he placed his glass back on the table.

"I understand that Julie and Oliver's funeral went well, and they had a beautiful service. I sent flowers to the crematorium."

George felt his pulse quicken at hearing the man responsible for their untimely deaths, mention their names, as if he knew them personally. The piece-of-shit was clearly goading him, looking for a reaction. He gripped his glass tightly as he took a drink, focusing his attention on the fiery scotch as it sat on his tongue. He allowed it to sit there a while, before swallowing.

If George had even the slightest reserve that this evening was to end in any other way than was planned, it evaporated the second the arrogant prick spoke his family's names.

"It was a very emotional, and touching service," George replied, containing his rage, "and it was very well attended. I'm sorry I didn't see your flowers, but I had a lot going on."

"Of course," Hightop replied, discounting the notion with a wave of his hand, "think nothing of it."

'How incredibly magnanimous of you, you insulant fuck-wit' George thought to himself.

The waiter returned, carrying a silver tray, on which sat two plates, covered by silver domes. He placed the plates in front of the two gentlemen, and with a well-practised flourish, removed the covers, before returning to the kitchen.

The two men sat in silence once more, as they savoured the delicate starters that had been placed before them. The plates were cleared away, and the wine had been poured, before either man spoke.

"So, at the last count, I am two associates shy, if you include Mr Watson," Hightop began, sipping his wine as he spoke, "and I have a sneaking suspicion that you know more about their demise than you are letting on."

George was surprised, both by Hightop's

candour, and that he was linking him to more than just Nic Watson's disappearance. He had no idea who the man seated in front of him was talking about, but he didn't let it show on his face.

"Whether you are directly involved, or their loss being a result of the intervention of your Talisman friend, I neither know nor care, but I hold you fully responsible either way."

George subconsciously rubbed his arm at the mention of the Talisman. The pain reminding him of the protection he was being afforded.

Both gentlemen sat back in their chairs, as the waiter arrived, pushing a small, serving trolley. Silver domes covered several plates, which the waiter removed as he placed the food in front of them.

"It's rather nice here," Hightop said to no-one in particular, "I think I might make this a regular dining venue."

"I wouldn't make any future reservations." George said, half under his breath.

"Sorry, what was that?" Hightop asked, unsure if he'd heard correctly.

"I mean, me personally. I won't be making any reservations in the future. It's a little out of my comfort zone, price-wise."

Both men ate their meals as they continued their conversation.

"Actually, it's interesting that you bring up the subject of money," Hightop said, with his veal-laden fork paused halfway between his plate and his mouth, "as that is one of the reasons for this meeting."

"Oh, how so?" George replied, feigning interest.

"Well, the way I see your situation, is this, you are responsible for the death of, at least one, probably two, of my men, which means, whether I can prove that or not, you owe me"

George looked up from his meal, and raised his eyebrows at Hightop, signalling for him to continue.

"I can't imagine what sort of damage it would cause your reputation, if news of your involvement in criminal activity, found its way to the local press, but I'm sure it wouldn't be favourable for you or your staff. I can protect you from this."

George put down his cutlery, and picked up his wine glass, allowing Hightop to continue with his monologue.

"I am not an unreasonable man George, so I

am prepared to do you a favour."

George coughed, nearly choking on his wine, as Hightop spoke.

"It seems to me, that given the right incentive, you are both willing and able, to make people disappear. I am sure your unique job provides ample opportunity for the disposal of all kind of things, should the occasion arise."

"It does present rather unique opportunities, I agree." George managed to reply, once his coughing had subsided.

"My proposal is this. You can carry on with your business as usual, and you won't have any trouble from me."

"If you don't mind me saying, that seems a little too simple, so what's the catch?"

"Should I ever have need for your specialised services, transfer and disposal of a body, getting rid of paperwork, evidence, that kind of thing, then you do what you do best and everyone wins. You will of course, be compensated for your time, and I think you'll find I can be a most generous employer."

"You mentioned protection, but as you are fully aware, I have the protection of the Talismen."

"No, Mr Mason, you've had the protection of the Talismen. Had! Unfortunately, having a Talisman working for you, does not guarantee your safety. Your Scottish friend may have the weight of the Talismen behind him, but you on the other hand, do not. What I am offering, is your safety, both personally and professionally. It would be a shame if anything untoward should happen at your business premises. A fire, for instance, would be devastating for you. The loss of your vehicles, equipment, and buildings would be very costly, not to mention the distress caused to those people who have entrusted their loved-ones into your care."

George listened to Hightop threaten his livelihood, then did something which caught Hightop completely off guard. He started to laugh.

"You are a very arrogant man Victor. May I call you Victor?" George continued without waiting for a reply, "I have sat here and listened to you gloat at the death of my wife and son, and now you are blatantly threatening the safety of my family business, as well as my employees."

Victor, now stripped by George of his gang-name, sat in disbelief that the man in front of him, dare speak to him this way.

"I can see by the expression on your face, that

no-one has ever stood up to you before, so this may come as a shock to you."

Victor sat back in his chair, and drank his wine. He was surprised at the size of the balls of the man across the table from him, and was interested to hear where this was going.

"You are a dangerous man, of that there is no doubt. You have injured, extorted, tortured, and killed people, both in person and by command. But what you are, above all else, is a bully."

Victor raised his glass in a fake salute as George continued his tirade.

"You sit there in your expensive designer clothes, with a stupid grin on your face, and tell me how my future is going to go. Why on earth do you think you have the authority to do that?"

Victor swallowed his wine, and started to reply.

"No, don't interrupt me, you've had your say, now you'll listen to someone else for a change. You're only used to playing with a loaded deck. Even now, you think you hold the best hand, but you don't. Not only are you blissfully unaware of the hand I'm holding, you don't even know what game we're playing. Quite frankly, it's laughable."

Victor was taken aback, and at the same time, impressed, by George's bravado. "Very impressive Mr Mason, I like your attitude. Not going down without a fight, eh? That's the spirit."

George looked over to where the waiter was standing, and nodded his head. The waiter approached the table, carrying a silver dome covered plate, on a tray.

"I ordered dessert for us both. It's the house speciality, I hope you'll like it."

The waiter placed the plate in front of Victor, and removed the silver dome.

The gang leader looked down at the plate, then looked up at George, with a confused look on his face.

"What is this, some sort of a joke?"

"Oh, it's no joke, Vic!" George replied, with added emphasis on the abbreviated name. "This is a Glock 19. In fact, it's the actual Glock 19 that was used to gun down my family."

Sensing that the situation was becoming untenable, Hightop raised his right hand in the air, and clicked his fingers. He then smiled directly at George, knowing that Deano, the man-mountain had been waiting for his signal. "I don't know who you think you are, or what you hoped to achieve by this uncharacteristic display, but to continue your earlier analogy Mr Mason, I always have an ace up my sleeve."

Hightop stared at George, and George stared at Hightop. Nothing happened. No scraping of chairs, no gasps from patrons, no light being blocked out by the imposing mass of Deano approaching. Hightop's eyes flickered, and his confusion was palpable.

George smiled knowingly, then raised his own hand in the air, "Losing your touch Vic? Here, let me try."

George clicked his fingers, and the whole restaurant reacted. The piano music stopped. There was a brief clattering, as every diner put down their cutlery, followed by a scraping of chairs from all directions.

Victor watched in amazement, as every man and woman in the restaurant, closed in around them, to form an unbroken, standing circle. So many thoughts ran through his head at once. He couldn't believe he had been set up, and on such an impressive scale.

"Our Scottish friend at work, eh?" He asked, as George slowly pushed his chair back, and stood up.

"In part," confirmed George, removing his jacket, and unbuttoning his sleeve, "but not alone."

George carefully folded back his sleeve, to reveal his forearm, lightly wrapped in cling-film. Although covered, the Helm of Awe symbol was clearly visible, etched into the Funeral Director's arm.

"You may have thought that you had an ace up your sleeve, but I knew all along, what was up mine."

Hightop rose from his chair, but strong hands pushed him back down by his shoulders. Before he could react, he felt a sharp scratch in his neck, and the world faded away.

Before the blackness took hold, the last words he heard were, "Goodnight Victor, ya wee prick"

CHAPTER 67

Victor Roberts looked quizzically at the white wall in front of him. Something wasn't right. It took his foggy brain nearly a full minute to work out what it was. The wall, was in fact, a ceiling. He was lying on his back, unable to move. His arms, legs, and even his head, were being held in place, but how or why, he couldn't tell.

He felt dizzy and more than a little drunk. He didn't know where he was, and couldn't recall what had happened. He felt cold.

"Ah, Victor, so glad you could join us!" The chirpy voice, was followed by a face appearing in his vision, then another.

Still feeling the effects of the Methohexital that had been injected into his neck at the restaurant, Victor found it difficult to focus at first. "Whasta hapn" he mumbled, confused at his apparent lack of co-ordinated speech.

"There's nothing for you to worry about Victor, you're in safe hands. I know what I'm doing, after all, I've done this before you know."

Victor blinked hard a couple of times, until his vision cleared a little.

"The thing is Vic, I know you were curious, as to exactly what happened to our mutual acquaintance, Dominic Watson, so I said to Tommy here, what could be better than showing you first-hand?"

Images flashed into Victor's head, a meal, and a crowd, plus something about a cake in the shape of a gun. No, the gun was real. The seriousness of the situation was just beginning to dawn on the gang leader.

The restrained man, coughed and spat, and after a couple of failed attempts, shouted "Deano!"

"No-one is coming to your rescue I'm afraid, especially your Mr Deano, you see, unfortunately, he ate something which disagreed with him. Quite severely, as it happens."

"Let me go, you fuckers!" Victor screamed, trying desperately to loosen his bonds. "I will burn you all to the ground!"

"Now, I don't know about you, boss," Tommy said, mockingly, "but that doesn't seem like a very good deal to me. If it's all the same to you, I think we should just take our chances, and carry on as planned."

"You fucking Scottish prick, you're the reason . . . "

Tommy's hammer-fist, made contact with the bridge of Victor's nose, stopping him mid-sentence. The sickening noise of his bone and cartilage breaking, echoed off the mortuary walls.

"With Dominic, I managed to get him prepared for the procedure while he was still asleep, but I know you were excited to know exactly what happened to him, so thought it best to wait until you were conscious, before I did anything."

George moved out of Victor's line of sight, and he heard a clatter of metal on metal, as medical instruments were removed from a tray, beside his head.

"Now, I'm not going to lie Vic, this is going to sting a little," Victor could see the scalpel in George's hand, as he brought it close, "but, on the plus side, it is also the least pain you'll ever be in again."

As the blade cut into the flesh on his neck, exposing his carotid artery, Victor shouted through gritted teeth, "You're a dead man, George Mason!"

George leant forward, until he was close to Victor's ear, then said, in a calm, steady voice, "Not going down without a fight eh Vic? That's the spirit! Unfortunately for you, you killed the people who mattered to me most, threatened my friends, and jeopardised my family name. I know a dead man when I see one on my embalming table Vic, after all, I *am* a Funeral Director!"

~~~~~~ ~~~~~~ ~~~~~~

ACKNOWLEDGE MENTS

First and foremost, I must thank my incredible family, for journeying with me on the adventure of writing this book. Hopefully my random rantings, and zoning out during conversations, as ideas were born and nurtured, will all have been worth it.

My editor, Theo Ridgeway. From berating me for capitalising words after possessive nouns, to ideas, re-writes, and for not being gentle with me. Thank you.

To all the guys at The Secret Sanctuary, thank you for allowing me to enjoy the peaceful solitude that you so wonderfully provide, and for the copious amounts of great coffee!

Thank you to Nick 'The Blind Embalmer' Smith, and Simon Dempsey, for their invaluable embalming knowledge.

The team at Book Cover Zone. The quality

of your work speaks for itself, and your cover design, works brilliantly to set the tone of this book.

Finally, a huge thank you, and ultimate respect, to the countless teams of funeral personnel, who work tirelessly, to provide an essential service 24/7/365. The dignity and peace of mind you provide to families, at their most vulnerable time, is a huge testament to you all.

ABOUT THE
AUTHOR

THE DIRECTOR'S CUT IS LUCAS TOBIN'S FIRST BOOK, AND HOPEFULLY NOT THE LAST

Lucas has several years' experience, working for various funeral companies, arranging, and bearing on, thousands of funerals, and has conducted hundreds of funerals, as a Funeral Director.

As well as going above and beyond, (as all funeral staff do), to ensure a person's final journey is dignified, respectful, and reflective of the person concerned, Lucas has also attended several interesting, bizarre, and horrific coroner's incidents, but, unlike Tommy, doesn't like to shock people by regaling (or embellishing) the stories.

Lucas lives in the UK, and is married, with three children, and one angel baby, plus a complete menagerie of both furry and scaly pets.

LUCAS TOBIN
CAN BE
REACHED ON
FACEBOOK

Or email tobin.lucas.books@gmail.com

Printed in Great Britain
by Amazon

39606859R00215